'Lone Hunter'
by John Clark.

This edition published 2020.

John Clark asserts his rights to be identified as the author of this work under European Law and International Conventions.

'Lone Hunter", Volume 1 of 'The Moses Hoffman Trilogy' is a work of fiction and any resemblance to characters living or dead are purely coincidental, except for references to people who are clearly in the public domain.

Bibliografische Information der Deutschen Nationalbibliothek: Die Deutsche Nationalbibliothek verzeichnet diese Pubikation in der Deutschen Nationalbibliografie, detaillierte bibiografische Daten sind im Internet über dnb.dnb.de abrufbar.

Herstellung und Verlag: BoD -Books on Demand, Norderstedt. This edition printed and distributed by BoD, Germany.

ISBN: 978 375 0413405

"LONE HUNTER"

by

John Clark

The Moses Hoffman Trilogy
Volume 1

A BERLIN PICTURE COMPANY PUBLICATION
2019

CHAPTER 1

For all Hoffman's sensibility to the Jewish heritage of his forebears, there is nothing Levantine in his appearance. He is a foreigner, north european, Herr Moses Hoffman, known to his friends as Mo.
The day had brought neither shootings, nor bombings, but he prefers to stay indoors.
He always has.
Exteriors spell danger and the hotel room's blue neutrality brings almost perfect privacy to draw. The evening air is warm and dry, with an aroma of spices, coffee and sun drenched stone, but there is no need for him to venture out. The room is clean and orderly, simply furnished, tranquil and pleasantly secluded. Almost relaxed, he stretches tired legs. A marble floor is cool against bare feet.
The old city of Istanbul seems calm and ever quieter, as it gradually becomes deserted. An air of tranquillity settles over the district. People are crowding onto the evening ferries which will take them across the Bosphorus to Uskador. A touch of wind ruffles the water, before the calm of night approaches.

Then someone on the street below calls 'Ali-i-i' in a plaintive, but assertive yell, a young man's voice insisting their friend answers the door, or comes to a window.

Later, Mo will phone down to ask whether one of the hotel people can bring him a tray of food from the café across the street. Before that, he turns his attention to graphics.

To begin, he will think about the drawing, only then, with a feel for the shapes and curves will he start to draw. His ideas muster as images, somewhere above, behind and beyond his pale brown eyes, but his speculations are a more, or less random affair, leaking through his mind with all the usual trappings of a fanatic's introspection.

Overhearing distant laughter, he is distracted, suddenly alert.

The grind of a lorry changing gear disturbs him.

Then a hurry of high heels click along the pavement and two dogs bark.

A pigeon flaps its wings.

Insects hum on by.

The swallows scream in pursuit.

Then the dogs bark again.

Then that is enough.

He settles down once more.

He is drawing and concentrating.

Once the dogs are finally silent, he can hear the modern city's distant fifty-cycle hum, as a moth flutters futile against the window-pane.

Sitting close to the open window, Mo's alert face and long fingered hands are self-consciously reflected in the acutely angled glass. While he's sketching, the pencil makes an audible swish as it touches the surface of the paper.

Looking down over an unrestored section of the ancient city walls, he leans forward and begins to concentrate again, carefully observing shadow, light and stone.

He draws.

When a shaft of light from the setting sun catches the Mosques, the domes and minarets glow rose red against the magic hour blue of darkening sky.

Mo draws and thinks his way into the form.

The colours are ephemeral, but these city walls have endured for centuries. They are astonishingly thick, bulging ruinously, primed ready to explode. A moment of structural failure, the inevitable triumph of gravity, and they will collapse into a heap of disordered masonry.

As if to confound his sense of the ephemeral, he realises that the rubble would be illuminated by the next day's pinks of setting sun, while the wall would be lost forever.

His hand quickens over the paper.

A visual imagination, the substance of his thoughts are murky, mainly monochrome, until his sense of form, uncoloured, floods with the flush of some carefully anticipated hue. Even so, his perspectives are of the traditional renaissance variety.

He knows how it would feel to hear the roar of collapse, then look down on disarray. He can perceive the slow improvement in visibility as the dust would settle. He can visualise the precise tints of blue and pink in his mind's eye. Then he reminds himself that the walls have not collapsed. They are quite intact and having survived the destruction, will probably stay that way for yet another hundred years. The earthquake had shuddered modern buildings into rubble.

Hit by the once-in-a-century catastrophe, all around Istanbul badly built blocks of flats had crushed and entombed a mass of people.

The sketched lines of his drawing accumulate for an hour, then touched by a presentment of his own life as history, he reaches for the computer to contact his girlfriend in Berlin.

Voice-mail is already waiting.

"Enjoy your thirty ninth, 'geburtstag kind'. I want you back. Mo, Birthday boy, I want you." There is a throaty pang in Inez'

voice as she repeats herself, "I want you."
As ever, it has the anticipated effect.
His reply is typically laconic.
An address, a click.
The affirmative, 'reciprocal with thanks', as he reminds himself of her skin, 'yes', the allure of her eyes, her breasts, "please", her feet, her voice, especially her voice, almost husky, almost a whisper, anything but virtual, 'I want you.'
'Yes - please.'
It's there.
He switches off the computer.
He's hungry.
He phones reception.
They promise to bring him kebab, stuffed vine leaves, white beans, 'chay' - tea - and a well chilled bottle of German beer.
'Becks or Köpi?' Why-ever is the Turkish thank-you, a very French, 'Merci'?
He lets his mind wander, unconcerned.
He needs to relax.
Then Mo realises, (a series of grey shapes forming an orderly pattern), that he belongs to the last generation of printers to have worked with moveable type in a manner that Gutenberg himself would recognise.
Half a millennium of print history is drawing to a close. First photo-lithography, then computer typesetting and finally the data networks have changed the printers' world, just as surely as the telephone overwhelmed letter-writing, before its e-mail resurrection.
The onionfish faces extinction.
Is that sufficient reason for this retreat into drawing?
Still intrigued by making marks on paper, the printer's devotion to mechanical reproduction no longer brings him satisfaction.
Mysteries of woodcut and drypoint engraving, acid etching and lithography absorbed Mo's youth, but the frustrations of fiddly

plates, corrosive acid baths, volatile inks and temperamental presses began to pall as he grew older, so he has returned to pencil drawing.
Paper is plentiful.
Pencils are ubiquitous.
Erasers are the biggest hurdle, sometimes smudgy, sometimes scuffing the paper.
The trace of their passage is inevitable.
Should he campaign for the survival of the onionfish?
Mo has always known he will never campaign about anything.
His ways are more subtle, he would claim, or is he simply shy?
Which was more significant? The invention of moveable type, or Gutenberg's innovation of printing on both sides of the paper?
The questions unfold in his mind, then fade. Last and first, second and penultimate, the masochistic cut and folded, sewn and glued, trimmed and sent for binding.
He glances cautiously across the waters of the Bosphorus.
Like a potter, whose glazes await the kiln before revealing their true hues, when he finally turns to colour, Mo thinks in terms of pigments. Each colour name evokes a precise sensation and a clear gradation of heavy metal tints, from unadulterated pigment to the faintest wash, chrome green, cadmium yellow, rose madder, viridian, or the old century's favourite, cobalt blue.
The last hints of sunset madder are leaching from the clouds.
The Bosphorus is lamp blackening past indigo in the gloom.
The colours must wait.
Mo is hungry. Moses draws and Hoffman erases.
He smokes a last cigarette before the food arrives. 'Merci.' A tip, quite generous.
Then, he eats.
As soon as it is dark, he sleeps.
The old city lies hushed.
The air clears.

The clouds disperse.
The city cools.
There are no new shocks.
No more aftershocks.
Breathing gently, he stirs in his sleep.

Over the Gulf of Marmora, navigation lights in red to red and green to green mirror the stars, as a blinking military jet flies off towards the west.

CHAPTER 2

At five o'clock next morning, the night porter nods wearily, as he notices the tall German leave the hotel and walk away towards the bazaar.

No heavy luggage, room 35, no unexpected overnight visitors, due to leave later that day, bill to be settled in cash. Cause for concern? Probably not, the porter concludes and writes that down for the security people.

He writes swiftly, and elegantly, forming each curl of Arabic script with élan, more interested in the shapes they create, than the message he is conveying. It will be noted on the security file that Herr Hoffman of Berlin has no known Kurdish, Saudi, or Afghan associates. Such is intelligence. When the phone rings, the night porter answers it and the early rising German is temporarily forgotten.

Neatly dressed and cautious, exploring the narrow alleyways of the old city, Mo steps aside for a line of porters hauling backbreaking loads of merchandise from the quayside warehouses uphill to the bazaar.

A handsome young man in a dark grey suit picks him out from

the crowd and begins to follow, unobserved. Instead, Mo has noticed a slender young woman in dark glasses and a deep blue headscarf, who is looking at a display of high velocity hunting rifles on show in a shop window. The Kalashnikovs and M16's she craves are stacked hidden behind closed shutters. Her cause is in disarray. Half a Soviet-built tank is concealed on the family farm near Ankara, where they keep most of their artillery. This year there is a shortage of hand grenades, but, thanks to the renewed global ban, a glut of relayable landmines. She notices the young man's good looks, his dark hair, the darker eyes and the whiteness of his teeth when he smiles at her. He has a mother and a young wife. A good son, she concludes, who will become a good father. She decides he looks Persian rather than Turkish. Then he passes on and after a few steps she forgets him, relieved that he isn't stalking her, but all too obviously shadowing the sweaty European.

Mo glances at the open stalls selling fabrics, tools and spices, alongside a thousand kinds of multi-coloured trash. Above all there is movement and noise, a swirl of people and chatter. As a visitor he can allow himself to find the effect exotic. The air is warm. Even as the fruit sellers welcome their early customers, a sense of heat and prayer runs through the crowd.

A thousand nagging details of disorganisation and indifference would enrage Mo were this where he came to work each morning, but it isn't and he doesn't, so the general impression is one of charm. The spices bring colour; the leathers a heavy sensual tanner's reek. The brassy gold glistens. The people sweat continuously. He is content to be distanced from the bazaar as everyday reality, the commonplace of business. Already, the cafés are beginning to fill up with men in search of news and deals, trader gossip, greetings and a fresh glass of tea for the day.

An old man clicks his worry beads and blinks. Smoke is making his eyes smart. He takes a sip of tea, inhales wheezily and turns to his companion asking why Bozorgnia's eldest son is following the nervous German in the Hugo Boss suit. "How should I know?" the other man answers, uninterested and the water pipe hubble-bubbles. He is tired. They are both tired, too tired for minor riddles.

After a rhythmic night at work on a Heidelberg printing press, morning is their evening and breakfast their supper. Their hands are wrinkled, but deft enough at the keyboard of the Linotype machine, as it clicks and clatters slugs of type into readable columns of metal to become clandestine news of shameful war waged against the Kurds. Their best journalists are in goal, some sentenced, others awaiting trial, but still they get the weekly paper out. Enough political prisoners die during their incarceration.

Last week, one of their contributors was shot as he drove from Istanbul to Ankara. Another confident has disappeared in Trabzond, after a EUFA Cup football match. The conflict is escalating, just as it has been for the better part of twenty years. So gradually had the war turned to genocide that only the victims and their families seem to have noticed and most of them are dead. It feels late, almost too late.

The old men catch each other's eye and notice the signs of worry they hope to hide from their wives. Their time is running short. The problems which have dogged their lives remain unsolved. Across the city, younger fingers tap computer keyboards, clicking and mousing their way through the internet, but the threat to their freedom is just the same and their hands will become old and wrinkled in due course.

The old men have no grounds for envy and are content to sip their tea.

"Bozorgnia has been acting strangely," says one, sighing, then drawing on the cool smoke of his second pipe, "He's getting old."

"Religion, he's been reading Steven Hawking," says the other,

"He told me it reconfirms his faith in Zoroastrianism, all that fire, but he thinks 'Big Bang' is a stupid name for something so awesome as 'Creation'. He's begun to look at necromancy too. Says that fifteen thousand million years doesn't seem very long." Both men almost laugh.

As a topic of conversation, neither of them is particularly interested in the old Iranian's spirituality, or his rekindled enthusiasm for flammable cosmology and they lapse into silence.

He is their enemy.

An informer.

Were he more effective, his life would already have been ended by assassination, but what is the point of murdering an ineffective opponent who tortures himself each day with the fear of dying? A violent death would only bring his troubles to an end. As their enemy, it has been concluded, it is better to let him live and suffer, disinforming whenever he tries to pass on falsehood as fact and rumour as news.

When the phone rings, the older man pulls it out of his pocket with a shrug of distaste. "Do we want to finance a lorry load of leaded petrol from Iraq?"

"How much?"

"One thousand, two hundred dollars. We get eight thousand litres at the end of next month."

"I have to go. The ferry is coming in. What calibre is the lead?"

"Nine millimetre."

"Yes, why not? Give him seven hundred now, the rest on delivery." A hand waves weary assent and they finish their tea.

"Do you think we'll ever see the petrol?"

"No, he needs to get food to his cousins. Their village was bombed. The houses reduced to rubble, everything gone."

They pay the waiter and rise to leave.

Then, nodding their respects distractedly to old acquaintances, the old men head for the ferries and home to sleep through the heat of the day. Were they to be arrested and imprisoned, no-one would be surprised, least of all their fellow inmates. Incarceration and death resemble one another. The old men would be missed in one place and welcomed by old friends in the other, but either way, they would dearly miss their wives.

Meanwhile, Mo has been threading his way along the alleys behind the bazaar and the autumn sun has risen two more degrees along its arc. The air smells of diesel fumes, turmeric and stale deodorant. When he steps onto a broad traffic free square in the heart of the old city, his eyes are momentarily dazzled by the intensity of the light. A film of adrenalin sweat dampens his hair, as his pulse races. Mo recognises these symptoms of his agoraphobia. This is when the young man taps him gently on the shoulder and says in English, "please, come this way, we have very fine carpets, please follow me, come this way," and ten steps on, he stops by a nondescript green door, "no-one was shadowing you" and politely shows him inside, which is always better.

Mo ventures in.

The air is cool.

The sweat evaporates.

His pulse slows.

He is in control of himself once more.

Two steps through the door and he cannot see, until his eyes gradually begin to adapt.

But for a hint of light at the farthest end of the long narrow room, the premises are unlit. The carpet dealer shakes his hand and manoeuvres Mo with the nimble gentleness of a very fat man. A faint scent of rose-water sweetens the dusty air, as Assad Bozorgnia leads him between the stacks of rugs, gesturing to the low stools arranged around the pool of light, where a single spot-lamp points directly at the polished parquet floor.

The shop seems centuries old and time stands still, as the sweet bloom of opium reaches Mo's nostrils and like a cat who smells a mouse, his nose wrinkles, his mind clicks in and eyes dilate, as he happily inhales.

Before his eyes can adjust a second time, a flick of Bozorgnia's podgy wrist sends a small silk rug spinning to hover a few centimetres above the floor. With each rotation, exquisite opiate colours flash as the spotlight alternately catches the pile from different directions, electric blues, ruby and gold, then silvery verdant greens and startling magentas, before the little rug flops motionless to the floor. Mo has seen the trick before.

Flying carpets.

He takes a deep breath and exhales slowly.

Not hard to imagine how the salesmen's gimmick becomes a medieval traveller's tale and the opium smoker's dream a myth of flight. Plied with another glass of cinnamon flavoured tea, Mo relaxes and lets himself be entertained. He has been here before and the two men begin a dialogue about colour, craftsmanship and form. A cloud of rich Caucasian tobacco-smoke fills the room, as Bozorgnia patiently describes how each region of Turkey, Iraq and Iran produce carpets of a distinctive style, village by village, thread by thread, silk, wool, vegetable and mineral dyes, rose petal pinks and aubergine blue.

"These carpets," he claims in a colonial English accent, "are a far cry from the output of those notorious child labour factories in Nepal and India."

Still, Mo is disturbed to see motifs of battle tanks, bombers and their dotted payloads incorporated alongside the age old silhouettes of camels, sheep and people.

War is died in the wool, spun into the yarn of conflict, then woven and knotted on the loom of battle. War in Punjab, Afghanistan, Iran, Iraq, Kuwait, Armenia, Georgia, Azherbaijan, Chechenia, Ossetia and Ingussetia, Nagorno-Karabakh, the Kurdish regions of Turkey, war almost everywhere, Serbia and Kosovo, Albania and New York, Iraq again and Palestine, all contributing to this new iconography, the dealer explains self-evidently, with a bushy browed frown of concern. The weavers make one, or two pieces a year. Everyone has seen battle, or suffered its consequences.

"I do not commission their work," he explains assertively, disclaiming responsibility, not to blame, "but simply travel from place to place, buying and bringing the produce to market. It is not hard to sympathise with their plight. I listen to their stories, but what can I do? I pay their price and buy."

Carpet after carpet are laid out for Mo to inspect.

He is less curious than the dealer supposes, indifferent to his selection.

Bozorgnia asks what he finds attractive, narrowing down the alternatives in a patient ritual of choice.

Eventually there are just two lying in front of them. He pauses for a moment before deciding.

Should he choose a piece out of solidarity with the peasants of Anatolia, or take the rug he likes most, an Iranian silken wonder that could cost him seven, or eight thousand dollars and set the dealer celebrating the day for a sale that means survival.

Bozorgnia mentions twelve thousand dollars, then eight. The piece took five years to complete.

Mo haggles until they agree a price of $7,600, reduced by a further 10% for cash.

"My dear Hoffman, you are a difficult man to satisfy," the Iranian complains with a little smile.

Then sixty-nine genuine US hundred-dollar bills exchange hands and Mo pockets fifty seven million Turkish pounds change.

Both men are happy.

Somehow they have kept inflation at bay, avoided the Euro and made a profit. Whichever carpet Mo had chosen, they both knew the price would have been the same. The market is hardly in good shape.

"Terrorism is not conducive to tourism," Bozorgnia declaims. Apparently the visitors had been staying away since a bomb exploded in the confines of the old bazaar.

"No sooner had the Americans overcome their fears of travelling after the Gulf War," says Bozorgnia, "when boom and in a matter of twenty four hours, there was not a prosperous Yankee in the city. That was ten years ago. Then we had another Kurdish crisis, the worst earthquake in living memory and there are fewer customers than ever. I have lived here in shock and awe since the Mullahs took over in Iran and never felt insecure until now that our American friends have doused the region in fear and loathing. None of us are Marxists any more, but on the day of the quake, as I looked at the world collapsing around me, I had to conclude that prosperity is theft."

Mo listens patiently, wondering why a one-time acolyte of the Shah's secret police should ever expect to be left in peace, or bother to pretend he had been a Marxist.

Bozorgnia promises that the carpet will be sent directly to his hotel. He's happy again and tells Mo about 'The Brief History of Time' and the 'New Left Review'. "I think our culture is carried forward by the scale of numbers we can imagine. Think of economics. Fifteen thousand million is not such a big number, even if we're talking about years. Take the knots in these carpets, then ask yourself how many carpets we have here. If I think of a year for every knot in all the carpets we have then it is a longer time than your Hawking thinks there has ever been. I think it's time they started looking for what happened before everything went bang. What sucked and blew us into existence? We talk of years and seconds, but what is the real unit of time that slips us forward from moment to moment? If a humble man like me can imagine all the time there is, there must be more to it than that, but who is to provide the mathematics?"

He snorts, simple and ignorant, but hardly humble, disdainful of the cosmologists' timidity, as his nose gurgles. Bozorgnia pours himself another glass of tea and Mo can take his leave, wondering why the man tortures himself with popular science, but never doubting the carpet will be delivered to the hotel in time for him to catch the airport bus for the afternoon plane.

"Enjoy your flight, Mr Hoffman," says the young man, as Mo steps into the street, half blinded by the sun.

Behind him the slender woman, still in her dark-glasses, but without her headscarf, steps unseen into Bozorgnia's shop.

There is shouting.

A shot.

Then, there is silence.

The printers' friends had changed their minds.

Four hours later, Mo is ready to depart. The taxi driver is waiting. He'd spent the day wandering through the elegant courtyards and pavilions they call the Topkapi Palace, dodging from fierce sun into cool shadow. Mo Hoffman pursuing his favourite indulgence, the study of walls.

The Topkapi is like a maze, mixing inside and outside in search of shade and privacy. Mo's nose had tickled to the chalky smell of hot stone. He had sneezed, as he let his hands run over the even masonry. The standard of workmanship astonishing him, he had sought the faults that should be revealed by three centuries weathering, but there was hardly a blemish. These curtain walls separated the servants quarters and gloomy kitchens from the inner sanctums of the Sultan and his Ministers, walls that doubled as the Seraglio's last line of defence against attacks which never came. The stone-masons had worked to ever finer standards as they approached the heart of the complex, until it was hard to distinguish the creamy limestone building work from sculpture.

The visitors were mainly local, either from the sprawling city suburbs, or the surrounding countryside. Mo had noticed that with the exception of three Australian women, the smattering of other foreigners were almost all earthquake familiar Japanese. Looking around, he drew comfort from the gulf that must exist between his thoughts and those of everyone around him.

He had listened uncomprehendingly, as a grandfather explained to a little boy of six, that Istanbul, then called Constantinople, or Byzantium, was once the centre of great empires and this had been the court of Suleyman the Lawmaker, the Magnificent, whose finery impressed the world. The cloaks and costumes on display in the Museum reveal him to have been a remarkably small man, which probably explains the magnificence of his vanities. The wide-eyed little boy had stared in awe at jewels and relics and swords and costumes, clutching his grandfather's hand with excitement and wondering how long ago was long ago and where was he when they were?

Mo wondered too, but he hadn't understood a word of their conversation. He had felt relaxed among this babble of unknown tongues. There was no-one there to notice him and even the romantically vulnerable schoolgirls gave him only shy glances, before turning away to giggle at their own audacity.

Wandering from building to building and courtyard to courtyard, he had lingered beside a pavilion, which fulfilled all his expectations of the pleasures enabled by a perfect disposition of walls. Each window graced an alcove with cushioned seats, couches and to Mo's delight, the most fragile of all walls, a finely carved wooden tracery of screens. Sitting high on a promontory affording a view across the Golden Horn towards the whole city, the pavilion is almost surrounded by a shallow pool, cleverly constructed as part of the terrace, to offer complete privacy and a cunning illusion of solitude.

Across the terrace stood a girl with coal black eyes and a mass of curly long dark hair. When she realised Mo was looking at her, she coolly put on her sunglasses, turned to look at him, and let her gaze rest on him accusingly.

"Do you like what you see?"

"Is that a question, or an invitation?" said Mo, meaning yes.

Then, without replying, she walked quickly away.

Walls, as terraces concealing entrenched pathways, also protect the laurel green hillside gardens, so unseen, the Sultans were able to welcome the women of the Harem after their journey by boat across the Bosphorus.

Mo had daydreamed the homeward flight away with thoughts of this Pavilion and the girl who'd turned away.

Where had she gone? Had he dreamed her?   How long ago was long ago?

His mind wandered through a catalogue of delights he felt sure were once enjoyed, rehearsing their potential in his imagination.

CHAPTER 3

Driving away from the polygonal airport terminal at Berlin-Tegel, the carpet carefully stowed in its plastic wrapping on the back seat, Mo feels a wave of exhaustion ripple through his body. His back aches, his clothes are sticky with the sweat of travel and his eyes are itching. As the car passes beneath a banner reading 'Wilkommen in Berlin', he sneezes. The early start, a change of time zone and the stark contrast between the two cities has left him weary.

Coming off the plane, he looked like a businessman and he looked tired. A bottle of arak, a box of Cuban cigars and a fine gold bangle for Inez to slip on her arm, or forget in her jewelry case, as she pleases. With an overnight bag slung from the shoulder, he carried the rolled-up carpet under one arm.

The German Border police had waved him through without even trying to read the Turkish script on the receipt Bozorgnia had given him. They weren't going to give him any trouble. A Berlin boy, like them. He's just come home.

Passport control were more interested in the Turkish passengers.

Born in Berlin, too, but do they have residence permits for Germany?

Were their great-grandparents registered as German in 1906?

Are they members of banned political parties?

Have the young men completed their military services in the German, or Turkish armies?

Do you aspire to martyrdom?

Are you a member of al-Qaeda, Hammas, the Christian Social Union, any of a dozen other organisations?

Customs officers from the 'Zollamt' were wondering how many kilos of heroin would get past the soporific sniffer dogs this time?

They are all waiting for a particular young woman, who is acting as a courier for the Kurdish separatists. She will be detained and questioned, intimately searched, before being allowed into the land of her birth. Arrangements are being made for her father to be deported, but she knows he will never leave the Neukölln cancer hospital alive.

Berlin looks grey with the coming of autumn, as Mo coaxes the little green Lancia out of the airport car park onto the motorway.

The carpet is safe now he's in his car. It is resting behind him on the back seat. Hoffman is happy to be back where he belongs, among the detritus of a different kind of decadence. Berlin, the air stale as ever, the promise of perversion and obscure gratifications in dark corners, corrupt and lazy behind closed doors. He still feels a twinge of nostalgia that the familiar French Armoured Personnel Carrier is no longer parked on the hard shoulder of the motorway as you leave the airport. Twelve long years have passed since the Allied Forces quit. Another kilometre and the Funkturm radio-mast hoves into view; an Eifel Tower in miniature that Einstein had opened in the nineteen twenties with a speech extolling the wonders of science.

Mo Hoffman dislikes the word 'billow', except when it is applied to sails, or skirts. In particular, he dislikes the word 'billow', when applied to a cloud of lurid green fumes being expelled under pressure from every crevice of a factory beside the autobahn interchange which he is about to drive across on

23

his way home to the apartment in Steglitz.

The building is billowing green - apple, olive, lime and slime.

Around him, drivers from all six directions are uncertain whether to slow down, or accelerate to evade contamination.

The green stuff is beginning to spill over the roadway.

Luckily, he's wide awake again, alert to the potential danger drifting into his path.

Mo grimaces, as he realises his hands are trembling.

Is it truly a gas, ugly and opaque, a mass of molecules free to mingle with the air it is polluting, as each billow builds the cloud? Depending on its toxicity, the impact might be felt over huge distances. Will it smother him?

The green is soup thick.

Maybe it is a smoke, in which case the solid microscopic particles will be carried on the wind, but settle as a fallout of powder green soot. That would clog the car's air filters pretty quickly and make the wipers shudder and squeak, but wouldn't particularly matter. Little would get through to pollute the interior. Filters can be changed and a roll through the car wash should splash away the rest.

Mo wonders how effective the filters really are? Against a gas, they might help, but only might. Who could tell what an unidentified green gas might react with?

Were the cloud an aerosol, he would soon know. A mass of tiny droplets will smear the windscreen, thick or thin as a coat of paint, when the wiper blades slide across. Will he be able to see?

He switches off the car heater, shuts down the ventilation and feels a little safer, but vulnerable, very vulnerable.

In this panic, Mo decides, other drivers are the immediate danger.

The gas cloud is twenty or thirty seconds away, 500 metres, but people are accelerating as fast as their cars will allow. Watching the traffic shuffle at speed, poker player Moses Hoffman anticipates the worst.

Lights on.

There are no slip-roads, no turnings-off, only one way to go, getting darker, gloomy, forward.

Flash a warning no-one will heed.

Changing lane to overtake a two-stroke Trabant at a hundred and thirty, he switches back as a black Porsche Boxster suicide ploughs through from behind. He hopes they're ignoring the traffic controls he knows are less than a minute's drive ahead on the urban motorway. The lights are about thirteen seconds beyond the cloud, but invisible, because of the tight curves on the interchange. Berlin roads take strangers by surprise at the best of times.

Any kind of queue at the lights and a pile-up is inevitable.

The cloud is already thick across the autobahn, a completely impenetrable bank of dull green shadow.

Mo guesses it will take four seconds to plunge through and hit fresh air on the other side. He'll need precious seconds to change down, brake and hope for the best. At this speed, the road will give him a second of reaction time, but no more.

Just one last time, Mo hopes the traffic lights are as green as the cloud.

Accelerate and flee.

Time to panic, is there?

A lorry changes gear.

Mo tells himself he should have stayed another day in Istanbul.

Faster.

Adrenalin floods his veins.

Now.

An aerosol vapour will be worst, he decides, millions of droplets to congeal against every component of the car and soak the deepest pockets of his lungs.

Too rational.

Stop thinking.

Do.

Now.

Depending on its volatility, the liquid will evaporate at some unpredictable rate, or react on contact with the engine's hot components, becoming what?

Over rational.

Scared.

Mo refuses to imagine the consequences.

He switches on the wipers.

He's on his way.

There's no alternative.

This is the autobahn.

No stopping, fear, no slowing, irrational.

He's about to hit the strangest wall he's ever seen.

The green cloud sucks in the Lancia like custard pudding round a spoon and he stops breathing. At a hundred and fifty there is no motion, till a hail of shattered windscreen glass rattles across the car. Someone nearby is in trouble, but the someone is someone else. What was that, the crack of metal on metal? What is this green? Sulfur dioxide? Phosgene, the black and white newsreel trench warfare gas of ninety years ago? Zyklon B? What colour was the Zyklon B. that killed his grandparents? What was that stuff that Saddam was supposed to have? How long can you hold your breath? No-one ever said. Can he sense bitter almonds? How long does Gulf War syndrome take to reveal its symptoms? A month? A year? How long can you hold your breath? No-one ever said. Can he sense bitter almonds? How long does Gulf War syndrome take to reveal its symptoms? A month? A year? How long can you hold your breath? How do you recognise Sarin before it does for you? Is there time to know you're dying before you've gone? Does anyone ever really believe that the very next moment will be their last? No-one ever said. One moment becomes another. The dead won't know what carries on, but the car radio clicks on with traffic news.

No death, no destruction. No need to panic, says a man reading a script with professional indifference. A small fire at a depot storing emergency flares is impairing visibility on the autobahn and roads will be closed until the blaze is under control. There is no danger from the fumes, no cause for alarm, the passive voice declares, but drivers are advised to avoid the area until further notice.

'That's exactly what I'm trying, Motherfucker.'

For three more quarters of a second, the cloud envelopes Mo's car. Then, just as an almighty bang makes him jump with alarm, the car bursts free, hurtling into bright sunshine and he brakes with all his strength. A pale blue Trabant speeds past, unequal to the task, its driver convulsed and choking. The little car smashes into the retaining wall of the elevated carriageway, before scraping sidelong amidst a banshee scream of shattering fibreglass and metal. A BMW, blue-black, Series 3, one lady owner, sunglasses, blonde, something silk and scarlet, glimpsed struggling at the wheel, slews into the Trabant and turns over. Locked together, a razor cloud, spray of red stains, they're gone.

Mo glances behind him in time to see a lorry hit the wreckage, a jack-knife roll and the cloud turns dioxin black as flames lick the misty fringe of green.

He takes a tentative sniff, then lets himself breath normally. He doesn't like to use the word billow about a plume of poisonous gas. He would rather dream about cotton frocks blown in the wind. The frock would be blue, rather than green and the seraphic girl who was wearing it would say, "Hello, Mo, I've been waiting for you."

The woman he's thinking about doesn't billow, she beams with intense nervous energy and he hasn't seen her in a cotton frock in all the years they've been together. Inez is small and dark-eyed with black hair that she braids sometimes and twists in ringlets. She wears T-shirts with short skirts and leggings to match.

When Mo reaches the relative safety of the autobahn's elevated section, he's heading south towards Steglitz. A posse of emergency vehicles, sirens blaring, race past in the opposite direction. He slows down to take stock. Nothing has adhered to the car. A glance in the rear mirror tells him that the gas is drifting west towards the Congress Centre and he wonders what the ambulance people expect to be able to do. The autobahn is deserted, apart from a small yellow helicopter coming into land behind him. There's no-one driving in his direction and the traffic going north has been diverted. A dull thump makes him wince. Explosion. A flash, then five or six seconds pass before the woompf and an even duller shock-wave thud that hammers on the door. Probably one of the crashed cars' petrol tanks.

There's nothing he can do.

The helicopter lifts off again, drifting slowly, as though the pilot thinks the view might be more attractive from the other side.

Mo slows the Lancia to a crawl, opens the sunroof and reaches into the glove compartment for his camera. Then he stares up in the sky and lets his head slowly tilt down until a mass of tiered concrete comes into view.

For the first time in years, he can take a leisurely photo of the building where he and Inez live. The road ahead is surprisingly calm, almost tranquil in the sunshine, a smooth stretch of blacktop, well-made, broad and neatly marked with clear white line, not a car in sight. The Albatross Hotel is still there to his left, accelerate, change up a gear and relax.

Survival.

Click - a picture.

He's running smoothly towards the high level tunnel that is home.

Click, again.

This tunnel is a building, testament to West Berlin's old guinea pig status before the Wall fell down.

Architects came and promised.

Then they built.

Then they went away and left the Berliners to live with the consequences.

Mo had grown up under the umbrella of occupation, when the Allies were content to let the West Berliners get on with their lives any way they wanted. Their military minds were focussed on the threat to world peace by mistake and the prospect of being first to frizzle in the event of nuclear war; incentive enough to minimise margins of error.

This bestowed a special kind of freedom on the city, a lawless, individual definition of freedom, but that was long ago.

Now, Ministry by Ministry, the Government has relocated itself from Bonn and the energies of anarchic self-will have been discreetly turned aside. The heart of the city is becoming a bureaucratic citadel, slow and ceremonial, a Bonn-upon-Spree. This public side of the city's life doesn't interest him at all.

The city is being sanitised, but the autobahn is still encased with homes and one of them is Mo's.

He remembers the cautionary words of Erwin Panofsky, 'The Germans, so easily regimented in political and military life, were prone to extreme subjectivity and individualism in religion, in metaphysical thought and, above all, in art.'

Five hundred years ago, according to Panofsky, Albrecht Dürer had warned about this sort of thing, "I have to take into consideration the German mentality, whosoever wants to build something insists on employing a new pattern, the like of which has never been seen before."

Now, a motorway runs through the middle of the house, like the gut of a segmented worm. Mo doesn't mind. The house is a wall unto itself, more than that, an island of seclusion and the sanctuary he's always sought.

As he turns off the autobahn to park, a lorry smokily changes gear and grinds into motion, then changing gear again, the motor begins to roar. A cloud of diesel fumes fills the garage.

Mo is relieved that the apartments face outwards and the autobahn is indeed encased by the high level tunnel.

In his most regular nightmare the structure of the building is cruelly inverted, so the balconies and windows look down over the roadway, grandiose monument to the noise and choking smells of traffic with a spectacular grandstand view of man's mechanical inhumanity.

CHAPTER 4

Waiting for Mo is less frustrating than waiting for Godot, but more intriguing. You always know that he'll turn up. The uncertainties, like the Cripple Creek lyrics of a rockabilly ballad, concern the shape he might be in.

His last trip, (to Norway by ship via Newcastle, returning via Malmo and Saßnitz to visit the restored farmstead home of artist Edvard Munch), had ended with a row of bruises beginning behind his right knee and ending in his left armpit. They had remained unexplained, but healed-up after a troublesome couple of weeks.

Sometimes, Inez switches on the news, just in case someone mentions that a German travelling on business, 'Herr Moses Hoffman of Berlin' has been abducted, murdered, killed, taken prisoner, or worst of all, caught in the act. Sometimes she just waits and sometimes she chats on the phone to her mother.

This time, she had spent most of her day at work in the tiny darkroom set up in the cramped oblong of their 4.040404 square metre bathroom (2.2222222m x 1.8181818m). Her ambivalence matched the usual anxieties of a woman who understands risk. Inez relies on observation, rather than intuition and knows that seeing is sometimes insufficient.

She had been feeling uncertain all day long, but without good reason. Ever since breakfast time, Inez had been repressing a well of foreboding that nagged her stomach, but she got on with her work as if she was secure in the knowledge that nothing untoward could possibly happen. That was before the green cloud began to billow over the city and her fears began to take on the mantle of reality.

Apart from the enlarger, the only illumination in the darkroom is an orange 'safe-lite' and whenever she comes out, for the first few minutes absolutely everything looks green. This time she'd gone into the kitchen to make some coffee and misinterpreted the odd colour that was creating the strangest sunset she has ever seen. As her eyes adjusted to the daylight, she was appalled to realise that one particular misty cloud has stayed tornado green and looked as if it was getting bigger and bigger.

Sonnenuntergang - the going down of the sun - green - oh, dear.

Is this art, or apocalypse?

If you can pose the question it must be art, or the two things simultaneously, inevitably twinned like culture and society.

By six o'clock, there is reason enough to be worried and she wonders why she tried to persuade herself otherwise.

Should she begin to panic?

Why not?

Inez is terrified.

Her hands tremble.

She wants to be sick.

Watching from the patio balcony, she starts taking photos out of habit rather than interest.

An arrow of geese (zoom in focus - click) are honking (wider-click) to each other as they're flying south, giving the lethal looking green a wide berth, (wait for their silhouette, then careful, wait for the moment and click), when she hears the apartment door open (clunk).

She has started shivering.

"Mo, come and look," she says, beckoning him to join her.
Looking lies at the heart of their relationship.

 For years, they have worked to attune their vision, just as
musicians synchronise their feel for rhythm and refine their
sense of pitch.

 When he sees the scale of the pollution leaching across the city,
Hoffman blanches and takes Inez protectively in his arms. Four
fingers of black smoke are rising out of the green into the sky.
Then he describes driving though the cloud. She is appalled by
his description of the accidents, but relieved he is unharmed.

 "I wonder what it really is?"

 "I'm sure we'll never know for certain and certain we'll never
know for sure."

 A moment of silence imposes itself between them, then passes
and she says a newly honed version of the words he has been
hoping to hear. "My darling Mo, I've been waiting for you."

 Their private cliché has its usual reassuring effect. She's
leaning forward, eyes closed, elbows resting on the balcony.
He's behind her, putting a hand to rest on her back, another to
cradle the back of her head, as she turns. They kiss and
embrace, affectionate and mutually dependent, contented by the
touch of familiar limbs.

 "Did everything go alright?" she asks.

 He shrugs, so she knows that nothing has gone wrong. After
being apart for nearly six weeks, they begin to set their world to
rights with a little sex, making love wrapped dark in the black
hammock that's strung across the balcony.

 "Mo?" she asks tenderly, while they're still cloaked warm and
sweaty in the shadows of the thick dark sailcloth,

 "Why do we live like this?"

 "Are you going to tell me?"

 "No," she replies, "It was a real question. Want to know. I was
wondering what you thought."

 "Because....we......you tell me," says Mo, his muffled voice resonating to make Inez flutter from within.

"Mo?" she whispers alluringly.

"A trade off," he suggests glibly, "Between the polluted city and the poison in our minds."

"You don't believe that," she says quietly.

"A proposition, discuss..."

Inez takes the notion no further. She had grown up listening to vague parental assertions presented as unalterable truths. Mo Hoffman's epigrams were an echo of that old familiarity, sometimes comforting and welcome home, longitude and platitude, but this time mildly irritating.

"Let's go inside," she says gently, "I don't want to inhale any of that green shit. My lungs are not immune and they're the only ones I have."

Mo begins the countdown they need to roll out of the hammock without risking broken limbs, 'three, two, one, go'. Flopping onto the nasty plastic grass, which was only put down when a neighbour had complained of the thumps their footsteps made through her living room ceiling, they can't help laughing.

Inez is thirsty.

Mo needs to sleep.

Now he is home, they both feel happier again.

"Who is Holger Nierbaum?" asks Inez, once Mo has finished his shower, "He phoned this morning."

"A cultural bandit," replies Mo, quickly adding, "He always wants too much. He's lazy and he's a snob. Works for one of the LandesBanks, sees art as money and wants to set up a bank of his own, a private little gold-mine, the 'Kredit Bank für Kunst und Kultur'. Theatres and Auction Houses will deposit their takings with him, angels will invest in funds, artists and musicians will mortgage their futures, while dealers and agents will use the bank to manage their investments. The City's cultural budget could flow through his bank. Money laundering in the best of good taste. He's not entirely stupid, but he behaves like a fool, which is probably worse. His real fault is ignorance. He underestimates his ignorance, but still makes demands."

"Don't do it then. Turn him down."

"I did, last week. Over ambitious. He doesn't care. He thinks that if he keeps badgering people, they will eventually agree to do his bidding. He's usually wrong, but he doesn't let that deter him, ever."

Inez turns to go inside, "Greed brings its own reward. Credit where debits are due. Where did he want you to go?"

"Almost everywhere. The Albertina in Vienna, then Salzburg, a private collection. The baby Guggenheim on Unter den Linden. After that, on to Venezuela and the Bibliotheca Nacionale, which was where the work would be done. Rumours of a Pre-Columbian manuscript. Holger has decided he wants it. The City has a scheme to encourage new investments. He would pay me forty three per cent of their value via the taxpayer. I told him last week, it's too far away and ninety nine per cent certainly a fake, so the value is nil and forty-three percent of nothing is a headache. Even so, stolen is stolen, whatever its worth. Half a day on the plane. Means they have time to discover the theft, contact the airports, check the passenger lists and have the police waiting to look through your baggage at the other end. Istanbul is only three hours away. You have time to make your getaway."

"Mo, you don't have to do everything people ask. Forget Venezuela. Show me what you've brought from Istanbul."

Inez closes the patio door carefully in case the wind might change direction and bring the cloud of gas their way. "Zappelduster" says a disembodied voice. It is five past seven. The neighbours radio is tuned to the children's programme.

Inside the flat, everything is grey, a monochrome scale from the charcoal carpet to the carefully selected pachyderm curtains, their private world.

Musicians live in quiet houses.
For Mo and Inez, extraneous colour is mere noise.
They don't have much space.

The apartment is really too small to be practical, their main room not much bigger than the patio, a product of the ziggurat terracing that comes with heaping housing over an autobahn. Apart from the 'big room', there's a bedroom that needs redecorating, the kitchen with its hissing gas water heater and the multifunctional bathroom, which is, above all, Inez' cramped darkroom. Everything has been strictly calculated according to a formula for social housing that allows only so much floorspace per function per person. Sometimes they talk of getting a bigger place, but Mo wants to stay in the autobahn house, so their choice is limited.

Like couples everywhere, their home is a product of shared tastes, but Mo and Inez have moved beyond a sense of style in decoration towards ambitious experiment, recreating the inner world of their imagination in the external world of this sequestered private space.

The home as a page.

Objects are acquired and discarded, arranged and rearranged, a nest of constant change, a domain of acceptance and rejection.

In an over serious mood, Inez will tell herself this is 'hyper-expressionism', her deliberate attempt to make metaphor material, but the precise terminology is irrelevant, because no-one apart from themselves is ever intended to share the experience.

When she's more relaxed, she simply calls it kitsch, a laughable pastiche.

No critics will be invited to appraise their work.

No articles will be written.

No seminars will be conducted to debate the implications of hyper-expressionism as a late twentieth century aesthetic, or a new foundation for art in the new millennium.

No monographs will ever be published.

Even her insistent Mother has never been invited to visit the flat, though she had arrived uninvited one Ascension Day, Himmelfahrt, when Mo was fathers' day drunk and Inez had threatened to jump off the patio to show once and for all that it is impossible for girls to fly.

There had been other false starts to their decorative efforts.

The first followed a trip to Weimar, where they'd visited Goethe's thematic home of polymath collections and carefully orchestrated rooms with their statues, etchings and plaster casts. They were impressed by the fakery of the pseudo-garden house, a replica created merely for tourists to visit, (which is what you get for being selected as a European City of Culture), but after a couple of dedicated shopping days, Inez and Mo realised that to emulate his style was impossible. The mixture of statuettes and tasteful prints simply remind you of a hotel, or one of Victor Hugo's overloaded Channel Island clutters.

Their efforts really began to make sense with Mo's attempt to create an imaginary library, a virtual collection of desirable books and documents. Its foundations lie deep in the gradual development of his slow, but insistent psychological crisis', rather than any strictly temporal founder's day.

Mo's library will be dedicated to the theme of walls. That much was clear from the beginning. "I will dedicate myself to the creation of a bibliographic archive devoted to the noble subject of walls," he had surprised Inez by pontificating one morning over breakfast. Thankfully she had taken him at face value and treated the project with the seriousness he intended, if not the dedication that he would eventually demand.

A library presumes an enduring collection of objects. Sometime soon, he will have stolen all he needs, so the virtual is slowly becoming unvirtuous reality, a four dimensional transformation of place and continuity.

Enough books have been written about walls to fill several

libraries, Mo had discovered soon enough, or even to build one, assuming a disinterest in information retrieval. The great mass of wall-centred publications are more, or often less sophisticated manuals about the bricks and mortar structural particulars of building. Building and construction is such a gigantic world wide industry that there are rafts of publications devoted to the worthy themes of insulation, ducts and cavities. Governments have their say in the form of thick tomes, loose leaf systems and computer programmes of norms and regulations. An even larger number, (unpublished thesis' deploying the rhetoric of deconstruction abound), concern the ins and outs of decoration and aesthetics.

Great caution, Mo reluctantly admits, would be required on the part of the theoretical custodians of this imaginary collection, if they were to avoid the temptations of roofs and floors, though their intimate relationship to walls and walling, specifically with respect to the ritual, symbolic and structural ambiguities of towers and turrets, would make the choice enigmatic as an extended arch. The allure of a buttress might be fatal to the integrity of the collection, but as inevitable as a cantilever, the question of walls bearing loads would arise like shame and guilt throughout the body of work.

Moses Hoffman knows exactly what he wants. From clues in Ablett on cornices and Tandy on cornerstones, he had tracked down rarities, like de Klerke-Starr's monograph on Tuscan lintels, Yorr on render, Mainwaring and MacDonald on timber framing, and only after much searching, Carter and Ebbs' three volume directory of nineteenth-century Bedfordshire brickmakers, which a grey haired Miss Kinnings of the Victorian and Albert Museum in London had assured him was the key to English Imperial thought and the global smattering of Lutyenesque red brick Brit-build which had ensued, before capitalism rediscovered concrete and the British empire floundered in the face of modernity.

'Apertures', as Mo terms them in his general classification, are holes in the horizontal, while chimneys and middens are altogether different, subject as they are to gravity, splashing, gaseous bouyancy and convection as demanded by their functional verticality. The literature of chimneys is a world unto itself, typified by Mo's favourite Canadian Swiss epigram 'If there's coal in the hearth, Santa Claus will get his trousers burnt', itself a distant derivation of the medieval Bohemian expression, which translated from old Czech approximates to 'Hollow logs make lousy chimneys, but are a great way to start a fire to burn your house down'.

According to Inez, almost as much shelf space should be taken up by the closely related subjects of holes in walls; whether they should be left open, mere absence of murality, demurely shuttered, or closed off by various forms of filters, the invisible fulfilment of glazing, casements and frames; holes as apertures appointed with doors, turnstiles, portcullis', drawbridges and such-like accoutrements of access.

A much sought after volume, long anticipated, but undiscovered, perhaps as yet unwritten, would provide a scholarly introduction to the closely guarded world of peep-holes in espionage, government, romance and erotica. Mo often wonders whether this should be factual material, or a version of literary criticism, even, perhaps, a collection of those luxuriously bound Sadean publications, so popular before the cathartic Freudian First World War.

The complex allure of these subjects would probably suggest ancillary works on balconies, passageways, landings and platforms, every divisive element already anticipating a budding Juliet and her Romeo to enact its circumvention.

Above all, Mo covets each and every scrap that refers to the destruction of walls. Peerless among these is Galileo's treatise on ballistics, startling for its accurate conception of the parabola, a momentous step in the history of mathematics, as well as a practical guide for gunners and commanders of artillery, a profession Moses Hoffman regrets he was unable to follow for geopolitical reasons.

The collection he imagines will overflow with images of cities, European cities, Asian cities, African cities, American cities, modern cities and ancient cities, each surrounded by the symbol of their autonomy, ring after ring of walls with gates and towers, ziggurats of deception, ramparts, defiles and declivities of death to the attacker. No exceptions are made in Mo's mind, except for Jericho, where far too many biblical mirages crowd in as Samson shakes its foundations.

Samson was dangerous, a loose cannon, primed to topple any settlement close to hand.

And so is Mo.

Moses Hoffman is a smuggler and a thief, a lone hunter, who specialises in the acquisition and appropriation of books and manuscripts.

How else might a humble printer be expected to fund the project of his life? Across the globe, city folk built walls to protect them from attack, defensive walls, but Moses Hoffman had been born in the only city on earth where, century after century, the walls were purpose built to keep its peoples in, Berlin.

He wonders whether he would like to die in Jerusalem, in sight of the Wailing Wall.

He is sure this death in Israel would be quite easy to achieve, but he wants to live. Death has yet to find a place in his agenda. The library had begun as fantasy and taken form as a project. Now, it is an ambition he fully intends to realise.

"So what did you bring from 'stamboul?" Inez wants to know, once they've eaten their way through a bowl of green pasta in creamy gorgonzola sauce and stacked the crockery in the dishwasher.

He's been waiting for her to ask, "I think you'll like them."

She licks her finger for a final reminder of the blue cheese flavour, as Hoffman takes the well packaged carpet and lays it lengthwise on the floor. They begin to unwrap it, ritualistically, together.

The clear plastic sheath splits away without any problem, then they both kneel to unroll the rest, after Inez has untied three green ribbons and cut free the smugglers' deception, a small blue wax seal with the image of a porpoise stamped in relief.

"Careful with the brown paper," Hoffman cautions.

The outer layer of paper comes away after three turns and Inez sets it aside.

"Now for the difficult bit," she says and Hoffman grunts agreement, as he's concentrating.

The next layers are wound up within the carpet. They work carefully, slowly unrolling the carpet until all five layers of paper have been exposed and they can lift them free.

"OK, get rid of the fucking rug," Inez says curtly to Hoffman and he pushes the offending silken textile to one side, where it lies in a crumpled heap by the mouse grey skirting board.

"You could give it to your mother for Christmas," suggests Hoffman and Ines agrees, "Yes, she likes that kind of tourist kitsch."

"It's silk. A bit gaudy. He gave me the full sales patter," Hoffman tells her, disappointed that Inez doesn't like the rug, though that's a secondary issue, "Took the best part of two hours, felt like two days, but at least there was some opium in his pipe to pass the time."

"And goes some way towards explaining your choice."

Taking one end each, they carefully lift away the last layer of brown paper, revealing a large sheet of unbleached linen beneath.

Ines cautiously inspects a corner of the linen and looks to see what's underneath. "Good. He's packed them the right way round."

Once the linen has been removed, there's just a single layer of fine tissue that Inez begins to roll away around a piece of dowel. Beneath that, a field of lapis lazuli blue soon comes into view. It is decorated with a fiery golden globe and silver crescent, sun and moon.

By the time they've removed all the tissue, three sheets of manuscript have been revealed. Each has the same extraordinary blue for the sky, though the images depicted under these astrological heavens are quite different. The pictures are unblemished, not a single crack in the delicate surface of the paint despite their age.

"Look as though they were painted yesterday."

"Are they quill-pen strokes, or did they use brushes?"

"Both, Mo. A mixture of inks and paints."

The first image is a forest hunting scene.

Trees and bushes surround a clearing that is obviously intended as a secret bower. A delicately drawn young rider has become separated from his companions, who are shown in the distance pursuing a stag with their dogs. The young man, dressed in the costume of a middle ranking courtier, has entered the clearing and discovered a maiden in need of rescue. She has been bound and suspended from the branch of a tree by her feet. The girl is naked, her clothes strewn around the dell, a plait of dark hair sweeping to the ground and the young man is portrayed sword in hand, as he presumably cuts away her bonds.

The second sheet of manuscript shows the same couple in the luxurious setting of a palatial house and polygonal walled garden where they are portrayed in seven different poses of sexual pleasure, comprising each of the main geometric variations of manual, orificial and penetrative stimulation. A peacock spreads its tail feathers to obscure the scene from a group of massively turbaned Marco Polo merchants who are passing by the house. Presumably there is a substantial retinue of servants to keep the house maintained, but the young couple's privacy is complete. Even the representation of the buildings is mainly symbolic, with a highly detailed small scale image of an almost Gothic house drawn in the centre of the garden.

The same two young people also feature on the third sheet. Once again they are portrayed in the forest clearing, though here it is the young man who has been stripped and bound, while the girl stands before him, a sword in her left hand. A group of ducks in the bottom left hand corner are swimming in a small circular cistern, which wasn't revealed in the first drawing. The girl is smiling, of that there is no doubt, though the sword is dripping blood and the young man's head is lying some distance away from his body, which itself appears to have been sliced open, spilling his entrails in the sunshine, which picks out every meadow flower, while dark clouds threaten a storm beyond the trees. In her right hand, the girl is holding what could be his smoking heart, while a pure white unicorn with a spiralling golden horn looks on beneath the spreading branches of a blue and purple tree with exotic fruit hanging in abundant bunches from two of the boughs.

"Persian, fifteenth century, with European influences," says Mo appreciatively, "That's for sure. Look at the house, almost seems to be brick."

"I wonder which order we're expected to look at them. The beheading, the third one, is obviously the last, but which of the other two should be first?"

"He might have been tying his lover to that tree?"

"Why not?" Ines proposes, "There's nothing to confirm that he is cutting her down, rescuing the girl, rather than stringing her up, but she has definitely done for him in this last one. Notice the angry curve of her eyebrows. Look at the tension in her arm muscles. She must have been so wild, a fury, a frenzy, carving him up in so many different pieces. Do you think there's a picture of her in action? A murder like that could set off an epic blood feud, vendettas that could last for generations. Look, there's one of his feet being carried away by a dog."

"Oh, I hadn't noticed that," Hoffman replies, with a shudder, "Perhaps it's just a shoe."

"No, there's foot inside, you can see a bit of ankle between the animal's front teeth."

"Oh, yes," answers Mo weakly.

"The inscriptions don't help," Inez adds, leaning forward to look more closely, "That just says that her father had sent the young man a message."

"The father did that to his daughter, then her boyfriend!"

"No, there must have been someone else. I don't think she inflicted all those wounds single handedly. Maybe the Venetians had been sent to help. Perhaps the girl's father covered the bills? Maybe she is from a Venetian family? Now that would be interesting. We are expected to know that her father lives many many miles away, even perhaps in a different province, or another country altogether. He would probably have had to employ a team of three or four. The main wounds are caused by sword cuts, but look - there is an arrow in the girl's back, just below her right shoulder blade. Presumably it is intended to imply betrayal."

"I hadn't noticed that."

"A symbol of mortality, assuming the girl is mortal, or could she be a goddess in mortal guise, filling in time with duties as an avenging angel?"

Hoffman sometimes finds Inez over-keen in her analysis of brutal detail, the fine traces of violence and aggression, though she rarely overlooks the grand design, or the mythological symbolism of gesture, character and object.

Then he realises that, rather like the peacock, this is a misleading generalisation.

Their's is a mutual obsession. His own interest is defined through graphic detail, layering and shadows, washes, infilling, line and hatching, the technical minutiae of representation, while Ines concentrates almost exclusively on metaphor and meaning.

They eventually conclude that the characters are all drawn from a middle tier of prosperous Persian society, neither aristocratic, nor in any sense royal, perhaps the prosperous peasant farmer, who has sufficient land to become wealthy and dominate the village. The sons of such a family would have completed their education in Teheran and quite possibly have served the royal household.

They also decide that the three images could be part of a longer series of illustrations, a story with many episodes. Whether they are the work of a single master, or the product of a workshop, it is too soon to tell.

"It's not just a question of order," Inez declares, "We really need to know exactly how many images made up the complete sequence, which would provide a clue as to the timescale of events. "

Inez fiddles with the wrapping paper, wondering if a full set of the pictures would make a complete biography.

"I'm surprised they have been painted on paper, rather than parchment," she says, "Dressing animal skins to make parchment began in that part of the world. Paper had arrived there much later, via Samarkand, from China."

Her heads bows once more as she leans over the drawings, "An interesting contrast."

"What?"

Inez cocks her head on one side, leans forward and smiles at Mo, "Which of them is the leading character? Are these pictures part of a series depicting the biography of a young man, who dies in tragic circumstances, or are we looking at a minor episode in the life of a great lady who lived on, much celebrated, oft married and respected, to a ripe old age, the matriarch, begetter of a dynasty with the scar of an arrowhead as testament to an adventuresome youth?" She rests her hands on Mo's shoulder, but sounds provocative as she draws the distinction, a clever diminution of the male contrasted with a feminine presence of mythological proportions.

"I don't know how we can find out," Mo replies, consoliding the legend of their discovery, "They were taken from a library in Basra, which is all he would tell me. I asked Bozorgnia if there were others, but he said not."

Mo knows his Hamburg dealer, Hagen, will be satisfied with the almost perfect condition of these rarities, whatever their provenance and the possibility that there could be more to come would only whet his customers' appetites.

The price he will get is difficult to estimate.

A Persian drawing Mo had seen in the Sotheby's Autumn catalogue had been estimated to fetch around a hundred thousand, so far as he could remember. Was it pounds, or dollars and what kind of price had it actually made at auction? What would Hagen look for? Half that? A quarter of a million for the three, Euros? Stolen goods? Services to be rendered. It didn't matter.

Watching the expression on Inez' face, as she peers closer at the illustrations, Mo begins to suspect the manuscripts are more unusual than he had realised.

"They've been cut from the same sheet of paper," she says, as she sets them alongside one another, "You can see a kind of watermark, a blemish in the paper that carries directly from one edge to another, and there's another mark here." She lays two sheets side by side and the third corner to corner with the first. "That suggests there was room for at least five other drawings, or even eight more than that, thirteen," she says sounding a little puzzled. "There could be sixteen images in all, or, maybe, whoever made them spoiled some, or used the other squares for something else, though it seems unlikely. No-one would waste such good quality material."

He gazes lovingly at the symmetries of her face, then she smiles and says, "Let's take a closer look."

Mo glances over her shoulder at the disembowelled headless man and wonders why anyone would ever want to sever their victim's foot.

Will Inez have to explain the symbolism of the dog and the foot to him, or is it one of those self explanatory little motifs, whose meaning will become apparent in due course?

CHAPTER 5

Hagen arouses certainty and doubt in the minds of everyone who meets him, not least the officials and judges of the criminal courts. They are certain he is capable of multiple ill deeds and doubt whether they should really have anything to do with the man, but all to often they find they have no alternative.

He shares their dilemma.

Each morning, as he takes a bleak look in the bathroom mirror, the prosperous disasters of the passing years glare back in resentful opulence.

There are days when Hagen would happily snub himself.

Does the lower lip droop as a result of sucking thick cigars for decades, or is this some premature failure of his facial muscles? Were the eyelids quite so hooded when he was a child, the stubble on his cheeks so thick and dark when he was a young man? Surely not. Had his lips always twisted into a scowl like that?

A black marketeer from the age of three, Hagen is as prosperous and unforthcoming, as the city that surrounds him, his adopted home, Hamburg. But, like the place, he knows that he too is a product of bomb damage. If the blast doesn't catch you, there's a better than even chance the shrapnel will.

Hagen's back is pitted with the black-scar signature of an HE iron bomb, dispatched by plane from rural Lincolnshire, that reduced the front of their house in Berlin Neuköln to rubble.

"Tell them I'll be round the corner with your sister when they come to bomb our bedroom," Hagen's father had said to his oldest friend and he was right, but when the air was filled with razor blade fragments of flying metal, Hagen's little brother had first been shredded, then evaporated by the heat of the blast.

Hagen glances at the gunmetal sky, then down over the docks, where the morning tide has swept in another row of cargo ships. He hears the back door close, as Frau Ozgenturk, who spends two hours cleaning the house each day, goes off to her next untaxed 'three hundred mark' job. Then he hears the garage doors open and close as she gets her bike.

There are three dark blue BMW's in the garage, but Hagen very rarely drives and they remain parked there unused and half forgotten for months on end. Off in the distance a lorry noisily changes gear. The wheels of her bike crunch along the gravel footpath, then he is alone.

Hagen likes solitude. He would invariably choose solitude and a desert island, were the offer ever to be made.

Moses Hoffman will get here just before the others, a little tired after the drive from Berlin, but expectant, as he always is when they meet to finalise their crimes. Hagen finds it hard to define the division between business and crime, no less so now that he is settled and comfortable, than when he was a scrap of a kid. He has never changed his ways, but over the years, amiable lawyers have urged him to legitimise his affairs. He heeded their advice, signed the deeds creating trust funds and companies, then paid their bills, until gradually, he has discovered to his surprise, he has become immune.

The villa is his.

It had not always been.

The clients are beyond reproach.

Their credit good.

His bills are promptly paid.

This was not always so.

Money is being made.

No-one is likely to investigate.

That had never been the case before. Almost unnoticed, a massive grey and red container ship passes up river and a pilot cutter surges in the opposite direction. Deep in the docklands, the clang of a forge echoes across the water. Hagen assumes the workers are toiling at their trades. He is old fashioned about that.

The sun is nearly shining, but there are thicker clouds on the grey horizon. At ten o'clock, the rest of them will begin to arrive. It is morning, the right time of day to do business.

A car pulls up outside the house.

Hagen listens as the engine is switched off and the car door closed. Then the boot is opened; a pause, before it too is closed with a perceptibly expensive clunk. One pair of feet click briskly across the paving towards the house. Heard for the thousandth time, the firm tread of Mo's footsteps are unmistakeable. Hagen is unperturbed, but takes the gun from his safe and loads half a dozen bullets. One each should be enough. He puts it in his desk drawer.

He and Hoffman will have a coffee together, before the others arrive and it is time to make a start. Then, in less than an hour, everything should be settled and he can think about lunching in one of the fish restaurants overlooking the wharves. A little smoked turbot and some salad would suffice, then a fillet of plaice, or maybe sole, with a glass or two of Riesling, cool, fruity and dry. Perfect on a warm summer's day; never too bad to be enjoyed, whatever the weather. Essential self reward for a man like Hagen, who has nothing to gain from the business he's addicted to, but who always needs something to do.

Realising he is already thinking about lunch, when there are important matters to be attended to, Hagen is disappointed with himself. Is well presented food his only solace against the tedium of daily acquisition? Better that than mere alcohol, he concludes, wondering why sex plays so minor a role in his catalogue of vices. It is scarcely nine forty. Hagen wishes he was still only forty nine, or thirty nine, like Mo. Then he laughs to himself. Why is Mo trying it on, this lying about his age? Surely Inez can't believe this nonsense. He'll be fifty soon and that is something you cannot avoid.

Then the doorbell rings and Mo Hoffman is there, predictable as ever, reliable, not quite smiling, a little tired from the journey, the portfolio under his arm. The sky is clouding over again and it looks like rain.

They greet each other like old friends, but only 'like' old friends. There is a lifelong pool of mistrust to ensure they will never progress beyond the courtesies of dependent exploitation. Friendship in any normal sense of the word is out of the question. The catalogue of their collaboration is full to overflowing, but they both want a clear conscience if it ever becomes necessary for one to betray, 'sorry old thing', or even kill the other, 'even sorrier, but really have no alternative, I know you'd do the same'.

Hagen accepts that he has been cast in the role of a father figure for this Hoffman, who is all set to play the Oedipus at every road they cross.

It had begun in the fifties, when Berlin began to empty. Despite desperate efforts on both sides of the city to rebuild on the ruins of the wartime rubble, more and more people came to the conclusion it was futile to stay. It was neither the East, nor the West in particular that was being abandoned. The whole urban area was being rejected, as fast as it was being rebuilt.

The post-war black market subsided quickly enough when reconstruction got under way and soon the city was full of cheap second-hand goods that no-one wanted to buy. Encouraged by Hagen, Mo discovered that all he had to do to steal a book was walk into a bookshop in search of American comics and walk out with a volume of Goethe stuffed under his several layers of pullover. As a little boy, he was too thin and scrawny for the booksellers to suspect there was anything but undernourished gristle beneath the threadbare clothes.

Too young to read, or write, he could draw and the plundered volumes were swapped for cheap unruled school exercise books and rows of coloured pencils of dubious provenance. The reds and blues were purloined from railway offices, the green ones from hospitals and the browns from a local laundry.

At first, Mo thought the orphan Hagen wanted the books to read. Once, he had even been foolish enough to ask whether Hagen had enjoyed a book he'd discovered in a locked cabinet, 'The Golden Fire', by a long forgotten author Hugo Schneider. His question had been met with blank amazement, then the news was gently broken that Hagen simply resold the stolen volumes to second-hand booksellers in Charlottenburg, on the other side of town. Mo became his very first hundred mark note. So began their partnership in crime, one of the most enduring associations in that divided city.

Hagen was a special kind of orphan, half an orphan, his mother scarcely stirring out of the flat after his father had been arrested for his wartime affiliations. Hagen's father, Gustav, had been driven off in an American jeep to the prison camp in Oranienburg, where the Allies filled the Sachsenhausen Concentration Camp with suspected Nazi's. He had never come home and Hagen had never asked about his fate.

Tobacco in the form of pungent French cigarettes had been Hagen's original currency. Then he was apprenticed to a forger, who taught him which of the Americans were interested in buying antiques and works of art. Eventually, they would become customers for the books that Mo began to steal for him.

By the time he was twelve years old and Kennedy laid claim to being a doughnut, 'Ich bin ein Berliner', Mo had lain his hands on material from every significant collection in the city, including the Russian depots in battle grey Karlshorst, the grey office ensembles in bleakest Normannenstrasse and sprawling Friedrichshein, where the National Gallery collection had been stored.

While art and literature provided bread and butter business, their best paid trade was sneaking wartime personnel files from the bureaucratic archives. The subjects of these personal histories would pay for possession of the original, then find that another of Hagen's accomplices would visit them three months later, armed with remarkably detailed information about their wartime enthusiasms and praise for their diligence which had never been properly rewarded. The ashen faced bureaucrats, de-Nazified or not, invariably paid up and Hagen profited without ever being vindictive.

The sums extorted were roughly calculated according to the victim's ability to pay. Only once was there a shooting and Hagen paid for his school friend's funeral. The other erstwhile fascists went on with their careers, living quiet lives in the shadier green suburbs of West Berlin, in Grünewald and Dahlem, while in the east they joined the Communist "Socialist Unity Party", which rewarded idealism far less than it cultivated crude ambition, taking the nationalism out of socialism to be replaced by democratic centralism.

To the best of Hagen's knowledge, there were only three suicides among his little Nazi conclave, testament to the resilience of the administrative assistants, personal secretaries and departmental officials, who had worn a deaths-head on their uniform, but felt no sense of obligation and responsibility, still less remorse, or guilt.

In the mid-sixties Hagen moved from Berlin to Hamburg and twenty years later he had moved into the opulent villa he now owns. Time has passed and he and Mo have both begun to lie about their age. Last week, the woodwork had been painted again in Hagen's nouveau riche favourite 'royal' blue. There's still a lingering smell of fresh paint and first thing in the morning, he'd noticed indelible fingerprints on the window frame in his bedroom. Of course, that concerned him, but he was not over worried. The thieves had obviously realised his alarms were good enough, or are planning to return once the paint has dried..

The big portfolio Mo had lugged out of the rented Mercedes estate and carried two-handed to Hagen's door (portico is only a shade to grand a word), is now lying open. The drawings have required twenty large sheets of thick hand-made paper, the graphite of two dozen pencils and approximately one percent of his life to complete.

Each man is dressed for his part, Hagen in blazer and bow tie, the recherché gallerist; Mo in pullover and jeans.

The artist and his dealer.

The patron and his performing monkey.

The last drawing of the series has been contrived from the Istanbul sketches, which Mo had made from his hotel window. The sheet is almost completely black, a wall of oppressive night fixed in stone.

Hagen takes each sheet out of the portfolio and glances at them one by one. Then he lays them on an old oak table, where Mo glares down with intense curiosity. In Hamburg, they look different. He had expected that. The daylight is bluer here than among the shadowy greeny-greys of Berlin.

There are big confident images on some of the sheets, speculative groupings of highly finished sketches on others. Hagen is bewildered by what he sees. The most difficult is precise and unmistakeably a layer of stucco rendered across the wall of an Italian villa, but apart from half a dozen lines on the paper, there are merely the vaguest, almost imperceptible areas of shading. Anyone would recognise this as plaster, but why? A little smaller than the original, there are no specific features to distinguish the surface for what it is, no window frame, or brick, no hint of the building, not even a weed, or a crevice to house a lizard, or a scorpion, just an absolutely clear impression that something abnormal has happened against the slightly weathered smoothness, which is all there is to see. Were people shot? Had some latter day Bernadette seen visions of the Holy Virgin? Hagen suspects that immediately adjacent to the part Mo has drawn, there is probably some monstrous stain, gore, blood, something unspeakably caustic, a sign of desecration.

He asks, but Mo prefers not to reply.

Hagen has the impression that were it possible to draw without paper, Mo could quite confidently scatter a handful of powdered graphite in the air and anyone looking on would be convinced they were facing an edifice in stone.

His hand shakes uncertainly as he makes the offer of a price, which Mo agrees without a quibble.

Again the doorbell rings and Hagen leaves Mo to count the forty-five thousand dollars he has already packed for him in a Gucci leather holdall.

The doorbell rings once more.

A quarter of an hour later, all four guests have arrived. The fifth is a no-show. "My StaatsSekretar has a meeting with the MinisterPresident about our representative offices in Berlin," she explains over the phone. Maya Hadron is Head of Department in a Regional Ministry of Culture. Germany is a Federal Republic, so each Region has it's own delegation to represent them in the push and shove of central government, a kind of embassy in Berlin, where they enter the administrative sump of lazy liars. She is anticipating a move, the chance she has dreamed about for a decade, to abandon Karlsruhe for Berlin.

Hagen provides dry sherry, which none of them would normally drink, but it establishes an atmosphere of gentile expectation, a necessary mask in this world of moderate wealth for the commonplace emotion they all share, the emotion which in children is called greed. None of them pay any attention to

Mo. They want to know what Santa Hagen has in store and to hell with the elf.

The visitors disguise their acquisitive lust according to their professions. Fr. Hildebrand cups the schooner of sherry in both hands and stands silhouetted at the window as she stares down searching the docks below to see how loading is progressing on one of the ships she owns. The multi-coloured containers stand out against the green and white superstructure of the cargo ship, twelve thousand tonnes of steel, all shaped and formed correctly so the computer controlled machine will wander the seas, enduring voyages without end, from port to port across the globe. Her vessels rarely visit Hamburg and all she usually sees of them are the scale models that line the company offices and the photographs of damage lodged with their insurance claims against the expensive policies at Lloyds of London.

The old man, her grandfather, had boasted that in four and forty years of peace-time trade, they had never lost a ship, though he had sunk a score of merchantmen from his U-boat in as many weeks during the war. Then, in the space of a year after his death in 1990, three of their container fleet had vanished under the waves. Mona's father was unable to bear the thought of paying widows' pensions to seventy five Filipino families and promptly retired himself. There had been a memorial service in the Sailors' Church, then a celebratory family lunch and following that, Mona had been officially installed as the company's new chief.

Her ambition was fulfilled.

There were no more sinkings and her father had gone to his grave haunted by the conviction that his own bad luck had led to the losses. He claimed the Tahitian Gaugin he had bought from an energetic Venezuelan widow bore a curse. Mona knew this was nonsense.

The naval architects subsequently reported that metal fatigue in a series of welds, the result of hasty repairs by cut priced contractors, together with an unusually vicious typhoon season in the Pacific explained the sinkings.

Deep in her heart, Mona believed this too was nonsense and she blamed her father for the catastrophes, just as she blamed him for everything else that had gone wrong in the jinxed decade since her mother committed suicide by crashing the twin engined Cessna into the side of a Polish fishing boat off Iceland.

The Poles, of course, had come off lightly, as the newspaper reports confirm. Their vessel was strengthened to withstand North Atlantic ice, but the little plane had splintered into ten thousand flaming fragments in the gloom of a winter's afternoon, a thousand of which were, till then, a person.

Mona knew exactly why the crash had happened and told her father half an hour before his death. The doctors in Reykjavik had confirmed her mother was HIV positive and had probably been so for two, or three years before the diagnosis was confirmed. AIDS was setting in. Mona had watched as the doomed woman settled at the controls of the aircraft, then carefully injected two grains of morphine deep into one of the veins by her ankle. They never said goodbye, just a shy grin, the wave of a gloved hand and the mildest of shivers at the shoulder.

The little plane had taken off, then buzzed the coastline erratically, before circling round the volcanic massif of Hekla, when looping the loop once, she had headed south into mid-ocean and from here to eternity.

News of the crash reached Mona at the hotel, but she showed no signs of emotion, or surprise. She simply invited the blonde bearded coastguard to share her bed and rebuked him sharply for ungentlemanly conduct when Lars Larsson, as he happened to be known, declined. "Dear Lady, I am not a gigolo. Maybe my cousin can help you. He is also called Lars. I'll leave you his phone number."

She had to spend three weeks on Iceland, assisting the

authorities with their enquiries. Officially the German woman's unmarried daughter, she was treated with courtesy and consideration by everyone in the courthouse. Each morning, she would stroll through the town centre, conscious of the local people's stares and their gossip across the supper table later in the day.

For session after session, she sat petite and patient, a model of prosperity, elegant in the spartan, but tastefully appointed courtroom. The magistrate settled the affair by awarding a substantial sum of compensation to the Polish sailors for the emotional hardship they had been forced to endure in the fifteen seconds in which the little plane was visible before the crunch and a lesser, but by no means symbolic sum, for the dent in the side of their ship.

She paid the Polish captain in cash and accepted his invitation to join the crew in their celebrations, which took them exactly four days and nights to complete.

As the judge anticipated, the money had indeed assuaged their stress.

It took her four more days and nights to recover from their attentions and complete the insurance claim, before flying back to Scotland and on to Hamburg. Six weeks later she went to a priest and asked him to pray for the Catholic soul of the troll like foetus which lost its chance of a life as the result of her pharmaceutically induced abortion. One day, she had promised herself, she would go to Gdansk and see how the boys lived back home, but she never has.

These memories were rarely far from her thoughts when she goes to meet Hagen and the skipping shadows of clouds across the dockyards threatened to rekindle her scarred emotions, so she turns away from the view and lets her eyes roam round the room. She had been here many times since that first fateful visit when she arranged the private sale of her father's entire collection of fauves and post-impressionists to a group of collectors from South Korea. She missed the Gaugin, but bought a container ship with the proceeds and sent it on a celebratory maiden voyage to deliver the paintings to their new owners. This morning, under the command of a South African Captain, the vessel should be loading in Shanghai. On board, there will be fifty kilos of heroin and twenty of raw opium, about which she and co-owners will never be informed.

Mo knows each of Hagen's guests has a history that he's better off knowing nothing about.

The Psychiatrist, he has seen once before, but they've never spoken. Inez' mother had made some disparaging remarks about him after reading an article the man had put his signature too. He smiles sweetly as he's introduced, but Mo merely nods acquaintance. They have nothing to say to one another now, nor will they in the future.

The Banker is well-dressed, Mo decides, the right clothes for a slender woman of forty five. She is Hagen's type, too. Perhaps they are lovers. If not, perhaps they should be. Her eyes are a careful shade of blue. There is something unusual about her demeanor that Mo recognises. She is shouldering a massive burden of guilt for something which will inevitably be discovered, but is for the moment known only to herself. Mo thinks she will try to run, when her crime is uncovered. He suspects she has an open ended plane ticket and a false but valid passport tucked away in some corner of her bag. Would Hagen go with her when she flees? No, Mo concludes. She is the kind of person who will be caught, however hard she tries. He decides she will spend her sixtieth birthday in prison, but he isn't sure in which country, or whether she will ever regain her freedom.

Without bothering to ask himself why, Mo registers the look of complete disinterest on each of their faces, as they shake his hand. He is one of Hagen's people. All that interests them are

Hagen's 'things'. Mo wouldn't want it any other way. If anyone ever asks questions, all four will say that 'one of Hagen's people' was also there, then give contradictory descriptions of his height, weight, appearance and the colour of his clothes. Mo has been careful to present himself differently to each of them. To the smallest person, he stood very tall, to the slimmest, he let his muscles flop portly round his middle. He gazed wide eyed, then squinted. Mo hunched over himself, then set his shoulders back. One will say fat, the other thin and all the interrogators will get is confusion. The only things he cannot vary are his eyebrows and these have already been smudged a little darker than their usual selves to match the indigo deep blue of his contact lenses.

With intentional slowness, Hagen goes to his desk and waits for the guests to gather before him. Then, with a flourish, he whips away a dust-sheet to present the Persian illustrations and all four visitors forget Mo to stoop in admiration over the teak and leather desktop. A wall clock ticks and tocks with the swing of a well-balanced pendulum and Mo relaxes.

The Banker turns away for a moment, covers her mouth with a fine cotton handkerchief and coughs, just as a trail of herring-gull shit slaps against the window. She laughs and glances at Mo to see if he noticed the coincidence. He ignores her. Soon it will begin to rain. The gull screams goodbye and wheels out high over the Elbe.

The grating squeal of a lorry changing gear interrupts Hagen as he describes the manuscripts' provenance. The guests, now clients, must be assured both of their authenticity and the legality of the transactions they are about to undertake. He tells them the precious sheets formed part of a collection in Manchester, which were bought up by a retired orientalist living in Paris. This is true, up to a point. The retired orientalist is Bozornia's sister and the collection was paid for by her husband in Manchester, who she divorced two years ago. That was where Mo had first played his part, some eighteen months before the journey to Istanbul.

Hagen says a private sale has been agreed with the family following the recent death. All lies, of course, but there are letters with a notary's stamp to prove they are authentic lies, that the Balzacian purchase was completed in the normal way.

He isn't content merely to legitimise the sale. Hagen wants to convince his buyers that they are behaving honourably, that greed is really virtue. He needs their faith in his version of events.

The former owner's grand-daughter, Marie-Juliet, he tells them, has been blind from birth, tragic irony in a family, nay a dynasty, of art historians, but she has no use for illustrations. She will use the money raised from the sale to create a sculpture garden in the small private yard behind her home in Montparnasse.

The Ship-owner's scepticism is placated by the saccharine sentiment of this smokescreen. She can visualise the clumsy walk of a seventeen-year-old blind girl, slender and pale with a sweet smile, as she returns from the local baker with a pair of phallic loaves under her arm. Hagen's lie is a consoling detail that Mona finds appropriate. She will buy at least one of the Persian drawings, she decides, maybe more, depending how keen the others are.

Then she swiftly commits every detail of Mo's face to memory. He's a rogue, that one. Why should a grown man want to dye his eyebrows? She glances quickly in his direction, shape of head, hair, size of ears, eye colour (also false) and eyebrows, nose, mouth, jawline. Eight details make a set, which she will never forget. Hagen is a crook, so this associate of his must also be a crook. Her grand-father had advised her to pay careful attention to every crook she met and never to overestimate a banker, or his uncle.

Hagen settles his guests in the leather library chairs around the marble fireplace. Admiration over, their glasses refilled, he leans against the mantelpiece, one foot resting on the wooden fender, relaxed as a nineteen century patriarch in their eyes. Mo listens carefully to their mild exclamations of desire. The Persian pictures have charm. They are attractive, well executed, in good condition. None of the clients will say what they really think in front of Hagen. Mo tries to measure the glint of greed in their eyes. Then Hagen spins another round of half truths about the subject of the pictures. A half forgotten legend, according to him, of which these are the only surviving illustrated fragments.

Younger than the others, the Genetic Engineer is least able to disguise his thoughts, but it is the Banker who buys the set. She doesn't offer a lot of money, nothing like the heap of banknotes tucked in the smartly tooled satchel by Mo's side, but more than three times the sum he handed over in Istanbul. Hagen seems happy. Only the Ship-owner is disappointed and Hagen will promise her something extra as consolation by the end of the week. Perhaps they are falling in love.

Everything has been settled in less than half an hour. A cheque will change hands later, but first there are others items to be discussed.

Mona is the first to speak.

Of all the many things she learned from her grand-father, 'enjoy sex', 'don't eat too much', 'wallow in wine, drink beer, avoid schnapps', 'pay your own bills', 'don't bother with murder', 'stay out of the Black Sea', 'learn to swim with your clothes on', she derives the most unexpected pleasures from his suggestion that, alongside the writings of Richard Haklyut, she should read about other people's voyages from ships' logs. There is one, in particular, which she has never been able to get hold of.

Hagen nods sympathetically, notching up the theoretical price. Mo feigns indifference.

The Genetic Engineer gives Mona a look of surprise, then

glances sheepishly at the others and modestly articulates his own interest in some reading matter that he has hitherto been unable to obtain. Of course, the Banker and the Psychologist also mention curiosities they would dearly like to possess, but Hagen dampens their expectations.

"You can't always have what you want, though I will see what is to be done."

As soon as they've gone, Hagen wants rid of Mo as well. They would never let themselves be seen in public together and Hagen's appetite is getting the better of him. He wants his dinner. The table in the corner by the window will have been laid for him by now. The waiters are ready for his arrival. The fillets of fish are ready for the pan. It will take ten minutes to drive to the restaurant. By then, the salad will have had time to lose its chill and the turbot's smoky aroma will have reached a perfect balance with the flavour of the fish itself.

"I'll be in touch," says Mo.

"The drawings are just what I've been hoping for," Hagen praises with a smile.

Against his better judgement, Mo is flattered, "I'll tell Inez."

Then Hagen undercuts his compliment, saying, "You do that. Maybe she'll be pleased. I don't know why you stopped making prints. Inez knows better than you how futile this project of yours really is. To recreate the inner world of your imagination in the external world of your environment. An impossible distraction. Why waste the money I pay you?"

"That's our pact, to explore the boundary between a mark and a sign, the objective becoming subjective, the benign becoming dangerous, the external world impinging on the inner."

"Or a brick becomes a wall," jokes Hagen, "don't forget your money."

Mo nods agreeably and drops the bag on the back seat of the Mercedes, "Or a wall becomes a heap of bricks."

Then they part. Hagen heads for his meal and Mo makes a brief calculation about travelling time. The clients have made plain their desires. All Mo has to do is decide on an itinerary, then work out precisely what must be done to achieve their objectives. Multiple theft, without detection, or suspicion. Routine assignments with routine requirements, but careful calculation. Cautious, Mo. Careful about precautions.

He will drive back to Berlin, via a small walled town set on a hill by the banks of the Elbe, one of his favourites, Tangermünde, a place that allows him time to think.

CHAPTER 6

The Elbe is a long and convoluted river, in places almost too long for its own good, as the thrust of the main flow threatens to slice through the looping meanders.

Driving from the north, Mo finds himself crossing the broadest stream at Stendhal, where Henri Beyle was shocked by the brutality of war and changed his name. Then he drives carefully across the lowlands of a meander to his destination. Local drivers overtake him all the time, reducing their life expectancy by the minute. There are fresh crosses by the roadside with wilting wreathes to commemorate the youthful recent dead.

There is also a wide expanse of farmland, green at this time of year, yearlings and heifers, a circus camel or two out to grass, then an industrial district, before reaching the next neater town centre. Though Tangermünde is little bigger than a large village, there are a steady trickle of tourists, so the arrival of a stranger goes unnoticed and unremarked.

The town is graced by a red-brick bastion built by the Kings of Bohemia, who wanted to control an outlet to the sea. Their power extended this far, but no further and they never achieved their goal. The sea was never won.

The strong walls buttress a sandy cliff to create an elegant defensive ellipse encircling the market-place with its Hanseatic trading hall, a couple of monastic cloisters and the most important building in the ensemble, a warehouse sized chancellery, where the Bohemians stored their wealth. Like Prague Castle in miniature, Charles IV's border town looks out over the river and its floodplain, a breeding ground for swans and deer, a feeding ground for black and white storks, big white cranes and elegant grey herons.

The next distinctive building is some ten miles away, after seven hundred years, still the most prominent landmark across the levels, Jerichow, that Jericho with a 'w' that is the oldest red-brick monastic church in Germany.

Mo leaves the Mercedes parked near the Church whose tower dominates the Tangermünde skyline. A little falcon dives off the tower and skims silently over the rooftops as Mo pops into one of the inns, a 'gaststatte'. He knows they serve his favourite soup, the left-overs from roasts and game stews, with offcuts of sausage, ham, all kinds of cold meat, cooked together with paprika and tomato, then served with sour cream and a slice of pickled cucumber and a squirt of lemon, soljanka.

He drinks one glass of the local beer, which comes in a simple glass with a decoration saying the brewery was founded in 1365, old as the town itself, then he rents a room for the night under the name of Herr Stefan Marutis, Diploma Engineer, Doctor of Biotechnology and soon to be Patent Lawyer, of Bochum.

Mo has only one reason for coming here, to cache the money Hagen gave him, but the tranquillity of this carefully preserved little backwater allows him the peace and quiet he craves to reconsider his options.

Very few libraries have comprehensive security systems and the custodians of archives all have different priorities. They are for the most part resigned to the pilfering that makes every collection a leaky vessel. Mo needs time to think where the leaks have already sprung and to work out a way to take advantage. He has wandered through cathedrals, cloisters and university colleges where thousands of rare volumes sit on open shelves. He almost fainted in Bayreuth. The music room in Wagner's old home, Wahnfried, is large enough to hold recitals for an audience of eighty, or ninety and lined with books it doubles as a library. Tourists can inspect Wagner's personal collection of books and manuscripts completely unsupervised. Shocked by their lax security, he had hardly taken anything. In England, Mo had swooned over the College Libraries in Cambridge and Oxford, where under-awed students no longer expect to find the books they need, but ladders are on hand to reach the loftier glass-fronted bookcases. A cloister in Prague carefully ropes off the baroque reading rooms from leaden footed tourists, but the visitors' corridor is lined with ecclesiastically dubious texts on medicine and black magic. Mo knows clients who would drool over an old Prague edition of their local seer Nostrodamus, but turn a blind eye to a bejewelled Latin Bible, or the New Testament in Greek. That that is is, as Shakespeare wrote of an old hermit of Prague telling a niece of King Gorbaduc, (until it isn't, amended Mo). He loves these places. But for the need to succour his own insatiable private yearnings and the professional requirement to satisfy the greedy clients who crave rarities and pay so much into the bargain, midway between the devil and the deep blue sea, Mo would never dream of taking anything.

By contrast, the worst thing in Mo's world is the corporate archive, where security consultants deem the costliest fireproof vaults be installed to house every sorry scrap of paper that management can scribble.

The older the archive the better from Mo's point of view and the same can be said for his cache.

The baker's shop, where Mo meets Tom's wife, Angela, is a

fairly modest affair, but they manage to make a living. It had been a struggle for them to get started after the fall of communism, but the locals had gradually accepted them, as a pair of well-meaning, if idealistic 'wessies'. That almost all the historic houses in Tangermünde stayed in private hands throughout the four decades of 'real existing socialism' had helped as well. In fact, the whole town had benefited from private ownership, because people had striven to keep their homes in reasonably good shape and following reunification, the banks had been happy to lend against the value of their property. Tom and Angela paid a fair price to the widow, whose family had owned the bakery since 1924. Less than a week after the sale was complete, she left for Chile to enjoy her old age living alongside her brother, the Major, in Santiago.

Now, most of their profits come from the Saturday afternoon business of selling cakes and microwaved pizza's to day-trippers. They sell about a quarter at the shop, but mainly Tom supplies the little cafes and restaurants along the High Street with bread and 'French Tom's home-made' cakes. They had tried pies and pasties, quiches and pastries, but the idea of wrapping pastry round a filling is unfamiliar to North Germans and Tom realised he was putting on too much weight consuming those that stayed unsold. He has reluctantly had to accept that one man cannot transform a nation's eating habits unaided, though he might corrupt their culinary traditions without even realising his success.

Tom had learned his cooking from the French garrison in West Berlin and his pastry was his proudest achievement. The business of using fresh cream in his gateaux, rather than the sugary mass of confectioners' cream the Germans expect had been a struggle that ended in compromise. The 'bit of both' approach had gradually worked. Eventually, even the most doubtful locals had begun to ask for the 'fresh cream' Schwarzwalder kirschtorte, partly Tom suspected because he sprinkled a more generous shot of alcoholic 'kirschwasser' on the chocolate sponge foundation of the 'fresh cream' variety.

With her freckled smile and reddish blonde hair, Angela had never been a skinny woman and Mo notices with a flush of lust, that since his last visit, she had turned a corner from curvaceous to plump. Angela has been living with Tom for almost fifteen years now. Her schoolgirl affair with Mo (and several of his classmates) ended two decades ago, but they'd never fallen out with one another and the quiet spirit of their affection remains.

"In the back, Mo," she says, giving him a hug and a lingering kiss that surprises one of her regular customers and leaves a tourist tittering to himself. Mo hears her explaining that he is one of her husband's oldest friends, as he walks past the wooden racks where the bread is left to cool. Out in the yard, Tom is fiddling with the engine of his delivery van and he looks up as he hears Mo's footsteps.

"Here again," says Tom as a greeting, statement, or question, difficult to tell. His tone is flat and matter of fact. There's frost in the air and he rubs his hands together against the chill. Mo smiles and tries to look relaxed. It doesn't work. He can remember the night when Tom took a baseball bat to a soldier in the Quartier Napoleon in Berlin-Wedding.

"I'll get the keys," Tom says without much of a smile and straightens up. A big man with hefty muscles and powerful forearms forged when he worked as a forester in Berlin's Grunewald, he now keeps in trim by kneading two hundred pound's of dough every day.

The bakery is really two distinct buildings leaning into one another. Tom and Angela live upstairs, behind the shop. An old and long disused bakehouse abuts massively into the corner of the city wall, where it runs up against the solid brickwork of the Watergate separating the town from the riverbanks. Mo has been renting this centuries old bakehouse from them for seven years.

The baker's anti-social working hours are Mo's security, better than any rented guard patrol. His money had helped Tom and Angela keep their heads above water in the early days and while Tom would feel happier if Mo were to pack up and go, he can't renege on the agreement that had been a Godsend when they needed it.

When he returns, Tom is in a better mood.

"Angela asks if you'll stay for dinner?"

"Of course."

"'tle be meat, real meat, chewy 'spect, cow, or sheep. Might be pig. That alright. You haven't gone vegetarian on us?"

"Roast?"

"Sure. Vegetables too, I would be surprised. Succulent turnips, my 'friend'. Have you ever contemplated Long Pig?"

A love of fine baking has induced in Tom disdain for the carbonised arts of the roasting oven, but encouraged a dangerous fascination with the temptations of cannibalism.

"Sooner, or later, I would like to try everything the world's cuisine has to offer, everything Mo, right down to the juiciest tender morsel you can imagine."

He has a flashlight with him, as well as a bunch of keys to open the padlocked bakehouse door. They keep it shut up, to create the impression of a building which has fallen out of use. Tom hands Mo the key. As he slips it into the well oiled padlock and turns the key, the whole lock seems to fall apart in his hands as it flops open, heavy. The door swings slowly on its hinges and Mo nods to Tom who shrugs and turns away, as Mo closes the door once more. Locking it behind himself, he shuts out the sun and prying eyes. Tom has never asked Mo what he keeps there and he returns to the infuriating engine, without asking any questions this time.

Inside is an old 'Dutch' oven, built of bricks, with a central fireplace and chimney, then a peppering of nooks and crannies making shelves and alcoved ovens, so the baker could work with different degrees of heat. Nothing has been cooked here for a hundred years. A rat has gnawed at the plastic cover of the cable he uses to keep track of intruders, but everything is secure and he disarms the hand grenade, that serves as his final, if self destructive, level of protection.

Once he's sure he is alone, Mo pulls the door to, then lifts a wooden flap in the brick floor, revealing a long dry cistern, sufficient at one time for a hundred litres of beer to brew contentedly in the even warmth of the fire. Instead of hops and malt, there's enough money here to start a small bank and Mo tucks forty seven thousand dollars into the American corner and picks up a few thousand francs from the French and a million lire from the Italian. He's thought about a trip to Switzerland, but he doesn't believe that banking secrecy is really as secret as it seems, though he's dreading their eventual demise following the introduction of the Euro.

The illicit world has lost its faith in the German government. Even Hagen has been moving his money around faster than before. The drug business officially accounts for eight percent of world trade, so criminal preferences must be able to sway the money markets. Mo fears the world will end up with just three currencies, the Dollar, the Euro and the newly promised Chinese something-else. Anything else will turn to plastic. Africa, Latin America, Russia, India and most of Asia won't have any money to call their own. He's fairly sure the Yen and the Rupee will fall into the nostalgic oblivion of stamp collectors and numismatists, another well of intrigue that he's glad he left behind.

Every printer who has ever lived has stared at the portrait on a coin, or the loops and lettering of banknotes, to wonder, if only for a minute, whether his skills could ever rival the sceptical eyes of shopkeepers and bank-tellers to make forgery worthwhile.

Later on Tom bores Mo with his loosely woven tales of rural

debauchery, as they spend the evening drinking in the Gastestatte.

Poor Angela, Mo concludes, as Tom passes from conquest to conquest, each less improbable than the last. He seems to have fallen in with some kind of club, which the farmers and local businessmen keep carefully to themselves. Wives, sisters, nieces, daughters. The lewder Tom's stories become, the more Mo feels uncomfortable. Why should rural life encourage the lurch to wantonness that Tom is describing with an edge of Clintonesque excitement that increases with each glass of beer? Soon Mo has heard enough and he doesn't even want to spend the night in Tangermünde.

When Tom decides he has to be back at the bakery, Mo pays his bill and leaves.

Two hours later, driving past the old monastery at Jerichow, he'd felt a tug of desire, but he took the left turn by the gates as fast as possible and drove on into the night. A spur of the moment theft would be absurd, yet Adler's nineteenth century classic, 'Mittelalterliche Backstein-Bauwerke des Preussischen Staates', is sitting in one of the Museum's plexiglass exhibition cases. It would take three minutes to steal. Yet.... The book he already has, in facsimile, but tacked on the wall is a photo of Friedrich Adler himself, a practical grey-beard, who lived to be over 80. Mo feels a wave of sentiment as he recalls the solid pile of bricks they've stacked in the museum to demonstrate the characteristic 3.2.1 of Gothic bond.

Mo no longer steals on his home ground. A professional book theft here would only draw the authorities attention towards his hoard, so Mo drives on and the Monastery rests undisturbed.

After a frustrating night-time journey in the fog down to Brandenburg and the motorway, he's home in Berlin. Inez is in a good mood, but there's correspondence to be answered.

He sets to work, then, next morning, when she awakes, Mo has gone.

LONE HUNTER

The first snow of winter has covered everything.
There's not even a footstep to be seen.

CHAPTER 7

Deep in the Jamaican library annex, half forgotten books stand side by side on old wooden shelves. There are mice and cobwebs in a half-lit gloom of dust and the dry smell of decay. The silence is almost complete, apart from the rare clatter of scurrying scorpions. A year must have passed, since anyone had removed a single volume.

A gloved hand reaches up carefully and selects a thick black bound manuscript and it is gone.

A door closes. The motes of dust settle as if forever. A mouse scurries back to its nest. A snake strikes. The steady velvet silence returns, as the layers of dust find an even depth.

The next five yearly stock-check should reveal the volume is absent from its place on the shelves, mislaid, purloined, or borrowed and never returned? Who might know? The librarians will be puzzled, irritated. The hand-written notes and original manuscript of a colonial autobiography are not in their place. Edward Chatham, the man who wrote hundreds of letters to his childhood sweetheart Jane and never posted one had bequeathed an unintended literary legacy. Hoping for its return, the librarians will probably conclude in vain, that one of their colleagues has borrowed the book without registering its removal. A theft will never be reported.

-:-

Lunchtime in the small campus office of a Danish university researcher. On the windowsill, two cactus plants, a tangle of lemon melissa; a stunted fig in a pot near the coffee machine. The computer is left on, a password already entered. Voices echo from the corridor. A file is opened. For some peculiar reason, the contents of the file are printed, rather than duplicated onto a disc, downloaded via a modem, or copied directly into a portable. Ten minutes later, once the printer has finished whining, the file is closed and the computer terminal is left on, as if nothing has occurred. In the corridor, there is an audible sigh of relief, as the office door closes. It has taken longer than expected. The battered old briefcase is full, but the hairy tweed jacket uncomfortable. A bus goes into town centre every eight minutes. Quite coincidentally, two minutes later a virus 'worm' emerges in the mainframe. Within the hour, picabytes of information have been irretrievably corrupted at Universities across the globe

-:-

The attic is surprisingly tidy, considering the turmoil that had engulfed whole villages on the other side of the border with Serbia. Until recently it was used as a hobby room by someone who needed natural light. Next to the sniper's rifle on its tripod, there are a rack of oil paintings and to one side a desk beneath the skylight window. At the other end, there are steamer trunks, hat boxes and an old wooden chest with a Chinese lock. When the chest is opened, inside are a set of identical cardboard boxes. In the first cardboard box is a stout object, dense and compact, its soft leather binding warm to the touch, a book with a single word written on the cover, 'Confessions'. The cardboard box is replaced without the book. The chest is closed and re-locked. Decades may slip by before anyone notices that something is amiss.

-:-

The bank vault in Hong Kong is clean and well lit, a sterile environment with an elaborate electronic security system and ultra precise air-conditioning to control both the temperature and humidity of the micro-filtered air.

Its walls have been painted a rather pleasant apple green for reasons which are only apparent to the technologists who installed the infra-red security cameras. Surprisingly, the figure moving through the vault is dressed in clothes of exactly the same hue. An invisible man revealed only by his shadow. The documents are stored in rotating filing cabinets, which are driven by electric motors that make a slight hum as the correct layer of files are brought into view. The hand riffles from file to file and selects a bundle of papers which have been folded and tied with pink ribbon. A typewritten label reads, 'Last Will and Testament'. More than likely, someone Scottish, a Laird indeed, will have to die before the papers are missed.

-:-

In a side gallery on the third floor of the Museum in Nîmes, a visitor looks into a display case, shrugs her shoulders and walks away.

The alarms tick quietly to themselves.

On a nearby wall, the paint is drying.

The guard sees nothing unusual.

A card inside the case says in several languages that the 'Rheims Bestiary', which was donated by an 'anonymous' collector in 1910, has been removed from exhibition until further notice.

This is a half-truth.

The Bestiary has been removed forever.

76

CHAPTER 8

For centuries, the Contrascarp lay on the very edge of Paris. The Roman road led south and the Rue de la Muffetard began just outside the old city walls. Even the stoney Pantheon and the revolutionary 'Grandes Écoles' are part of the city's overspill. Those fields where Rousseau wanted to retire to 'cultivate his garden' are long built over and lie within the motorway ring of the periferique, where the newer suburbs of cars and concrete poverty now begin.

A stonesthrow from one of the few surviving sections of the red-stone medieval city wall are a seventeenth century farmhouse and a line of stables, a relic in the heart of the city, which have been converted into quiet rooms around a chestnut shaded garden, Mo's favourite French hotel.

No-one there is surprised that a guest should spend most of his stay sitting quietly in his room, drawing and reading, singing to himself from time to time. The Grande Écoles are nearby. Their libraries attract all kinds of visiting scholars. For decades the hotel had catered for students, who lodged there all year round and the mother and daughter who still own and run the place, enjoy old-fashioned guests like Mo, an echo from the past amidst the elderly and middle aged American tourists, polite parents with considerate grown-up children, who are the mainstay of their trade.

Mo has arranged his new books on two shelves. The computer print out is left in his suitcase. Apart from the formal application for Letters Patent, all it comprises are rows and

77

columns of the same letters repeated in seemingly endless combinations of the four letter alphabet A,G,T and C which will be popped in the post to Hagen in the morning. AAGT GTAA AGTA AAAT TGTT TAGG GTAC CACA CCAC GTAC etc, GGTA CGAT TAGT, etc, etc, CCCC & TTTT. Mo has no ambitions to read genetic code, but he is content to browse through the rest of his haul, skipping at random from chapter to chapter, or, in the case of Gerard 'Jed' O'Kelly's account of his Caribbean voyages, from entry to entry in the log of the East-Indiaman under his command. In the distance, Mo notices the noise of a lorry changing gear, then begins to read.

  While loading a cargo of silks in Macao, the then fifty-year-old Gerard, somewhat overweight and suspecting he is past his prime, has turned whimsical, remembering an earlier voyage and the phase of his career as a seafarer, that brought him fame and notoriety.
  'Following my orders to the letter, the men offered no resistance when the pirates boarded us, after a pursuit lasting three days across the open seas. We had spied the French held island of St. Martin and knew there is no better place to capitulate than in sight of inhabited land. Hand to hand fighting would have been more futile than is customary, since their frigate had canonry primed and we were broadside on to their guns. I estimate the 'capture' was completed within ten minutes, their men running swiftly through each deck to station themselves at well-conceived and pre-arranged vantage points. Only Joris Sweelink was hurt in the attack, when a cauldron of boiling water was upset and his legs badly scalded. I saw to it a cutlass quickly ended the agonies and his screams abruptly ceased.
  The young rogue who led the boarding party immediately informed my crew that they were free to join the pirate group, or would be allowed a jolly-boat to make for land at their

leisure. We were, thankfully, less than a league from the shore of Anguilla, which meant there was little prospect of their failing to reach safe haven. The other officers and myself were told to prepare ourselves in readiness to meet the pirates' leader, who had remained on board the enemy frigate.

So it came to pass, with these preliminaries that on the eighth day of April off the Antilles, I came face to face with my cousin, the notorious sea brigand, Tomas Oqueli, so known in Hispano-Irish, but acquainted equally to his men in the name of Captain Paddy Crookleg, firstly on account of our Irish ancestry in the County of Connaught and secondly owing to the unfortunate illness he had suffered in childhood, which rendered his knee joints immobile and bent like a prop in one of New Castle's coal mines, as second mate Geordie Shafto was wont to inform us, after regailing the entire company with musical tales of his silver buckled cousin 'Wor' Bobby and the wenches in those dark and dusty districts.

Taken under armed guard to the 'Blue Zephyr', as the 'Maid of Bristol' had been renamed under her piratical commander, I came face to face with my kinsman and we immediately fell to drinking toasts to each other's health in pure Irish spirit, soon after which, Tomas came directly to the point and made a suggestion which I did readily and well accept, being mindful it was a proposition I could not refuse.

Weary of the constant trials and perilous nature of commercial voyaging, I agreed to the compact, whereby we would sail together, my own vessel sporting the colours of the Merchant Venturers' Company. Thus we determined to intercept other vessels of the Company, plead our downfall at the hands of pirates, then turn the tables, taking control of our luckless victim's vessels, bloodying the waters and proceeding to bring their cargoes to market in the Florida ports and on to the rebel cities of New England, or the French stronghold of New Orleans.

Thus, it came about that I took to piracy, every one of my officers and men loyal to the skull and crossbones, as it was hoisted in celebration of our freedom to trade and profit from the energies of our own collective endeavours, a project which has sustained our prosperity these last fifteen years.

Only lately, due to a surfeit of our preferred spirit, rhum, as it is known to our French associates, has my cousin and brother in arms, Paddy Crookleg succumbed to the physical and spiritual decline which followed our passage round Cape Horn and afflicted him during our recent seasons of plunder in the Pacific and I have commended his body to the deep, as the sun rose above the yardarm. The knife wound that punctured his spleen remains the work of an unknown hand, so the necessity of maintaining good discipline gave me no choice but to see to it that the sixteen fellows now swinging by ropes from the crosstrees pay the final penalty for this heinous crime. Before the seventeenth was hauled aloft, the identity of the perpetrator was at last revealed and it is the Freisian, Petrus Leon Braun, who, tied across the mouth of a cannon, was at the touch of a match from my own hands, broken into a myriad meaningless fragments by the shot so fired and became the first of my dogs to make a shark's breakfast. Somewhat to my astonishment, no sooner had these monsters gathered to feast on those shabby Lutheran morsels, than a flotilla of Chinese fishing boats gathered to haul the bloodthirsty beasts to their doom and I have no doubt that soon after sunset this evening, we shall be offered some of that Oriental delicacy 'shark's fin soup' to set a seal on this grisly affair.'

Mo notices the next brief entry is written in a slightly paler ink and reads, 'The soup was excellent, as ever, but I have recently discovered that the so-called 'hundred-year-old eggs' are in fact aged for no more than a few months before being served at table. Enough to satisfy any curate, I should hope! I have arranged for a set of the shark's teeth and its widely hinged jawbone to be preserved as a memento of this sad affair and a reminder to my lads of the risks they undertake should anyone be so minded as to make an assault on my person.'

Later in the memoirs, Mo realises that this O'Kelly had become embroiled in the nascent opium trade and found favour once more with the British, who were already pushing to make the island of Hong Kong a base for imperial ambition and eventually rewarded their man with a knighthood, 'Sir' Gerard and a pension, 'to preserve his comforts after such distinguished accomplishments in Her Majesties name.'

He hopes that the Ship Owner will not become favourably disposed towards the modern flood of drug trafficking as a result of reading this survival from that altogether more callous age. A more callous age? There seem no grounds for generalisation. Perhaps their behaviour was more open, public displays of gangster style domination that would nowadays be resolved by a drive-by killing, or the quiet disposition of a hit man. Those pirates were as much a law unto themselves as any Los Angeles gang, but there weren't the police and 'law enforcement agencies' to be kept at bay, merely the representatives of maritime imperial power. After all, O'Kelly had been supplying the Parisian markets with silk throughout the Reign of Terror, without ever being intercepted by a Vessel of His Britannic Majesty's Navy, a privilege which had cost him a great deal of money to arrange following a prolonged negotiation carried on through the good offices of the overseer on Nisbet's Island, who had 'congenital' good reason to rely on the support of Admiral Nelson.

There are American voices out on the secluded terrace, where a row of white tables entice the hotel guests to eat the snacks and pastries they buy from the patisserie across the road, or drink a glass of the cheap wine they inevitably purchase from the supermarket by the cafés on the square. The sunny hotel garden is calm and tranquil, golden brown under the boughs of a massive horse-chestnut tree.

"Another book about surveying, I'm afraid," says a fifty year old male, a college professor to judge by the confident measure of his put downs. "First Umberto Eco with that preposterous overblown metaphoric ticking ship full of clocks, next Longitude, which had at least the merits of freshness, then Pynchon comes along with the interminable Mason-Dixon line. Now this, 'Oder, oder?", a German view of cartography during the Napoleonic Wars seen through the eyes of a feminist camp follower, contrasted with the experience of German soldiers propping up the dykes during the floods of '97. Well, I'm not going to teach this to the sophomores, even if they have seen the floods on double-u, double-u, double-u,wetnetdotgov. I want proper thematic development, not just people wandering around measuring and wittering about El Nino."

A Philadelphian female voice backs him up, "We at the 'Institute for Measuring and Testing' always find these literary appropriations lacking both in style and veracity. From a purely personal perspective, Monsignor Timmins, I also find the cheap jokes about 'dykes' and 'dykes' equally unprepossessing."

"Ambrose Bierce started it, that short story, 'Theodolites in the Civil War' or whatever," adds a younger voice, male and pre-doctoral. "Surveyors are the unarmed dogs of war. You always find these guys are practical, yet high minded men caught up in deeds and deals beneath their lofty ideals of scientific training and authors can let them be shocked by the barbarities around them. I see the attraction, especially to snipers. At least one of the heroes must get shot."

"Do you, indeed?" replies another voice in camp disapproval.

"Shut up, Manson," says someone else.

Sitting at his desk, about to open the 'Confessions' for the first time, Mo wishes he'd included a few maps in his current haul and could present himself before the tourists as the author of a sprawling novel about the Cartography of Mass Destruction, featuring perhaps, a couple of pathfinder navigators in a World War Two bombing wave, the mapping of ocean trenches by U-boat commanders and a 'Star Wars' technician in the Reagan years who must compute the anticipated trajectories of hostile thermonuclear missiles before breakfast, but is interrupted by the completely unexpected news that suicide hijackers have flown a brace of planes into the World Trade Centre. The story would be deconstructed by his Mother, Magdalena, known as Lena, maiden name Vonnegut, as she tries to calculated a safe wall-hugging route home from work during an Anglo-American daylight air-raid over Berlin.

Instead, just as another voice asks the tourists if they would like to see 'Foucault's Pendulum', he shuts out the conversation and opens the volume in front of him.

The leather binding is in poor condition and the pages slightly 'foxed', but the 'marble' end papers have been hand made. On the title page, in an introductory paragraph, the author claims to be a friend of Voltaire, having met the philosophe during his stay as a guest of Frederick the Great in Potsdam, which may, or may not have been the case. Mo has a soft spot for Voltaire. Depressed by the goings on in militaristic Brandenburg, the Frenchman had left without warning, which infuriated Old Fritz, who had him arrested at Frankfurt on the grounds that Voltaire had stolen some books from the Library in Sanssouci. Well, Mo had also purloined a piece or two from the palace, without being apprehended, which put him one up on Voltaire, who probably hadn't pinched a thing.

The 'Confessions' are a family history of an epistolary nature, a couple of hundred pages spread unevenly over three generations by a 'dutiful' grand-daughter, though Mo can't work out whether the mixture of printed text and hand written missives which have been bound together are a literary concoction, an elaborate forgery, or some genuine relics of a not so guilt ridden seventeenth century conscience examined by an enlightened, but Sadean eighteenth century mind. The paper feels right, ranging from old to very old and the letters themselves are tucked and folded, so the reader has no sense of their being other than the original. Mo wonders what the Banker will make of her acquisition and who she might read them to. The first chapter, 'kapitel eins', introduces the author as one Veronica von Beelitz-Harburg. Mo wonders whether this is already a falsification, Beelitz being a village outside Berlin and centre of asparagus production, in particular, 'spargel' of the priapic and aromatic thick stemmed white variety. The only Harburg, Mo has heard of is a suburb of Hamburg.

Her first set of correspondence is initiated by one Albrecht, who seems to have fled his family sometime during the Thirty Years War.

Unfolding the letter without causing a minor tear in the paper is tricky and Mo is tempted to removed the white cotton gloves he's been wearing, but he perseveres. Sweat is bad for the paper. A trail of fingerprints and DNA is bad for Mo, who is careful where he sneezes.

The printed introduction is commendably brief, yet enticing.

'On the day that Frederick the Great's grandfather was born, Albrecht wrote to his sister with a warning against the wartime temptations of depravity.' A clever combination of famous names, scandal and intimacy, reminiscent of the popular press several centuries later.

"Gentle Sister," the letter begins, once Mo has turned the book sideways on, so he can read the carefully formed old handwriting, "My knowledge of your humours and emotions may never reach such pinnacles of delight as we enjoyed together before my departure from our Father's house and the beginnings of your own residence in the community our Mother has described in her letters as 'The Sisters of St. Margaret', but news of a disturbing kind has reached me from an unexpected source, relating, as I have heard, to the employment of various companions whose duties it has been to care and comfort soldiery of Queen Christina's army. Knowing how formerly you thrived on my daily attentions to your needs, I implore you to consider joining me here in Antwerpen, rather than submit yourself to trýals born of a deluded sense of charitable works.

Your daughter, 'Immaculata', is now a maid of thirteen summers and much taken by the exercises we two perfected together, which I have been privileged to introduce her to, much to my own satisfaction and spiritual upliftment. My own considerable pleasure, notwithstanding the expenditure of great energies in the performance of these services, is nevertheless tempered by the knowledge that our own especial legacy in the pursuit of virtuous enlightenment stands incomparable, a nonpareil, in accordance with the rights and duties of sibling affection, which I would, unreservedly resume in pursuance of the duty which befalls me as a brother and 'nuncle', as your daughter is so fond as to call me.

Even as I write, my fingers are heavy with the rich scent of self anointment, while my left hand is free to smooth the fair mane of hair as her head rests gently suckling at the font of my contentment, which was thus freed and animated for the purposes of her amusement."

Mo skips the succeeding paragraphs of this ornate pornography to discover what kind of reply it had elicited. He isn't surprised that the handwriting reveals signs of haste, the (forged?) reply, supposedly, having been penned the moment Albrecht's letter had fallen into his sister's hands.

"My dear fondest Brother," she began, "Little can you imagine the joy with which I read of your devotion to my daughter and the place she has assumed in your fatherly affections. The education of a tender hearted child should be the priority for parents in all lands, though sadly, I fear, the true expression of parental affection is much frowned upon by those hectoring guardians of impudence masquerading in the guise of priests and censorious Bishops. Your devotion to duty aroused in me the sweetest of sentiments, memory, and I felt moved to reflect not only on the enchantments we shared, but also to recall the consideration shown me by our Father, whose valiant efforts were in every way a true demonstration of paternal affection. Any less considerate attention to my appetites and affections would have been intolerable and I exhort you to overcome any tears, or tantrums to ensure her pleasure may be complete. May I commend the practice of chastisement, painful as I know it to be for the sensitive bestower, who may reflect on the knowledge that our flesh is but the outward expression of God's will and to refrain from this practice only at such times as your own feelings and sensibilities prefer not to confront the iron tang of blood."

Mo wonders for a moment what the visiting professor would make of this as an alternative to novels about surveying and decides that these 'Confessions' would have an equally hard time getting onto a mid-west college reading list, unless a film was produced starring John Malkevitch as a distinguished censor much disturbed by what he reads and a frowning grey haired Jeremy Irons, post Lolita, as the sensitive if profane protagonist caught as it were 'red handed' pursuing a dalliance with Julia Roberts only to be dragged kicking and screaming in a dignified kind of way through a tyrannical investigation, the whole being resolved by Malkevitch falling for the good woman's extraordinarily arrayed teeth and her responding with renewed virginal commitment to the wholesome holiness of his vocation.

Three days go by, as Mo reads carefully through the fifteen acquisitions he has made in this journey through Europe.

Very much against his expectations, the Bank robbery had

turned out to be a very simple affair. Mo hadn't even set foot on their premises. An unhappy young woman, who had been working as a temporary secretary at Credit Mayonaisse was probably sunning herself on a beach by now. When Mo had approached her, via the recommendation of an old friend in the securities business, she'd burst into tears of joy at the prospect of leaving Luxembourg. The 'Will' he asked her to look for in the bank's archive had been sent to his hotel by motorcycle courier, following a couple of phone calls.

"Would you like me to burn the Bank down?"

"An interesting thought, but no, that won't be necessary. Perhaps you should talk to your boss about it?"

"He wouldn't want to torch the Bank. He loves the Bank. I'm sure he loves the Bank, more than he loves me and I know he loves me, more than he loves his wife. That's why I don't think he wants anyone to burn down the Bank. If you asked him to torch his wife, the answer might be different."

His most difficult moment had been on the roof of the Vatican Library. Mo found himself silhouetted by an unexpected change in the cloudy weather that allowed a massive moon to spotlight St. Peters and encouraged tourists to peer in every shadow. Fearing discovery by an observant and unbribed Swiss Guard, he had lain prone in an autumnally damp gutter for two hours, until it was safe to lower himself through the pre-arranged open window.

The volume carefully stowed in his rucksack, as Mo retreated, he had triggered the alarms, but his favourite precaution had worked as well as ever.

When the Guards arrived, they discovered a pigeon flapping around the reading room, where someone had carelessly forgotten to close a window. By the time they captured the bird, Mo was in Trastevere, eating thin slices of veal cooked with an even finer slice of ham in a sauce of sage and gentle Marsala, 'saltimbocca', which he was delighted to discover in rough translation means, 'jumps into mouth'.

However much he tries to persuade himself to enjoy Rome, Mo has always found it a difficult city and he had taken the first train for Vienna next morning. The ancient Fiat he had driven south from Turin was left abandoned at the airport. Eventually the previous owner would be traced and forced to pay a fine and collect the vehicle, but he would still have made a hefty profit and could sell the Fiat a second time. The papers were all in good order, neatly folded in the glove compartment where they would be found quite easily.

So far as he could tell, no-one knew Mo had even set foot in the Eternal City. At least three years will pass before the Jesuitical Treatese, a Critique of Freemasonry in Franco's Fascist Spain, will be missed.

From his haul of material, this is the only book he has had any qualms about taking. Mo suspects that Hagen's client in Madrid is trying to get hold of all the surviving copies and will destroy the book, once it has been delivered. Before that can happen, Mo will ask Inez to microfilm each page for posterity.

On his fourth day at the hotel in Paris, Mo leaves early and takes a fast train to Brussels that spits through the rain and arrives on time at the heart of the European Union. After calling into one or two bookshops, he returns to the station and finds a train that is ready to depart. Then he perambulates on the local railways, drizzling by half a dozen towns on his way back to Paris in the early hours of the following morning.

The books have been bundled into packages. Each one contains a postcard to himself which reads, "Dear Mr. Hoffman, here is something I hope you will find complements your collection."

He sends them from Eindhoven in Holland, Brussels itself, Ghent, Bruges and Lille, which is windy as well as wet. Two are dispatched by normal letter post, another couple as packages, then three others are consigned in the hands of commercial courier services, TNT, DHL and UPS, of which one is sent express, another 'next day' and the third by the standard 'sometime soon' service. The last of the packages, he has already dispatched by the railway parcel system and must be collected in a week's time from a station, 'the Ostbahnhof', in Berlin.

All this was very much in a day's work for Mo and he's in a good mood. There's a little manuscript he'll carry home in his luggage, 'The spilled ink business and loathing ready stead man, fear soft scarf burrowing machine shooting back yard Kentucky Jaspar targets tacked on the garden wallio...' Forty unpublished pages of cut and paste from the artist's studio near Rochester, a snip to appropriate now the Channel Tunnel carries trains from Paris to London and back inside the day.

He awakes refreshed at nine next morning, enjoys breakfast in bed, then settles his bill in cash with the ladies at the hotel. Kindly as ever, they wish him a safe journey and ask if he will be paying them another visit around Easter-time, as in previous years. As in previous years, Mo tells them he will send a fax to confirm his intentions.

Then he heads for the Metro, pausing to buy a croissant from the bakery opposite the very private gates that hide the hotel from prying passers by. He travels a couple of stops, changes trains to go north to the Gare du Nord where he can join the fast train for Charles de Gaulle Airport, until finally, after a delay for air traffic congestion and an argument with airline security, who confiscate his Swiss Army knife as a precaution against him running amok at ten thousand metres, 'many of our passengers are quite mad, M'sieur', he boards an Air France flight to Berlin-Tegel.

Once they have landed, the stewardess returns his knife in a brown paper bag, which a curious German customs officer insists on searching. Then Mo picks up the little green Lancia from the long stay car park and heads for home in Steglitz.

This time, there is no green cloud to drift across the autobahn interchange, but it's raining and there's a queue of traffic by the Exhibition Centre, so he turns off the motorway to stop start at all the lights along the ever seedier Kantstrasse, then he takes a right onto Leibnitz, crosses the Kurfurstendamm and rejoins the motorway by Konstanzerstrasse, which means this final leg of the journey home ends up taking him more than an hour. The Albatross Hotel is still there. He's glad about that. Sometimes he wonders how many albatrosses chose to holiday in Berlin.

Before he can get the front door open, one of the neighbours traps him in conversation.

A cat. A visit from her daughter, who brought the grandchildren, which cannot be the case.

The woman is childless.

The price of everything.

This is all news from another continent, so far as Mo is concerned, but he smiles, if only bleakly, as the old woman rambles on.

The man with a black dog.

Could he be, by any chance, an alien?

The man, or the dog?

How is his wife?

Will the world really end on Thursday?

"My husband is dead, you know. He had an affair with my sister in 1955 and dropped dead. Some say he was poisoned, but the police said I stabbed him with a kitchen knife on Christmas Eve. Good day to you, Mr. Hoffman."

The widow talks to everyone she meets as an antidote to loneliness, then goes home and weeps behind closed doors.

She had enjoyed a more varied social life in prison.

Neither Mo, nor anyone else is sufficiently interested in the old girl to alleviate her predicament and Mo harshly, but fairly concludes that her tears are completely justified.

CHAPTER 9

Early in the morning, one wintry day, as blackbirds are singing messages across the city and the magpies hop and chatter over the rooftops, Inez is watching Mo. A black and tan crow caws three times to announce the coming of spring, as it struts along the balconies. Mo is in bed, exhausted, unconsciously soothed by the song of the crow.

The neighbour's dog is bellowing refusal and the local babies caterwaul in unison, but he doesn't stir. The noise doesn't disturb him.

He is sleeping like a child, legs apart, arms thrown back, but he snores like an old man.

She is taking photographs. The Hasselblad is on a tripod to one side of the bed. The pictures are intended for an exhibition she's devising.

Once they're printed and framed, a group of four or five will be entitled 'Mo in bed', with a soundtrack looping his more violent snores to amuse the public. Some of them might mistake her efforts for 'art' and gaze on seriously, then Inez will be expected to decide. Unless she denies it publicly and categorically, her pictures will become art by default. Even if she protests, the serious critical gaze might steal them away from her.

The pale grey bedclothes are tangled beneath his arms. His hair looks lighter than usual against the dark grey pillow and his skin is more papery and paler than ever before. The pictures will be black and white, but in colour, Kodachrome colour.

Something in his expression has changed since the turn of the year.

Her last set of photographs show no sign of the little frown that has become a feature of his appearance. There's a hint of tension making a tiny knot between his eyebrows, the beginnings of a furrow on his brow.

Inez is both an idealist and a sceptic, which leaves her feeling suspicious about herself and the world in equal, yet opposite proportions. She has harboured feelings of suspicion almost all her life. They have become habitual. Usually she senses their onset and decides her doubts should be ignored.

Things are to be done, not worried over, so she shuts herself in the darkroom and processes the film, twisting it into the spiral and flooding the tank with chemicals. The sour smells of developer and fixer make her nose itch.

Inez' suspicions had begun to breach the boundaries of clinical depression through the uneasy cohabitation of materialism and mystical thinking that entrapped her mother long ago. This kindly woman succumbed to a very Germanic self-delusion in which worldly temptations may only be resisted if the house is a mansion, the garden an estate, at least one of its perimeter boundaries the shoreline of a tranquil and pellucid lake with a landing stage and boathouse, as appropriate.

Only then, confided Inez' mother Indira, is it possible for the German 'mystic' to live a life of simple self sacrifice. Usually male, a younger son of good family, she confirmed, usually in their fifties, usually divorced, usually with half a dozen children they never see, but send birthday presents of symbolic rather than material value, this Germanic 'mystic' seeks nirvana with the loyal help of a carefully selected group of acolytes and assistants, the majority of whom are, more often than not, young and female. A proportion will become pregnant each year, as the coterie evolves into a commune.

Of course, the petty squabbles and distractions of the unfeeling world are carefully screened from the mystic's attentions to be replaced by a luxurious sense of omnipotence. In these self centred confines, the Guru is arbiter to petty squabbles of a domestic order, which are never treated as distractions, but as key indicators to the successes and failures of personal development. Then, having attuned himself to the resonance of the universe, the German 'Mystic' begins to publish a series of books on 'self-healing and sexuality' for the psychologically fragile, in particular, pre- and post-operative cancer patients. There is no promise of a cure for their ills, but the readers will be convinced that they are personally to blame for their predicament and must assume a degree of guilt, both for the traumas and the pain they will endure as their afflictions progress and for the anguish they have brought into the lives of their families and loved ones.

As the nineteen seventies wore out and Inez had learned to read, her mother had decided to challenge patriarchal convention and establish her very own devotional assembly. Like the medieval abbess Hildegarde von Bingen, Indira has a preference for green robes and white wine.

Astonishing Inez, after more than a decade of concerted effort, from the humblest beginnings Indira had managed to succeed. She is even threatening to begin a therapy programme on afternoon tv. People from 'The Philosophy Channel' have been in touch and suggested a programme on the internet that would be sandwiched between crystal gazing (point a camera at a highly illuminated piece of rock, rotating slowly on a turntable

JOHN CLARK

in time to ethereal, computer generated music) and their hottest programme segment, the astrological phone-in. We need someone to wake up the audience between the stone and the phone, an executive had explained.

A great many people, all over the world, have an over-inflated opinion of their own worth, Inez had concluded long ago and nowhere was this so marked as among her friends and acquaintances in Berlin, an overwhelming proportion of whom convince themselves they possess exceptional talents and superior intellects. Their smug sense of self satisfaction would be laughable were it not for the embarrassing reality that they are convinced of their own perfection.

Thus, for many years, Inez' mother had been perplexed by the curious minor 'research' professors, oddball dentists and worst of all state sponsored artists and their creative bureaucratic keepers, who arrived at her yoga classes convinced that it was she who would learn from them as they basked in the glow of their own egos. It took, on average, six months of yoga before they telephoned the flat to ask if they could register for a course of psychotherapy, after which they would arrive for their weekly hour of self abasement with Inez' mother in which tears and blame were sprayed around with the abandon of grapeshot, friends and family vilified, parents and educators abused, colleagues and employers pilloried, all without invoking a shred of self criticism.

Inez had heard her Mother soothing these bruised and battered egos, but never once had she overheard her telling the clients her real opinion of their woes. A doctrine of truth without honesty. She told Inez instead. "Self-centred, foolish, vain, the lot of them, Inez, but we have to pay the rent, however humble the abode God wills we should inhabit. All very reminiscent of Bombay, should you be inclined to wonder."

Pay the rent, they did and God apparently willed that Indira and her daughter should live in a succession of progressively more

94

desirable abodes, so by the time Inez was ready to leave home, her Mother was preparing to re-establish herself in a spacious villa on the expensive shores of the River Havel at Wannsee, not far from the grove where the poet Kliest and his terminally ill girlfriend had killed themselves in Germany's most celebrated romantic double suicide.

No sooner had the lawyers rubber stamped the purchase of Villa Nothung and renamed it in the name of her company the Centre for Growth and Spiritual Renewal GmbH & CoKG, than the search began for a suitable group of impressionable young men who would take up residence with her and render their services as acolytes.

As the good sons of Stuttgart and Hanover, resident in Berlin to avoid military service, had offered themselves as 'Candidate Pilgrims', Indira's manner took a turn for the matriarchal, rather than maternal, reminding all her old friends of Margaret Thatcher during her war with Argentina over the Falkland Islands. This was a self-development programme too far for Inez, who firmly refused the role of 'assistant saint and handmaiden', preferring to stay on at school, where she could learn some real chemistry.

As a child, Inez had proposed all kinds of different lives for herself, in the full knowledge that only one would be chosen. Why not become a fisherwoman on the shores of the Bay of Bengal? "I'm sure I can do anything, but you cannot be everything everywhere. The privileges of a profession depend a great deal on the circumstances of place."

"Oh, to be a pig farmer in Ireland, a shopkeeper on the island of Tristan da Cunha, a librarian in Canada, preferably in Winnepeg, or one of the Klondike's half abandoned mining towns." Reluctantly, Inez accepted that she was attracted to exotic place names for their own sake and wondered if she should consider literature. Chittagong, 's-Hertengebosch, Saskatchewan, Kalamazoo, Lvov and Ipswich, anywhere with an excess of vowels, or a novel row of consonants evoked the kind of life she dreamed of leading - the Sage of Salamanca, that would do. The day to day experience presented by these vocations was a secondary feature of her fantasies, which presented a dilemma when the time came to think about leaving school and decisions were required that would define her future. Would she really like being a shepherd? All that wool and weather? The endless baaing? Narrow unfeeling eyes? Dogs and dips?

Her teachers were perplexed by the pairings she proposed. Inez' equated a dentist's training with life in the Caribbean; an electronic engineer's diploma would be essential, she concluded, were she to live in India. A banking qualification, according to her, would be an absolute necessity for Brazil. The permutations seemed endlessly compelling, her indecision resolute and ultimately fruitless, but one thing she learnt was that lots of things that might seem like fun for a week, or a month, or a summer, become a living hell if they are the only thing on offer for a lifetime.

Then she met Mo, rejected God in favour of reality, here instead of there and now instead of sometime, at which point, she prevaricated, concluding that reality was circumstantial, experience therefore conditional on situation, time and place. In common with many young people, Inez decided the less conformist the context, the more probable the potential for revelation, given that everyday life, so far as she could tell, brought most people little more than mind numbingly predictable repetitions and unaccountable bouts of misery. Her outlook was anything but optimistic, so she left school without bothering to register herself as a student, like most of her friends, or taking up a place on a training programme, like the rest. Within weeks, she found herself in limbo and was almost ready to accept her mother's offer of assistant sainthood, when Mo changed her life and she his.

They met by accident, during an accident, in the midst of an almost random sequence of accidental events.

Equidistant from the point of impact, where an old-fashioned manual typewriter landed on the pavement in front of them with all the force of a cast iron object that has accelerated under the pull of gravity from a lawyer's fourth floor office and disintegrated into a cloud of shrapnel made worse by the massive glass splinters of a shop window that cascaded around them, as the typewriter's rigid frame spun and sprang into a travel agent's office, their eyes met and immune from the chaos around them, bells rang.

Almost, but not quite, the first thing Mo did, was to lie about how old he was, knocking ten years off his age, while persuading himself this girl made him feel ten years younger, so it probably wouldn't show and maybe it wouldn't really matter.

"Hello"

"Yes"

"Would you like....?"

"Is that a question, or a suggestion?"

"Yes."

"Now."

The meeting didn't change her life, since Inez had been on the look out for Mo, or someone very like him for several days. He presented her with a Berlin permutation of a career option that might be accepted by the people around her and open up a world of opportunities to indulge her fantasies.

She would train as a photographer, she decided, as the typewriter parts were still tinkling all around her and a suspiciously sharp shard of glass came to rest against her ankle, instantly cutting a neat line into the leather of her lace up shoes.

"Careful, let me move that."

"Let's get out of here."

Mo would serve as the lifelong model for her work, a period

97

she anticipated, by the look of him, that would last between eight and ten years, by which time she would be in her late twenties, internationally famous and ready to move on.

She informed Mo of this decision within an hour of their first post-coital cigarette. He seemed curiously unmoved, agreeing with her and accepting a series of propositions she made about their forthcoming life together.

After a two minute pause, which followed the lie about his age, Mo warned her that he might live a year, or two longer than she expects. She is equally unperturbed, twisting a sheaf of curly hairs round her fingers and telling him she wouldn't be too dogmatic about the odd year, convinced as she is that there's no way he'll live beyond forty. Forty is a contentious number, but in those days world wearyingly remote, (as all benchmarks are once you've passed them), so Mo had taken a deep breath and suggested she stay awhile, which is what she did, having first corrected his 'awhile' to infer the 'foreseeable future', or 'til your death do us part.'

A quarter of an hour later, the negatives are ready and she unwinds the wet film from its spiral and leaves it to hang in the bathroom. Mo is still sleeping deeply, but he's finished snoring. Her archive is almost complete. She has recorded every detail of Mo's body as it ages from season to season.

A study of feet might be interesting.

She has about a hundred and fifty of these foot pictures, some single, others pairs and she decides to assemble them in a group to see what is revealed. Unlike faces, breasts and genitalia, feet are under-represented in the annals of photography. As ever, there is less than a year before Mo's next birthday, in this case the supposedly big four-o and Inez is already twenty six and a bit.

When he finally awakes, Mo squints and notices that Inez is squatting on the floor, her left leg outstretched, while the other is tucked neatly beneath her to make a seat. He stumbles out of bed and kneels behind her, kissing her neck, then caressing her breasts, nipples gently aroused, before letting his hand rest heavy and warm against her thigh. The hem of her skirt lies like a black line across his wrist, a fold of cloth cutting off the back of his hand at the wrist, as though in homage to ancient taboo.

"We should be photographed together," she says, her eyelids drooping half closed, as the words begin to slur.

"Yes."

Their favourite word.

Mo has come to expect her moments of reverie, though he can never anticipate them. Inez has enjoyed these erotic trances, as her mother had described them to him, since she was three years old. Mo had been astonished that the Mother of a seventeen-year-old should be so direct about her daughter's sensuality. He was equally bemused about her intentions. She had been quite specific using the word erotic about her child.

"Infantile sexuality should be acknowledged, but never abused," Indira had emphatically affirmed, "What you must discover is how to explore that self contained ecstasy within the world of your shared emotions."

Never having tried to fathom the feelings of anyone in a trance, Mo had half expected she would offer him advice about the kind of insights he should anticipate, but Indira had said no more and dropped several hints that he would be unwelcome at her weekly classes of erotic therapy. This was much misunderstood course of profession training for young women intending to become prostitutes and apart from Indira's exhausted, but ever smiling resident assistants, men were not required, unless they were prepared to make offers in cash.

Inez' mother, Indira Schmidt, soon to be tv guru, was brought up a Calcutta Communist with Hindu leanings, Buddhist principles and a pragmatic sense for the inevitable. She had somehow managed to end up married to, then divorced from an

East German physicist called Misha Schmidt who crossed from the old East Berlin, hoping for work at a Max Planck Institute. Misha had made one useful contribution to her development, explaining how the spirit of Christianity and Capitalism are inextricably linked in Germany through the single word 'Messe', which serves simultaneously to mean 'Mass' and 'Trade Fair'.

Long before she bought the villa in Wannsee, Indira had brought her daughter up single-handedly in a succession of communes and collectives in West Berlin's Kreuzberg and encouraged auto-eroticism, as an alternative to the dependency culture of husbands and lovers.

As Inez leans back in his arms, Mo feels the gentle curls and twitches of her body as the trance begins to pass. He has come to expect her moments of reverie, though he can never anticipate them. Mo has learned only two things about Inez' trances. First and most important, she insists, is that he must never interfere, or attempt to join in. Her trances are quite separate from the concrete personality who shares her sexuality with him.

Mo wondered whether it was quite so simple to distinguish between the different aspects of her sexual psychology and decided he was not the right person to ask. Then he realised that if he couldn't ask, then no-one could and the world would have to wait for Inez to explain herself voluntarily.

No doubt Indira would transform Inez' revelations into a tv programme for the Philosophy Channel with a subsequent phone-in to mop up the perverts and entice them into the costly confines of phone sex chat-lines, or better the premium charge digital meditative channelling on the 'revelation on-line' franchise.

He had also learned that Inez rarely remembered anything about the contents of her dreams, if that is what they were. In the moments of reawakening, she is happiest when she realises that Mo's arms are around her and she can lean luxuriously against the warmth of his body. She simply recovers herself and describes her awakening as though reviving from a pool of well-being. "Were I a Christian," she'd said, "Perhaps I could describe myself as a bride of Christ, but as it is, I've no idea, who, or what begins to move me so. Perhaps it is the male half of my ego, that bears down on the female in myself."

When Mo hears expressions like this, he too shuts his eyes, at least metaphorically, and hopes for the best.

Inez expects that her half-remembered trances will not come into conflict with the exceptional, almost exclusively visual, sympathy she shares with Mo, but she can't be certain. That is a paradox, but it will hardly prove fatal. Only the passage of time will achieve that inevitable ending, however unexpected and whatever the eventual motor of its execution.

He envies her the special state of mind, her 'transport of delight' and is waiting as the years accumulated to see where it might lead. Inez realises that in an earlier age, these little trances would have been sufficient to condemn her to incarceration in an asylum, or the worst fate of a witch. She is thankful for Mo's arms and sighs, opening her eyes, then she turns her head to look at him directly and stretches like a cat in the sun.

As she begins to mumble and murmur his name, the doorbell rings and they shrug away their fantasy to take delivery of a small book sized package.

The delivery man in a brown uniform proffers an equally brown hand-held computer for Mo to sign using a little electric pen, which he does.

"At last," says Mo, "Thank you so much, I thought it had been lost," as he accepts the parcel, but the delivery man is already on his way.

"Beware the ocelot," Mo shouts after him, but the man has gone.

A catlike growl comes from an apartment two floors down.

The footsteps quicken, the growl subsides and Mo gently closes the door.

Inez watches intently as Mo peers closely at the package, turning it this way and that, a puzzled expression on his face. It should have been delivered weeks ago.

"Funny how parcels always seem different when they finally arrive."

"You always say that," Inez reminds him, "It's the battering they take in the depots, all that rolling along conveyors and plopping into skips. This one was obviously left lying around in some obscure corner of a delivery van."

Mo opens the parcel calmly and removes the handwritten note which reads, 'Dear Mr. Hoffman, Here is something I hope you will find compliments your collection.'

Then he takes out the carefully protected volume, unwraps the bubble plastic and drops the book, as if he has been burned.

"Don't touch it!" cries Mo with alarm and looks at Inez with an expression of complete amazement.

She waits for him to say something more. Is the binding impregnated with poison? Is it about to explode?

"Inez, this is the wrong book. This is not the book I packed in Paris; not the book I took to the delivery people."

Suddenly, Mo twitches.

Inez isn't sure if this is the right word to describe the strange jerky convulsion, as every muscle in his body seems to contract simultaneously.

She wonders horrified if he is having a fit, or a maybe a brain haemorrhage.

The twinge leaves him curled forward, cat-like, first nosing out, then staring down its prey before the pounce.

"That", he stammers, in a voice filled with bewilderment, "is not the note I wrote. I never spell complement with an 'i'. But, the handwriting, the wrapping paper."

This mimicry is worse than anything Mo had ever expected.

Arrest had been an ever present danger.

Inez and he had understood that through all their years together.

Disappointed clients had often to be placated. Arguments over money had been won and lost, while there had been even more violent disputes over rights of ownership.

But this tit-for-tat substitution was a violation of an entirely different order, a gross intrusion of his most precious asset, his jealously guarded reputation, the hard won credibility he had garnered for authentic irrefutable theft.

The entire basis of theft as a customer service is to steal a particular, otherwise unobtainable, object. Sometimes this can only be achieved at great expense, the costs often rivalling the commercial value of the object to be obtained. But who would be interested in commissioning a thief who delivers fakes and copies? That would be to compound the criminality of theft with deception.

What would be more ludicrous than a thief, who can guarantee the theft has taken place, but because of this surreptitious substitution, the location of the objects, which have previously been defined in the category of 'whereabouts known but unobtainable', must tacitly be reassigned to the exceedingly odd and difficult to define set of objects defined by the words 'whereabouts unknown, mislaid in the course of theft'?

In circumstances such as these it would be foolhardy to expect to be paid.

"Pass me those," Mo says flatly and Inez hands him a pair of transparent medical gloves, which he puts on, then tentatively starts to open the cover to reveal the title page. No sooner has he begun to lift the book-cover, than his hand shakes and he lets the pages fall shut again.

Inez reaches out and takes Mo in her arms, as real fears,

illusory fears, forgotten fears, repressed fears, new fears, old fears and worst of all remembered fears, flood out.

He is cursing and crying and she is scared, as the terrors of a childhood spent dodging border guards, police and bullies is re-lived before her eyes.

"I was twelve," he says, "And the sun was blinding bright. The train rolled straight over me, where I had fallen from the wall of the Pergamon Museum. It was a foolhardy errand. We should have known better. The railway tracks run along embankments and bridges through the city centre, bisecting the Museums. I'd been climbing from the roof, like some alpine mountaineer. I wasn't surprised when I fell. I was merely dropping. In fact I felt a sense of relief that whatever the outcome, the silly climb had ended. I fell. I was falling. I fell onto the railway tracks, but stayed conscious all the time, or I would undoubtedly have been killed.

The driver didn't stop, or try to stop. I'm not even sure he realised anyone was under the train. I doubt whether he could have stopped.

There were hooks of metal skimming my hair, tearing my jacket, trying to pick me up and pluck me, as I was trying to lie flatter and flatter until all the carriages had passed. The live rail flashed a massive blue spark each time the carriage's contacts passed. I was burned on the cheek, but I didn't dare move.

Hagen was watching from the trackside, but he turned his back on me. I suppose he thought I was being killed. Later, he told me he couldn't move, but he couldn't watch either. He thought I was being shredded. I should have kept my eyes closed, but I was too frightened to move a single muscle and the fear hit me with my eyes open. The trains go through there every couple of minutes and as soon as the first train's carriages had rolled past, I knew I had to get off the track as fast as I could before another one came along. No-one can be so lucky twice. When the last shadow passed and the noise began to roll away, I sat up and turned to the left, just as an express from West Berlin thundered through on the track to my left. There were two more tracks to my right, one with a live rail running alongside, so I dashed to the side where a parapet ran alongside the track and walked along. Then I realised that I was on the bridge over the canal that runs in front of the Museum. I could see my shadow on the wall of the museum reflected on the surface of the water.

The next train was going really fast and the wind almost sucked me back under the wheels. Hagen had turned to watch. Our eyes met, then I looked away. I crouched on that parapet, hanging on by my fingers, then without even looking, as soon as the train had gone, I jumped. A sudden silence, falling again and I dropped straight into the water with scarcely a splash. Of course the police came, but they never realised I'd actually been inside the Museum. Hagen had the painting we'd taken. He'd rolled it up inside his jacket and once he'd seen I'd be fished out, he was off.

The next time I saw him he said he expected I would crash into some underwater obstruction, getting skewered by a steel rod, or broken on the cracked spar of a girder. The canals had been filled with all kinds of debris as the war came to a close, bombs and artillery shells, rails and shattered tram lines. Hagen didn't think anyone would have bothered to clear things here, because the ships never used this spur. He was right. He said my dive would have won a medal at the Olympics, so fine was the trajectory, so controlled and perfectly executed the splashless entry into the water. I was lucky, that was all."

Two hours pass before Mo is calm enough to take another look at the book. Outside it is beginning to snow again and the birds have fallen silent. Inez has learned more about the dangers of a Berlin childhood than she thought possible for a youngster to live through and thrive. The habitual alcoholism and brutality of life in the deepest hinterhofs, those gloomy courtyards surrounded by scores of flats, leaves deep scars, the kind that seem to heal, but never cease to itch.

When Mo spoke of his Uncle Ulrich's binges and the knife attacks he perpetrated to finance them, Inez recoiled. The murder of an American soldier and his girlfriend had only been the crime that got him caught. Mo lived his childhood in the rock and roll years of the fifties and early sixties, but he lived them in tenements where for a century and more, people had pitted their humanity against the brutal facts of penury and deprivation.

"We'd better have a look at this thing," says Mo eventually, a little saddened, chastened, a touch morose.

He sits down at the workbench, puts on the gloves and opens the book.

" 'Ars Muralis'," he reads aloud, " 'The Art of Walls' - A studie of the Meckanickes and Diverse Meanings Governing the Conception, Construction, Creation and Maintenance of Walls and Walling. Revised According to Ancient Principles by Marcellus D. Hadrian and printed at the sign of the Crossed Keys and Compasses, Antwerpen, 1669."

Inez says nothing. The subject is precisely calculated to strike at Mo's heart. 1669, the year of Rembrandt's death.

"It begins with definitions," he continues, the cramp in his stomach biting harder as his eyes slip from sentence to sentence, wondering where the printed page had really been set up in type.

'Consider a line drawn in the sands of the desert and you have conceived the first basic tenet of walling. The boundary, a border to be respected, one side and another, or to be crossed and in the crossing breached. Hold in your mind too, the rage of a storm across the desert erasing all trace of its presence.

Consider then a cave carved as a volume in the very rock of a cliff and its sides provide shelter, the second fundamental function of walls.

Consider thereafter, the combination of these features and their elaboration whereby all manner of strukturs ensue, from the constructs of Babylon to the hand that wrote its fateful message to deliver the Jewish people from captivity.'

Mo considers the elaboration of this subterfuge and is impressed. Whoever perpetrated the substitution has gone to extraordinary lengths not only to deliver the book in a credible package, but to seek out this even more extraordinary volume, a text which may prove the keystone of his collection, the fulcrum around which the entire edifice of his imaginary library might be assembled. He's elated and appalled.

A diabolic liberty.

The perverse humour of a spiteful child?

A Mephistopheles?

A Faustian parody?

Where had the volume been unearthed?

He has never seen the title in the antiquarian's catalogues.

The author's name is new to him, though Hadrian, of course, is one of the most wallish names in the world.

Inez suggests they run a search through the internet. Has the book ever been catalogued? A scan of the 'Staatsbibliotheek' in Antwerp reveals nothing, nor does the Library of Congress Catalogue in Washington. Mo logs on to the 'Not Extant' catalogue of books which are known to have been printed, but so far as anyone is aware have failed to survive the ravages of time and the slipshod habits of bookowners and their heirs. Three hours of searching from database to database brings no hint.

107

The author is unrecognised by Google, or Alta Vista.

No record exists of a printer working under the sign of the Crossed Keys and Compasses in Antwerp in the seventeenth century.

A mass of books and pamphlets were written and published in 1669, but none of them even remotely resembles this 'Ars Muralis'.

By the end of the day, when Inez takes over and follows some clues of her own, the only trace of the book's existence is the trail of requests that Mo himself has made.

"Do you realise," she says, "There's a reference here on the 'Not Extant' update, 'Ars Muralis', Author: Hadrian, M.D., 1669, requested. That's you. Asking for a book that you seem to have the only copy of worldwide. This morning, this book was completely unknown, yet somehow you've managed to bring it into existence. Virtuality."

"There's nothing virtual about the book, it's as real as you and me, even if it isn't genuine. That doesn't matter. If this really is the only copy," Mo says, taking the book in both hands and waving it in front of Inez' nose, "then whoever sent it only has to check, 'Not Extant' to know their trick has worked."

"Mo?"

"Yes"

"Which book was originally in the package, before the substitution was made."

Mo sighs, "It was one of my dummy packages, just a harmless old second-hand book, that's the point. I always send two or three times as many books as I steal. I think this looked rather interesting, something about voodoo medicine. I found it in a second hand shop in Lille. As a matter of fact, I'd been looking forward to reading it. Thought your Mother might find it interesting too. There was a second volume, too, 'The Irish Faustus'. I'd found that in Bruges. Now we've got this little mystery to deal with instead."

CHAPTER 10

Mo's anger is mediated by despair and cunning.

For ten long days and nights, he cuts himself off from the world and locks himself in the bedroom with only the book for company.

Even Inez is excluded.

She leaves a plate of food outside the door twice a day and ends up sleeping on the sofa in the living room, seeing Mo only fleetingly when he goes to shower, shit and shave. He doesn't say a word. A note requests chocolate, soft Pitt pencils in sepia and sticks of 3B 2900 pure graphite.

When Hagen phones on the third day, she tells him that Mo will call back later. By the end of the first week, Hagen is getting upset, so she has to invent a better excuse. "He's away on a trip." Hagen refuses to believe her. "Then why is he ignoring my e-mail, Inez? We have a contract to fulfil. He's already been paid. Why won't he talk to me? What happened to the delivery?"

She leaves him with the impression that Mo is ill, which on the ninth day is the way he looks, furtive and haggard, his face drawn from lack of sleep, his hair lank and greasy. On the tenth day he leaves a note asking for multivitamin tablets and mineral water. Instead she buys fruit, fresh Turkish apricots and a bottle of Montrachet, which the man at the wine shop insists is as good a French white as you can get. Her ploy works.

When Inez wakes up on the morning of the eleventh day, she

can smell freshly made coffee. The bathroom mirror is steamed over and Mo is sitting in the kitchen smelling of hot water, expensive shampoos and bath oils. He's eating toast and lemon marmalade, while skimming through 'Die Zeit'. The birds are chattering, as a thaw sets in. Down by the bins a rubbish lorry changes gear and showers a deafening stream of bottles from a skip.

Inez can hear Gisela Zimmer's morning programme on the radio, storm over Croatia.

"Nothing of interest," he says looking up with a smile and folding up the Feuilleton, as if the last week and a half has not involved perverse and self inflicted stifling incarceration, "I don't know why we keep getting it." The newspaper is delivered every Thursday morning.

Inez sits at the table and drinks her coffee slowly, waiting for Mo to explain himself.

He has shaved, washed his hair and changed his clothes. An old cord shirt and a pair of faded jeans. He no longer looks eccentric, but she wonders if he might be insane.

"I put some new sheets on the bed, the others were getting a bit sweaty," he says after a while, "Come and see."

Inez hopes these are not the ramblings of a madman. Where lies the borderline between merely mad and the criminally insane? Must blood be shed before the definition is explored?

A glance in the washing machine confirms that the sheets are charcoal black.

There's a long pause, as Mo finishes the coffee.

Then Inez wonders whether Mo mad might be a refreshing change to Mo obsessed. Artistically, at least, it should be possible to record and catalogue his descent towards insanity. Maybe she can concoct an exhibition from the results, 'Footsteps on the Road to Incoherence' (private title: putting your foot in it).

"My incarceration was a necessity," he says unapologetically, folding up the travel section of the newspaper and taking hold of the long knife they use for cutting bread.

Inez eyes the sharp blade nervously.

His hands quiver, but rather than embarking on a psychopathic rampage, he clips it to the magnetic band on the kitchen wall, Mo neat, and takes Inez by the hand, Mo gentle.

The bedroom door is open and so is the window. In so small an apartment, having the room returned to general use is a relief. The air can circulate again.

If Mo had considered himself immured, as the days dragged on, for her part Inez had begun to feel cooped up, especially when the smell of acetate fixer seeped under the bedroom door like a decaying bowl of sweet and sour pears. The quadrat metres had shrunk around her, while her wardrobe had lain on the wrong side of the bedroom door. The washing machine had been full when Mo shut himself in, which was lucky, but the permutations of mid-wash coloureds eventually runs thin. At the end of the first week her credit card had come in handy to stock up on tights, a very fine knit pullover she'd had her eyes on for months and a slinky dress she'd decided not to buy at least seven or eight times.

As they stand outside the bedroom door, Mo says "wait there" and for a horrible moment Inez wonders if he is going to lock himself inside again. She waits, then the door opens and she steps into the gloom.

Her foot crunches something into the carpet. She knows the feeling. One of the thick sticks of graphite Mo uses for his drawing has just cracked to a gritty powder. She takes her shoes off, then looks round the room. The furniture is intact. A relief. Inez had feared an orgy of destruction. He might have deconstructed the bed, the wardrobe, or her favourite object, a Chinese cabinet they'd bought in Singapore, but Mo has been more predictable. He has constrained himself to visual amendments.

There are drawings on all four walls and they are drawings of walls, walls which are Japan paper thin and walls that are honeycombed subterranean metres wide. There are dark inscriptions and mythical beasts, all set in an intricate network of perspectives. Where-ever you stand the perspectives are sustained, but lines that are unimportant from one direction, assume a new significance to lead the eye from another. Mo has created a compound image, one set of details forming the outline of a totally different surface, which itself becomes the defining form of another space entirely. Inez sits on the bed. She's been wanting to sit on the bed for more than a week, then shutting her eyes, she lets herself lean back to rest.

"Look," says Mo.

Opening her eyes again, she does.

Her bedroom ceiling is no longer as it was.

Shutting her eyes again, she gives herself a couple of minutes to become accustomed to the idea of a bedroom Raphaelised as a Papal apartment.

Then she looks properly.

First there is a jumble of disordered impressions. Then from the morass of a thousand entwinements, she gradually begins to recognise the details that create a new order. A revolution, or perhaps a revelation from above. The ceiling is a portrayal of their life together. A hundred figures, more, sit, stand, run, jump and lie their ways through all the times they've spent with one another, from Inez eating an ice-cream on the Leaning Tower of Pisa to Mo pissing against a tree in Wales. There are couplings she can recall with pleasure and contortions she remembers with discomfort. The green socks he had worn one Easter Monday in Prague had attracted their attention by fitting exactly over the knobs of an old fashioned brass bedstead and she can find them drawn in graphite grey by one of the architectural cornices Mo has used to evoke a sense of height.

After they had made love for the second time on that Prague

spring morning, Mo noticed that a small boy was sitting under an apple tree in the garden, replaying the scenes of their love-making on his father's video camera. Mo had gone to remonstrate with the boy, but returned laughing. He bought the tape for ten dollars and the boy had offered him others, one of his friends playing football, one of his father mending their car, one of the sea in Portugal with waves coming right up to the shore and one of his sister in her wedding dress and one of the dog with its puppies and one of the cat eating a fish's head his Aunt had given it.

"What's so funny?" she had wanted to know, as a squirrel hopped onto the open window sill and stole a hazelnut from the fruit bowl on the table. Even now, Inez can remember her surprise at the length of the little squirrel's furry red ears.

"The boy asked me what we were playing," Mo had replied with a chuckle.

Inez looks round the ceiling to see if she can find the boy with his camera and finally spots him tucked in Mo's armpit that time when she had been kneeling down in church and Mo had lifted her skirt and reaching round her, leaned his arms on the pew in front for leverage. Her face reveals an expression of religious ecstasy in the drawing, which Inez doubts was really how she looked. She can recall a not unpleasant sense of surprise and remembers looking round the basilica wondering if any of the priests would notice what they were doing. The drawing shows them as a monumental statue in its own alcove, a pair of sinners kneeling in mutual devotion.

As she looks, Mo stands to one side, then squats on his haunches to watch her. There's a smile on his face. A wicked smile that Inez likes.

The dome effect is a old trick, which works only when you look at the image from a particular vantage point. Two years earlier, they had spent a morning looking at Andrea Pozzo's painted dome at the seventeenth century church of Sant' Ignazio in Rome. Mo had been struck by the precision required to create an illusion such as this on which to build a fantasy. Perspectival painting, he had declared, commits the viewer to illusion, before inviting allegory. The viewer's imagination is opened up by the visual tricks and devices, so their mind is susceptible to mythical propositions and absurdity. Truth is an illusion, but the geometric veracity of the image convinces us that the illusion is in some unalterable way, true.

"I wondered whether to leave gaps for our future," he says, "Then I remembered the other room, so this is a depiction of our past. I don't like unfinished work."

Inez isn't listening. She's looking at herself. The image is less than two metres above her head, but the furthest she can see herself is a figure leaning nonchalantly against a cloud with her feet dangling daintily in mid-air. This pleases her. Inez is vain about her feet and Mo has depicted them in petite detail.

The fragments of exploding typewriter have also been exploited to make little platforms and balconies for their figures, while the shards of glass carry images in reflection.

The speed of Inez' memories seems unrelated to the rate at which she recognises the scenes Mo has recreated. Because the ceiling is so low and the image is intended to be seen from the bed, which is off centre, with the bedhead by one wall and a little towards one corner, the drawn figures are grotesquely distorted, curved and twisted to comply with the demands of three curving axis', which turns each straight line into an arabesque. She is quietly surprised to remember just how many times they have made love. Each image reminds her of a dozen other situations, when this way or that, they've fucked with abandon. How often has it been, a thousand, fifteen hundred, two thousand times, between the same two bodies. Mo has managed to visualise forty, or fifty variations, so far as Inez can recall, given that her own recollections are defined from a different point of view. Noticing the strains and contortions, distinctive stresses and expressions Mo has given himself, Inez decides that she will buy a mirror to help have a better view of Mo's body as he burrows and plunges his way inside her. Then she snaps out of this pleasant array of fantasies and asks Mo the question he's been waiting for.

"Mo, what about the book?"

"Oh that," he says evasively.

"Yes, that. What have you done with it? What was in it?"

"I haven't thrown it away."

"Where is it? Can I look at it?"

"Yes, but first let me tell you about it. Inez, it is a wonderful book. I hate every page of it. I could destroy it, once, but then I would no longer be able to admire it."

He unlocks the Chinese cabinet and opens the outer door, which is decorated on the inside with a painting of the red brick walls of the Forbidden City in Beijing. Then he opens the inner doors, which are illustrated with one of the Palace buildings. He unlocks the top drawer, before pulling it slowly open. The book is wrapped in a green cloth and taking it in both hands, he passes it to Inez. The gesture is formal, like that of a server handing the sacrament to a Catholic priest. Then he leads her to the bed, caresses her neck, strokes the fine hairs behind her ears and kisses her shoulder.

"Look for the drawing on page two hundred and three," he says, "it's about half way through."

Inez leans on her side, resting the weight of her body on her left arm, as Mo lies behind her, slipping his hand under the hem of her pullover and cupping her breast in his palm. She can feel his knee pushing between her legs and she lifts her right leg to let it fall again and rest easy on his thigh and calf, a comforting pleasure. The scent of arousal wafts as private perfume between them. Mo's erection is firm against her, but tranquil, content to bathe in her warmth.

Then she opens the book.

The page numbers are printed on the top corner of each leaf of paper as they open. The sevens, threes and nines are especially elegant, elongated so the eights, ones and fours nestle into their open curves. The zeros and ones have two styles, upper and lower case, while the twos and fives are more compact than usual.

Page two hundred is text opposite an illustration on page 201. The next page is blank and unnumbered. The illustrations have been printed individually then bound into the body of the book. Page two hundred three is the beginning of a new chapter. The first paragraph is set in small type, six point perhaps and consists of a series of subject headings, under the title, "On the Topicke of Nature, the Supreme Being and the Handicrafts of Mankind". "Beetles, Birds and Bowers - The Labours of Creation - Of Rocks and Minerals - Of Living Beings - The Sentient Being and Synthetic Action - The Lord Protector - A Quarrelsome Discours with Master Burgess Wilson - A Mason's Freedom - Mr. Newton's Optimism - The Skirmish by Tangermünde - Fellowship in Shadowes."

Inez decides the list is as uninformative as it is obscure.

The page has only four lines of full text, which she reads aloud.

'So as the crystals resonate, do reckonings and calculations of the finest subtlety form stratagems in nature. We may imagine that which cannot exist, yet harness its presence as a factor in the mesh of naturs engine and bring forth all manner of forms and structures, that once elucidated may then be rediscovered in the symmetries of living tissue and fossil stones alike.'

Inez turns her head and say, "I don't understand a word of this."

"Turn the page."

She does so and sees an even more inexplicable array of symbols and numbers arranged in four groups, like a set of formulae. On the page opposite are a numbered group of diagrams, which Inez assumes are expressions of the formulae she has failed to decipher. They are patterns, similar to the outline of different types of plants, a fern, an elm, an oak and a pine tree.

"So the book is a fake," she says.

"Why," asks Mo.

"The symbols are just a set of squiggles made to look as if they might be credible."

"Surely, if someone had made a discovery, then they would have to create their own set of symbols to express it."

"Of course, but I'm sure these drawings are copied directly from a computer programme. They've been simplified a little, but these types of calculations only make sense with a computer. They have to be repeated over and over again, before the shapes begin to make any kind of sense. Anyone working three hundred years ago would have to spend months just repeating the same calculation before any kind of shape would emerge. The only kind of person who might do that would have to be obsessive to the point of madness and locked up somewhere, like a prison, or an asylum."

Mo seems to sink a little within himself, "Inez, don't you think that might have been possible?"

"But, they would have to have an unreasonable amount of information, to have been aware of people like Leibnitz and Newton?"

Inez isn't exactly sure what she means, but she's been reading paperbacks about science and computers.

"Think of the little mansions across Germany and Poland," Mo proposes, "frozen in for half the year and quite cut off, hardly a town to call a city between Amsterdam and Warsaw. I can imagine some young aristocrat with a little talent, fresh from a couple of years at University, Heidelburg, or Prague, maybe with a young wife already expecting the first of a dozen children. They're stuck in the deep cold winters, there's no internet, hardly any kind of link with the world beyond the boundaries of the estate and he's sitting at his desk running through calculation after calculation, getting lost in an ever longer sequence of numbers and wondering where it will take him. What we think of as isolation was quite normal all over Europe."

"Your 'he' could be a 'she', of course, but it's too improbable, like knitting a computer programme by chance. It's even more improbable that their efforts would be recorded in a book like this."

Mo takes a little time to work out his reply, then with a hint of anger, or panic in his voice, he says, "But I find it less improbable than the notion that someone has spent the last few months faking the whole bloody book, just to send to me. An assassin would have been cheaper and quicker, come to that."

That is, of course, a sentiment with which Inez can sympathize, not that she would have wanted anyone to make an attempt on Mo's life, not yet, though the evidence that the book has been specially concocted to undermine Mo's credibility is beginning to seem more and more likely.

Looking round the room at all the drawings, Inez realises that the book has driven a deep wedge in Mo's identity. He had begun to draw in a desperate attempt to resist his feelings of defencelessness. Inscribing himself on the walls, he has been securing a breach, reinforcing his fortifications. None of his previous drawings have been conceived under duress. They were all outward explorations of his inquisitive imagination. But these new images are symbols to ward off intrusion. She wonders which she should examine more closely, the book, or the drawings? Then she decides that the only way to discover the answer is to ask Mo himself.

She beckons him to curl up in her arms, offering refuge in the warmth of her embrace. As he snuggles against her breasts, she wonders what Mo would fear most.

Then he tells yet another version of the oldest fantasy he has shared with her.

Eight years old.

The boy wandering through a bomb disfigured city street on his way to somewhere, stumbles upon a door that swings open at his touch.

The first time she'd heard his description, there were gloomy adjectives, which he subsequently exchanged for the hard edged brilliance of an amphetamine high and alternated with the mellow gold of late summer softened further by the gentle glow of old red wine.

This time, he simply describes the streets as they once were.

"Visualise a line of houses five storeys high, the rooflines a uniform twenty-two metres above the ground, Inez, with narrow pavements and an equally narrow roadway running east to west. The buildings are so high that the sunlight never shines below the second story and the footway is always paved with shadow. Towards the west, at the far end of the street is a school, red brick, dark with windows that allow no light to pass. When the sun sets in evening, it casts a massive shadow and consigns the road to a premature twilight, though the sky above is still bright." Mo sighs before continuing the story.

"Would you like something to drink?"

"No thankyou, Mo."

"The only vehicles to be seen are a black Auto Union sedan, a hand cart and a lorry delivering brown coal briquettes. The district was too poor to be worth carpet bombing during the war, so despite the ruinous gaps, the general pattern of run down decrepitude has endured to imprison its inhabitants for another hundred years. Evenly spaced along the treeless street are three gas lamps mounted on cast iron posts. They're painted the same dark green as an old hand pump that stands outside the school, a relic of the days when horses needed watering and the houses had no plumbing. There is no evidence of the city centre grandeur that begins a few hundred metres away, but to the east, there is a simple junction, where a bar dominates one street corner and a laundry hogs the other. They face nothing apart from a stretch of blank grey concrete wall a little higher than a tall man's outstretched arms might reach. Just behind the wall is a high concrete lamp post topped with a rounded metal housing that directs a bright sodium light downwards away from the street and behind that is a tower, higher than any of the houses, from which men in uniform gaze over the rooftops, using binoculars to watch every move that people make.

The boy has played football under their gaze, chased dogs and watched his friends' sisters with their dolls, but the men in uniform have never once come down from their tower to walk along the street and greet the people they watch from dawn till dusk and all night long, as the seasons shift from warm to cold and colder still until the winter plummets into February, then waiting for spring through March, their cycle of surveillance begins again."

Mo breaks off, "I wonder how many times I've dreamed this dream? Do you remember the rabbits? They colonised the death strip hopping to and fro between the Wall itself and the wire-fences on the eastern side. At first it simply looked as if the grass was uneven, with little hummocks, then you'd see there was movement and only after a few seconds of bewilderment was it clear there were hundreds of rabbits."

Inez has no answer. Of course she can remember the rabbits. When the Wall was finally breached, they scattered throughout the city and most either starved, or ended up as road accident victims. Apart from the slow moving military patrols, the poor animals had never seen a car.

Mo frowns as he returns to the tale.

"The boy is always surprised that the door is never there when he looks for it, either as an entrance to one of the old houses, or anywhere along the wall. It is simply there when he pushes and beyond the door is a dark spiral stairway that he is always surprised to climb and find that once he's rounded the first turn, it has no walls. Once he's climbed enough, the boy sits on one of the steps and eats a green apple. Then he too can pick up a pair of binoculars and gaze across the city."

Mo doesn't seem quite certain whether the boy is himself, or someone else. "It could be me, but needn't be, because I can watch him, I can see him seeing like me."

But this is his version of the city, of that there is no doubt. And Inez would like to free him from its nightmare.

Mo describes being high enough above the clouds to look down and see the sprawl below as if it is a whole, an almost logical array of streets. Then he will descend and district by district the relics of destruction emerge. Improbable wastelands cut a swathe where the branching lines of railway sidings are over-run by woodland, only rusting water towers breaking the impression of broad green spokes radiating as parks from the city centre. There are other open spaces, sandy and barren, with different kinds of towers, like the one at the end of the boy's street. A little lower and the unhappy shells of buildings gutted by conflict deceive the eye, a cruel mockery of habitation. The boy can glide lower and lower over the bombload rosettes, until the scampering figures of destitution, the greedy and desperate, flit furtive on the make, waltzing through a cheat and cheating the mazurka of murder. The sedative of repression has becalmed one half of the city where the dance of panic has subsided into listless melancholic drift.

The people's faces are pale as his mother's. Mass misnourished, too much of this and more of that, pink, fat as a bow-tied porker and diabetic, the eyes watery and pale. There are nearly three million faces comprising statistics of ill health. When Mo begins to describe the fear in their eyes, Inez makes a decision.

She will get Mo away from Berlin, but first she wants him inside her, so that he is completely embraced and can begin to forget his troubles. They don't need to move much. Her gentle rocking is enough to make him come. Then, as she's standing at the handbasin to wash, she can feel the warmth of his body against her back and she leans forward. His soapy hand is warm against her breasts, then warmer still as it works away between her thighs. Then he slides himself gently inside and she flushes with pleasure as, with one hand on her shoulder, the sway of his body gradually builds up a rhythm.

As Inez begins packing the green overnight bag she likes to travel with, Mo asks her plaintively to look at Chapter Eleven. His sadness has not been alleviated by their love-making and improbable as it might seem, he's showing symptoms of post-coital tristesse, a tear in the corner of his eye and an uncertain hand ruffling through his tousled hair. Inez loves Mo like a wave of hot chocolate welling through her veins.

"I'll read it when we get there," she explains, "No-one will know that we have gone. So, no-one can know where we've gone."

CHAPTER 11

"The Illusions of Wellbeing - A Period of Tranquil Deception - Hiding and Running - The Spirit of Another Age - Fortunes of Politics - Bastions - The Varied Strengths and Weaknesses of Siege Defences - The Gates of Heaven and Speculations thereon pertaining to God's Protection.

'The exposition of mercantile esteem and self-confidence conjoured by Master van Rijn, known also as Rembrandt, and his fellow portraitists in the prosperous city of Amsterdam and towns across the 'Low Countries', or Nieder Lands, as they are known by the inhabitants of those parts, was no sooner established and codeified as painterly convention, than in the year 1651, the model of man's insular condition, independent, resourceful and self reliant was dealt a terrible blow by a notable tract produced on that coaly island whose windy shores provide our North Sea with its western coast.

Were Master Hobbes the member of a less populous society, spending his time in streets less congested and foul than those of the Grete Wen, so perhaps his insistence on the Social nature of the Leviathon he describes in these writings may well have been less inclined towards catastrophe.

The roaming armies, whose engine of destruction was as much the motor of consumption without production, plunder, brought destitution to many North European lands and through death and deprivation saw the population reduced by one third of its previous numbers, so should we not be surprised that Master Thomas considers the life of man in time of war as 'nasty, brutish and short'.

The recent conflagration which set about Thomas' city and proved unstoppable as it consumed alleys and cathedrals, hovels and palaces alike should not mislead us into believing that all cities share London's sad vulnerability. The city walls had been much neglected and the flames sprang from district to district with complete disregard for the efficatious barrier provided by a system of walls had they been maintained in good repair unencumbered by the flammable shacks and 'lean-tos' erected by the press of habitation.

As the prickles of a cactus from the Spaniard's Potosi will give protection against the foraging goat, or the spines of a porcupine render the creature's soft body inaccessible to predatory fangs, so can the earthworks and structures surmounting them, make a great city unattractive to the roving mass we call an army, whose very mobility denies the necessary engines for swift and certain victory."

Inez has been reading for only a few minutes, but has already begun to jot down a list of words she suspects are inauthentic. Beginning with the word 'codeified', adding the phrase, 'painterly convention', she likes the idea of a sea being given a western coast, a suitable maritime inversion, which makes her suspect the author may have genuine connections with ships and seafarers. Most suspicious, she decides, is the conjunction of production and consumption, especially in this negative variant, an almost certain anachronism, fake, but still she isn't certain.

With pictures, Inez is always confident, but these are words and she doesn't entirely trust her own judgement. Her Mother had once warned her about Indian mystical texts, after one of their arguments about God and not God, or never God and not any more God, all in sing song Indian English. They hadn't got as far as 'will be someday God' and never did. If it wasn't for the calligraphy, her Mother had warned her, you'd be surprised how these ancient seers pen disturbingly modern ideas.

Then Inez asks herself when London might have been known as the 'great wen'. It sounds Dickensian, but she wonders whether the diarist Samuel Pepys may have used the phrase. Then she remembers that while Pepys was a Government bureaucrat and very much a city dweller, he worked for the Admiralty and had all kinds of dealings with the Navy, taxation and merchant shipping, which is maritime enough. Without really thinking that this is a long lost Pepysian essay, she discards the notion. Her Mother had filled her childhood with extraneous detail. Nevertheless, the book had supposedly been printed only three years after the Great Fire of London and she is more than content to believe that the aftermath of conflagration was very much a talking point, as King Charles engaged his architects to replan and build a new city on the ashes. So? Maybe the thing could be genuine after all, couldn't it, well, maybe, maybe not, but, you can't help wondering, can you?

Inez is sitting in the warm glow of an open fire as she's reading and a tingle of excitement trickles pleasurably down her spine, while the finest hairs on her neck stand up. The book has begun to work its magic. Issues of authenticity and age, of authorship and provenance are suddenly irrelevant. All Inez wants to do is read, snug and secure, where no-one will disturb her concentration.

Mo had built the fire as soon as they arrived at the cottage, using old newspapers as kindling to light the logs, which Inez herself had split and stacked to dry the year before. The cottage had been closed up since then and while there was no damp, the tiled floor was chilled with the lingering reminders of deep winter. While Mo coaxed the flames, Inez had unlocked the wooden shutters and opened the windows to let the cold air escape and encourage a draft to help the chimney draw. She opened the linen closet, letting the sheets and table-cloths air. Then Mo lit another fire in the cast iron stove they use for cooking and the big kettle slowly began to warm. Only then did they think of unloading the car.

As Mo carried the last of their bags inside, Inez parked the little green Lancia away from the lane, where it couldn't be seen. The colour gave it camouflage against the pine trees. When she switches off the engine and steps out of the car, something seems to go click in her head and she feels her whole body relax.

Away from the city, they have relinquished noise and she begins to hear sounds clearly again, the whir of a wood pigeon's wings, the sigh of turf as she walks back to the cottage, the faint rustle of leaves on a murmur of breeze and the scamper of a half awoken squirrel trying to remember where it cached its stock of juicey autumn acorns.

She wants a lot of sex and almost as much sleep in the next few days. Flush with the oxygen of rural air, she wonders if this might be a good time to conceive and her daydreams are filled with visions of little Mo's coveting books and building bricks in their kindergartens.

The journey had begun after a shopping binge at the HavelPark hypermarket on the outskirts of Berlin, frozen ducks, cheap wine and all. Mo had driven north for three hours, but the journey had brought them less than half way between Berlin and Rostock.

They'd travelled from village to village along the country roads, rather than the motorway. They stopped twice, once for coffee at a little café that calls itself the Toll House and once to look at Frederick the Great's country house at Rheinsburg, where he had lived as a young man. The restoration work on the Schloss was almost complete, so it no longer looks like an ill-used minor baroque masterpiece with rising damp, but is coming to resemble the set for a third-rate television costume drama. Inez noticed that the phrase third rate also has a nautical provenance. First rate, second rate, third rate, the quality of ships of the line. Mo wonders how long the paint will continue to look new.

Their intended destination could hardly be more different.

The sideroads from village to village around Fürstenberg, Lychen and Templin are little more than cobbled farm tracks, weaving around a landscape of shallow lakes and hillocky woodland. The three roomed cottage had belonged to Inez' grandfather and nothing had been done to modernise the place since the winter of 1945, when he had insisted the whole family get on their bikes and ride away from Berlin and the advancing Red Army troops. A generation later, Inez had loved the place as a child, learning how to fish with rod and line and trap rabbits using a loop of wire. She could shoot as well as her father, but the shot-gun had been left to one of her father's friends in his will, hence the supermarket ducks. Shooting is one thing, but Inez had never enjoyed plucking bloodied birds, so she wasn't at all disappointed and the local wildlife could enjoy another season of partial tranquillity.

Mo works at a drawing board set up by the window. He's been drawing now for a couple of hours. A lukewarm cup of coffee balances precariously on the sloping top. His hands are deft and precise, as he lays out the beginnings of a preconceived plan.

He turns towards Inez as she speaks, letting his hands rest in his lap, while he twiddles a pencil between his thumbs, but he can't answer her question about an author called Villard de Hounecourt, who wrote about human proportion and art.

"Never heard of him, but medieval painters certainly constructed their figures according to a set of formulae, which were supposed to correspond to a sense of proportion that defined beauty. They didn't look at real people or use models for their Madonnas, just as they didn't look at flowers, but copied the forms that painters before them had conventionalised. It wasn't laziness, just that the painters were interested in symbols, not a slavish reproduction of objects sitting in front of them. Looking was one of the wonders of the renaissance."

Mo laughs.

He and Inez have been over this ground a hundred times before, he usually proposing that representation of all kinds is delusion, while Inez prefers the word illusion.

"The infernal question of self-deception," says Mo latching on to the subject, "Your 'illusion' proposes the perceptual deception of a rational mind, but my 'delusion' is a greater mystery, less the pragmatic assumption of human sensibility, than a scream in the face of a creation that refuses us anything that the eyes cannot see, or the ears hear, or the fingers touch."

He sighs a little with contented sadness.

"Weighed in the balance....I wonder," adds Mo, with a hint of nit-picking to come and the threat of an argument about mathematics as truth or description. "It was no accident that Pozzo's painted dome in Rome was commissioned by the Jesuits."

"Commissioning an illusion to confirm our illusory sense of God and nature," says Inez, half wishing she could resist the temptation to argue. They had wasted April 1997 bickering about this.

"But proclaiming that wonder is no delusion," Mo replies emphatically. "Optimists!" Then almost as an afterthought, he asks, "Have you got through Chapter 11?"

Inez decides not to embark on a debate about photographic reality. Her cameras work. Yes, admittedly they have been designed, principally by Japanese engineers and are to that extent anthropic, part of a system made in the shadow of human perception, but the little lightproof box is a functioning object with its shutter and lens projecting from three dimensions into two in a thousandth of a second and the picture she develops will reveal all the qualities and quirks of Pozzo's painted dome. Anyone wanting to create the impression of a dome on a flat ceiling need only take a photo of a real dome, print it up to the desired size and paste it on; or even better they could simply project the image.

She takes a half stolen glance at Mo's undomelike drawing, then returns to the book. He has begun to shade a decorative border and is concentrating on the pencil's imitative curling tracks.

The next passage that catches her eye comes towards the end of the chapter.

'In the space of a few short decades of years, the Projekting Societies founded to undertake specific schemes of work, or Projekts so called, such as the construction of bridges, drainage of districts prone to flooding, or the settlement of distant lands, soon discovered the need for a new and altogether novel forms of organisation, that is societies, or associations dedicated not to the pursuance of particular schemes, but devoted to the interests and activities common to those who would from time to time discover themselves in the circumstances of Projektors, much as the Guilds of an earlier time had represented the interests of Masters working in those trades. The Conclave of Königsburg in 1641 was but the first of a series of more or less clandestine confrérences arranged in towns and cities from Pau and Albequerque to New Virginia and that Yerichowe by Tangermun, where it was decided that written money and credit and monies written down be deemed the 'capital' of this newly coined territory, a borderless commonweal of commerce and construction overthrowing the tyranny of coin and gold. Thus it may be said that those who build are citizens of a new country whose boundaries will nay be defined on a map, but only by the journeys and undertakings that will in good time surely criss-cross the globe, graced by our efforts in the Glorie of God, Größ Arkitekt.'

Inez' knowledge of seventeenth century economic history is nil, though she imagines the first stirrings of the industrial revolution were probably underway, whatever that might mean. She realises intuitively that these 'Projekting Societies' must have been some type of company, a firm or corporation and the bewigged Projektors dependent on the dealings of 'men of affairs'. What exactly was meant by a 'Chemical Wedding' besides a general sense of Rosicrucian bullshit? She remains unsure.

Inez has no trouble imagining the charred reek of London after the fire, as new building work commenced and the sweet smell of freshly worked timber competed with the corrupted stench of ordure and decay. In a fuzzy sense she recognises that the era of London's greatness, which came to an end with the first world war, had been evolving for only two, or three generations when the fire swept through its streets. The fire defined the city and is still, in a curious way, the template on which each redesign is laid.

It is not enough to have a city, Inez' mother had told her, it must also have money and for London, 'The City' had always meant money. Even though it is growing old, New York is still the world's greatest city and Wall Street a challenge that Mo has only rarely overcome. None of its larger cousins, like Cairo, or Sao Paulo have measured up. Berlin has never enjoyed such an era of pre-eminence, though the megalomaniacs often tried to force its attentions on an unwilling world. Had that something to do with what she reads next in Chapter 11? With the Government's arrival, had Berlin leapt up the rankings?

'The circumvention of convention in these times, has encouraged a general enthusiasm for obscure and occult rhetoric. So impenetrable is the dogma of established thought, that a feigned adherence to pagan gods, the pantheon of Norse and Egyptian cults, pre-eminently Osiris, the Greekish Mysteries of Ephesus and the Oracular Cults of Delphi, has driven the Societies to meet in dark and hidden corners, under a cloak of ritual, alchemy and gothicke intrigue. There will learned men spread despondency among the simple minded, while pursuing for themselves the newest and most effective ideas of mechanics and construction. Moreover, in the guise of charity, do they exchange contracts for works to be undertaken and from the excess monies thereof do they assure themselves and their families against the uncertainties of old age and decrepitude. Death do they hope to overcome by means similar to those that bring them worldly comfort.'

Their 'speculations', Inez supposes, are therefore more in the character of a mutual fund investment, than the subject of spiritual enlightenment and the 'Gates of Heaven' referred to in the chapter heading seems little more than the prototype for a benevolent society, or the sketchy beginnings of a primitive insurance company.

She tries to work the thing out from two points of view.

Firstly, if the document is genuine, as she hopes the book will prove to be, she will seek a direct interpretation; then she will ask herself the same questions from the point of view of a forger, hoping to uncover the kind of message its forger's paymaster might be trying to convey.

She decides to read on and begins to skim her way through Chapter 12, which enters the realm of prediction and prophesy -

a town planners' Nostrodamus, 'in the two hundred and eighth quartier, a rhombus envelopes an egg, but sloughs itself of glimmering scales upon those innocents parading below'. Inez is astonished. Only a few weeks before, she read how the new Galerie Lafayette in Berlin's Friedrichstrasse was having problems with dislodged windows and walling panels – the address 'Quartier 208'.

The city it describes remains unnamed, but is in the throws of reconstruction and redefinition. A city of guilt and hatred. A city of oppressed minorities. A city of lies. A city turning its back on all history, except to lie about its history. The descriptions are over-elaborate, the commentary a cynical critique of government and speculators hand in hand to despoil the historic heart of the city and impose a new pattern of streets and buildings that will shut the people out of the centre and deny them a role in their own affairs. This too could be the Berlin of Gerhardt Schroeder's Beidermeyer Social Democrats.

Such as it is, her conclusion is simple. Inez does not believe in prophesy. The description of the city is far too like that of Berlin since the Wall was brought down, an event whose consequences no-one had predicted. She concludes that the book must be a mixture of original material and newly made forgeries. Whether the original material might also have sometime been forged is another issue, one she won't bother herself with. How old must a forgery be before it acquires a representative degree of authenticity? A genuine antique forgery, typical of its period, when mendacity and literary deception motivated the passions of gentlefolk in every corner of Europe.

Sometime, while she was engrossed in her reading, Mo had stopped drawing, though she hadn't noticed. She can hear him rooting around in the kitchen, so she takes a quick look at the drawing board to see how far he's progressed. He has made a pretty accurate sketch plan of the cottage and its gardens, but it's purpose is unclear.

Mo's plan is more of an aerial impression than an architectural drawing. He's got as far as smudging in the line of pines that make the northerly and north east boundaries.

Almost hidden among the trees, her cottage is a simple single storey timber affair, built as a weekend retreat by city people, who wanted to pretend they could get back to nature. Surprisingly, they more or less succeeded. There were no near neighbours then and there are none now. You reach the place along a sandy track through the woods that leads down to the water's edge. There, next to a wooden boathouse with a shingle roof is a rudimentary landing stage.

Inez had always wished the lake was deeper, so you could dive crystal cool off the landing stage, but the water is only waist deep and it's a ten stride wade before the sandy bed falls away and the water deepens enough to execute a pearl fisher's surface dive. Maybe she could persuade Mo to extend the landing stage a little further towards the deep water.

As for the boathouse itself, there is a much used old rowing boat and another hull of about the same size, a model that her grandfather had spent many summers building, but never completed. The engine parts are stored in the cottage, wrapped in oily rags. One day, she hopes, they can get the little steamship working. There should just about be room for two people to ride in her, though she expects the paddle wheels will splash enough to soak them through, smoke from the brass funnel will sting their eyes and smuts of soot will cling to the white cotton of her summer blouse. No idyll is ever quite as it seems.

The garden has an unusual shape, because the parcel of land the cottage had been built on was hexagonal. Inez' great-grandfather had been a successful industrial bio-chemist and he told the family they owed all their little luxuries, of which the cottage had proved the most enduring, to the extraordinary properties of carbon when combined in the form of a benzine ring. He also told them that a hexagon is the geometric figure within which to inscribe a circle to make the Jewish 'six pointed' 'Star of David'. Originally, the cottage had been named Little Israel, but after 1931, they had changed it to Hexagonhaus, which attracted no unwelcome attention from the uninformed uniformed village thugs, who assumed there were 'new' owners.

One by one, the people who had brought the cottage to life had grown older and died, even if they were lucky enough to avoid the genocide. The presence of these little houses in the woods, were one of the reasons why the city's Jews had remained so placid in the face of deportation. There are thousands of them around Berlin, sometimes clustered together as idealistic colonies, sometimes built in isolation. From Inez' cottage, the nearest village is Himmelpfort, site of a medieval monastery and a busy tourist centre for weekenders and families. A terminus on a network of single line railways, the Ravensbrucke concentration camp is only four kilometres away and Inez thinks that the victims half dreamed that they would be allowed a decent life in the reduced circumstances of a sylvan arcadia. If anyone had genuinely harboured such hopes, they had been fatally wrong.

The Hexagonhaus eventually fell to Inez, after the death of a paternal uncle in Israel in 1992. He had only enjoyed six months in his adopted land, but her father said he had been happy, so Inez was content to accept the inheritance and considered selling it, (an offer from her Mother was politely, but firmly refused), but the moment she saw the place, she became determined to hold on to it.

When Inez goes into the kitchen, Mo is peeling Cilena potatoes and she leaves him to it. The cottage is warmer than the day before, regaining the specially snug feel you only get in a sun-drenched timber building.

She goes onto the verandah and finds a catlike spot of sunshine where it will be possible to read the book and bask in comfort. Skimming through the book again, she tries to see if there's anything resembling a story, the beginnings of a novel, or any evidence of fiction. Even the slightest resemblance to Thomas Mann or Virginia Woolf would expose the book as a fake, but she finds nothing, until her fingers discover a page thicker than the rest, one that is folded in upon itself.

The page is really a little envelope with three flaps to unfold, and as she does so, a square of tightly folded silk no bigger than the palm of her hand, drops onto her lap. For a moment her nose is sensitive to the aroma of sandalwood oil, then it is lost. Intuition has brought Mo to Inez' side, without her needing to call him.

"Let's go in and open it on the table," she says.

She turns the square first one way, then the other. The gossamer fine silk is as long as Inez' outstretched arms and the height of a good sized book. The fabric ripples under their breath and threatens to float aloft in the slightest draught, but it bears the faintest traces of pattern and colour, a series of eight rectangles. Only with a magnifying glass do they discover tiny particles of blue pigment, lapiz lazuli powder, clinging to the threads. Under the glass, Inez notices sparkles where minute granules of gold and silver have caught between warp and weft. The reds have been reduced to a rusty shadow and the greens are little more than specks.

Their conclusion is unavoidable, however improbable it might seem. The pigments are identical to those of the Persian manuscript drawings, which Mo brought from Istanbul. At some stage in its history, this piece of silk has been used to protect them from damage. In transit? A cover sheet in a library's display? Simple protection, centuries ago, while the drawings were cut in preparation for binding with the text? If the drawings themselves were an enigma, this was the ambiguity they'd been wrapped in.

Inez spends the next three hours trying to decipher the images, but the traces are too indistinct for her to unravel the patterns in any coherent way. She had hoped to trace the sequence of episodes, to decipher the story beyond the three situations they have already seen. Her hopes are soon dashed. She can find nothing recognisable at all.

"What if they're just samples from the same workshop. Craftsmen using the same materials. They needn't have been our pictures. Wouldn't that be possible?" she asks Mo.

"I wish we still had the originals," he answers.

"You could ask Hagen?"

"Not worth the bother," say Mo sounding regretful for once, "He'll have sold them on by now. I wonder if they really were originals. Maybe they came from the same workshop as the book? Surely, the bookmaker would never gamble that we would recognise the silk for what it is?"

Inez laughs, "You could always steal the pictures back, couldn't you? Then we could have them properly dated."

Mo smiles at her suggestion, but he says nothing at all.

It wouldn't be hard to steal the pictures, but it might be more revealing to uncover the forger's workshop.

CHAPTER 12

The little terra cotta bricks are no larger than Mo's thumbnail, but they can be laid and cemented like the real thing.

They come in expensively packaged kits. You can buy them from the sort of shops that sell educational tools for budding genius', rather than toys for children; the kind of place where Grandmother asks the shopkeepers what she can select as a present for her son's youngest, the dubious little angel who will be seven soon, but is astonishingly gifted in Latin, Greek and violin and piano and never picks his nose, so he must be a prodigy, because the Mother, herself a trained music teacher says so and his father, who is also a very highly regarded teacher but one specialising in classic languages, agrees.

Given a fair chance, Mo expects the bricks themselves will survive for centuries, before they eventually crumble into dust. They are far too good for children. But, in his heart of hearts, he knows that anything he constructs will quickly be undermined by seedlings, shoots and roots, the passing feet of voles and rats, a trampling badger, or the autumnal fungal snufflings of the local wild boars.

Still, he's interested in the patterns the little bricks might leave as traces to confuse some future archaeologist attracted by the hexagon, which, barring glaciers, is sure to be recognisable far into the future. These quizzical folk should have to ask themselves if this was some rare sylvan temple, a shrine of some kind, a monument perhaps? But a monument to what, a strange event, a defining moment in human experience, the unknown deities of war, or peace? The hexagon might symbolise the meeting point for obscure enthusiasts, the expression of a hitherto unknown religion, its traces ready for decipherment.

What kind of an illusionist would build with the archaeological future in their thoughts? Mo is intrigued by the obscurity of his own handiwork. He'd spent another three days working on the drawings, before he began preparing the site.

Now, a couple of well squared stones provide a solid and level foundation covered with a layer of fine alumina cement before he begins laying down the first course of bricks, which are to be firmly embedded in the mortar. He is already anticipating the directions in which the bricks might eventually scatter as the passage of time wreaks its inevitable destruction. Mo wonders which, if any, of the miniature structure's original geometric character will survive as a layer of highly compressed colour, or as scratches scored into the weathered surface of a stone. Could the residual evidence of his efforts outlast mere history to survive in geological time to be recognised in the strata of a yet to be created layer of sedimentary rock?

Is this a game, or is he toying with fate, tempting retribution, outstaring the calendars of entropy and time? So much for theory. In practice, for the first time in several years, Mo is beginning to have doubts about one of his own visual concepts.

The effect he is striving for can only be achieved by the gentle action of wind and rain, a decade or two of persistent, but selective erosion. That saps his confidence. Drip and grow. There should be a place for liverworts. His drawings anticipate at least a century of weathering and biological activity, including moss and lichens, marks of colonisation that loom oversized against the tiny bricks. Maybe he should bring in a sand-blaster to work on the bricks. There are no guarantees that nature, or the increasingly unpredictable climate, will allow the necessary species to establish themselves. He could paint the wall with some nutrient rich gauno to leech into the stone and encourage the process of colonisation. The growth rate of lichens is notoriously slow. One good sousing of strong sour fox piss can set them back a decade. A speck of plutonium dust from the power station and they could be lost forever, or replaced by a pool of mutant strains.

As his doubts grow stronger, Mo continues laying the tiny bricks and three hundred are already in place when he decides to go inside and take another look at the drawings.

Should he deliberately introduce that speck of plutonium at the very core of the structure, a beacon for the geological timescale, a star radiating at the heart of his conception?

What guarantee can he expect that the building work will ever match the grandiose concept he has devised on paper?

At long last, he is beginning to recognise the dilemmas every architect must face.

The contrasts of scale and concept.

The clash of materials and effect.

The conflict of two dimensions becoming three.

The simple errors of execution and their consequences.

The overwhelming sense of place dwarfing the carefully conceived patterns of detail and decoration.

The seasons.

Colours.

Chaos, Difference and a hundred other temporarily fashionable terms.

The delicate traceries of prevailing fantasy.

Moreover, he recognises that he has had a completely free

hand, untrammelled by building regulations, or planning decisions. Mo is his own client. He can do as he pleases, or as well as he's able and he isn't even constrained by the dogmas of form and function, modern and post-modern, training and fashion.

The little edifice he has erected is no taller than his ankle and about as long as his arm from wrist to shoulder with a distinct corner where the bend of his elbow decrees a turning point. The corner is open, because Mo had defined it by the creation of a roofless double pointed arch, gothic in inspiration, if not in execution. It is like a gateway on the corner of a city wall.

Grinding the miniature bricks down to the wedge shapes he needed had taken half a morning and he's laid them out on a full scale drawing before beginning to build. However the drawing is illustrative, rather than technical. The four piers curve together to provide the skeleton of a tower. Then from opposing sides, the walls, half built, half complete, spread like wings at right angles. They serve as buttresses for two of the piers, but the trial and error nature of his construction made him wonder if the other two piers might burst apart under the pressure.

He eventually makes a simple wooden frame from two pieces of floorboard and a length of spare timber for the vertical. Using them to build the piers against, he has invented a crude, but effective form of scaffolding, a brace which holds everything in place until the mortar has had time to set.

He would like the miniature to be a friendly and welcoming object; attractive, yet enigmatic; uncomplicated, but unknowable. Perhaps it should embody some mysterious mathematical formula. It's not to be, or rather if there is some credible formula its definition is out of his hands. He's been too busily concentrating on keeping the thing upright to bother too much about the niceties of theoretical proportion. Even so, the idea that Gothic architecture was inspired by the notion of a woodland bower has always attracted him. There are long trunks and bisecting branches in his mind's eye. Leafy boughs of intertwining foliage overlap to form the roof and fronds of hops and creeper trail along the aisle. No sooner does he remind himself of the idea, than a vision bursts throughout his imagination, overwhelming all his other thoughts.

He envisages an avenue of tall trees intertwining high above the woodland floor as they changed their hue from season to season, the light all dappled by the leaves, ripe for transformation into stone and stained-glass. A old forgotten rock, a boulder from the glacial drift, becomes an alter.

The very thought gives Mo an insight into the motivation of cathedral building. That the greatest edifices of Christian worship derive from the old forest rituals for woodland gods astounded him. Were the Cathedrals built to atone for the deforestation that stripped Europe bare of its primeval green? If so, it beggars belief and Mo is glad he has none.

Like the cathedral builders, Mo is denied a suitable avenue of trees, or the decades to plant for the maturity of future generations and he accepted the need to work in brick and stone with good grace.

Luckily, the small scale work allows him to ignore the greatest drawback of working with brick, - 'backstein', baked stone, as the Germans say. The Great European plain that runs from the North Sea to the Urals is short of quarryable building stone. The main source are single rocks which have been carried by the glaciers then dumped as the ice retreated.

Almost all the medieval buildings around Berlin use massive glacial boulders, but they are of uneven size. The biggest are reserved for the lower courses, then as the height of the building increases, smaller rocks are set in place, but the result is uneven. Collecting and shaping sufficient material was a nightmare. Hence, the Germans turned to bricks, which were usually made from local clay in a kiln near the building site. But unlike the rocks they were familiar with, brick has very unpredictable strength squeezed under compression and to add to their uncertainty, every new kind of brick had slightly different qualities according to the local clay and the effectiveness of the furnace made to fire them. With each extra course that's built, the pressure below increases. Eventually, they fail. A point is reached when the pressure is too great and the bricks simply pulverise. Then the whole edifice collapses from the ground up. Somewhere, Mo has a postcard from Venice, the photo probably faked, showing how the tower of San Marco had collapsed from bottom to top.

The ancient builders' answer was to build ever thicker walls to spread the load, so North German Gothic rarely meets the soaring wonder of French and English minsters. There are exceptions. The cathedral at Köln, Cologne, stone cladding around a frame of iron, mainly nineteenth century and very French, is celebrated, but Mo's favourite is a fine south German church made from the shattered fragments of a great meteorite, perhaps the only building on Earth of extra-terrestrial provenance.

Mo is squatting on the ground, dreaming of a meteorite's arrival, (landing as always near New York, or near enough to drench the city under an obligatory tidal wave after the fiery wind has toasted Manhattan), when the sun breaks through a bank of cloud and a flock of wild geese honk along on the springtime air. They're working themselves northwards for a season of sex, eggs and soon by summer, the next generation. Mo likes geese, envying their autonomy and the physical stamina that keeps them on the wing for weeks on end, airborne for eight, or ten hours a day.

The building work is going to take at least two, maybe even three years, just to finish the structures he's already thought out and drawn. There are bound to be hundreds of new ideas to incorporate and amendments to the overall plan. When Mo tells Inez that, she seems relieved. He is inventing a future for himself. The birthday, which she has always guessed should be his last, is drawing closer every day. Will it be marked by doom, or celebration?

Inez thinks that Mo must decide.

Of course, Mo has a different sense of time's passing and more importantly its consequences.

He is indifferent to destiny, or the odd decade, impressed enough by the fluke of existence to worry about the outcome.

Up to his fourth birthday, he had assumed himself be immortal and the truth only really sank in, as he watched a friend die in the tangle of a cable spinning machine in a local factory. They had both been fifteen, about to leave school, when the accident happened during a visit to see who from their class might be given a job as a trainee technician. One grew no older. The other aged ten years in a few short minutes. Till then, Mo had never dreamed that a playful push in the back could have such catastrophic consequences, but after that, his nightmares were filled with endless repetitions of the deed and the odd way his friend's pullover had changed like a traffic light from green to red.

Even as he's sitting in the sunshine, watching the first shadows cast by his little mock gothic building, he can visualise the rotating cables being spun together, as they twisted and cut through his friend Christof. Had any of the schoolboys more experience they would have shut the machine down before he came to grief, but the supervisor was standing on the other side of the cable spinner and only noticed something was wrong when the boy screamed. His fist, instinctively, hit the red knob to halt the machine, but by then the damage was done and the last half turn of the spinner sliced Christof up like leaky cheese.

Mo was surprised that any of his companions should accept the company's jobs, but three of Christof's old school-friends still work in the factory today, more than a third of a century on.

After half an hour of rumination, Mo finally admits to himself that he's never tried building anything before and it is much more difficult than he expected. The geese have flown on and he's losing his concentration.

The little bricks come in an assortment of different colours, so his new walls are already taking on curious polychrome patterns, the deep reds contrasting with yellowish light ochres creating an impression of Aztec playfulness to his Gothic forms. Were the Aztec's playful? All Mo can remember is that they hadn't invented the wheel and practised ritual human sacrifice, but who's to say that the rest of them didn't find the sacrifice business immensely entertaining, with betting and feasting, sideshows and dancing? Was it the Aztecs, or the Mayas who played football with the ball bouncing off their hips in a kind of extended tennis court. He can't remember. More likely, he never really knew.

The next stage of Mo's building work is going to need full sized bricks and he's decided that half of them should be new, freshly baked direct from the builders' merchants, while the rest will be rescued from building site rubble and ruins. Original medieval bricks would be ideal. Important buildings like the Cloister Church at Chorin have heavy, well squared, bricks, but in the local farmhouses and outbuildings they are usually flatter and a little broader than modern bricks. Like a very thick tile, they're often slightly warped with inevitable consequences for the texture of the building, another reason why very old buildings seem to have more character than newer places.

The big problem with medieval bricks is laying your hands on them legitimately. A reputation for stealing bricks is hardly something to get yourself known for, especially if you're professionally established as a specialist in the appropriation of maps and manuscripts, bound volumes and printed papers, by unofficial appointment to crowned heads and corporate emperors alike.

While Mo has no qualms about stealing books, he respects their integrity and tries never to damage them. He despises those dealers and booksellers who break down books to sell the plates and engravings for framing as decoration in bars and restaurants. The restaurant people pay through the nose for decorations that might just as well be photocopies. The engravings are damaged beyond repair after a couple of years in the stinking atmosphere of tobacco smoke and cooking fat. Once the books have been torn apart, no-one can put them together again.

Mo has always been angry about the undervaluation of old books.

Now in his fourth decade as a book thief, he is beginning to believe that taking books from all but the most cosseted collections is a morally correct act, enhancing the book's chances of long term survival.

While there is no National Library of Bricks in Paris, nor a London Library of Bricks on the Euston Road, in principle, he sees bricks in a similar light. Remove a single brick from an ancient building and the whole suffers, its integrity irrevocably compromised. Look at any over-restored old building and you'll see the spirit's flown. Once prised away from the wall, as victim, the brick is no longer part of the whole to which it belongs and the whole is no longer fully itself.

Hopefully, he can find a barn, or a cow-shed that's being modernised. This is his doctrine of minimal addition destruction, (MAD); sometimes known to himself as Mo's Law of Conservation. When-ever improvements are made to farm buildings, some of the older building materials are discarded and there's nothing he can do about that. Many the medieval detail that ends up in a pigsty wall.

The older farm buildings are usually wood framed affairs, with brick and tile infill. A trailer load of medieval rubble shouldn't be too expensive and he might even be saving the superfluous masonry from total destruction. Farmers like cash. He decides on a trip to Mecklenberg, or Polish Pomerania between Stettin and Gdansk. He should go sometime later in the year, perhaps September, even October, after the harvest, but before the winter freeze sets in, the time of year when people get on with this kind of reconstruction and repair work, securing their outbuildings against the weather.

When Inez brings him a beer, he gets to his feet and they look down on his little building together. Mo is puzzled. Inez looks on with a sense of curiosity, mixed with a schoolgirlish kind of pride that Mo has proved that he can build a wall. She would like to applaud, but Mo would think she was being cynical.

What kind of wall exactly is it supposed to be?

The form is neither enclosed, nor in any traditional sense could you categorise it as a boundary wall, or a curtain wall, or an external wall, or a dividing wall, or load bearing wall. It is neither a tall wall, nor a wall of death. Could it be a monumental wall, in the manner that a statue can become a monument? Neither abandoned, nor decayed, it cannot be defined as a ruined wall, or a ruinous walled folly. The arches are somehow too complete and the pair of walls lack that random sense of lost material that denotes genuine abandonment. The other thing that strikes him is the size. It is too small. He wonders whether to start again, aiming for something knee high, rather than this itsy bitsy ankle and a whisker thing that's lying at his feet.

Mo hasn't much to say, by way of explanation. He depends on intuition. Inez hopes he isn't going to intuit the whole garden into a building site.

Despite his momentary loss of confidence, Inez realises that the double arch is really well made, obeying all the structural rules and the work has been completed with the same care and attention that Mo gives to his drawing. His doubts are unnecessary.

If this is the way he wants to spend his energies, she is happy

146

enough. The sun is rising earlier and earlier as the weeks pass. This spring becoming early summer is the best time to get things done in the countryside. Because of the lakes there is a mosquito problem and the insect population slowly builds up through the summer, until late August, when it is impossible to spend more than an hour or two outdoors without being bitten to distraction. By then, Inez expects the situation will be clearer and they will have returned to the flat in Berlin.

The next round of thefts won't even be planned for another two months and they won't be carried out till later.

Mo is always busier in late summer and early autumn, especially those first weeks when clocks around the northern hemisphere move to winter time and people hurry home, resenting the reminder that cold is on its way. Hagen closes the order book at the end of June and promises delivery in November, which gives Mo sixteen weeks for between twelve and twenty well planned operations.

Then everything will go quiet for a few weeks, until he has a sudden burst of activity just before Christmas, when people are distracted from work by social and family obligations. Cupboards are left open, doors ajar, people forget the window-locks and burglar alarms are left inactivated because visitors are expected. Best of all there is music and dancing, so no-one pays attention to stray creaks and unexpected shadows.

Back in Berlin, anyone who asks Inez will be told that Mo is out looking for Christmas presents, which, in a sense, he is.

Clients, especially the really rich ones, often ask Hagen to drop by on Christmas Eve with his goodies, but he puts them off. You can't be in two places at once and Hagen doesn't want his face seen by customers' families and friends. He thinks people should at least be able to do their own giving. Hagen and Mo have already taken care of the taking. Nor does he want to risk the indignity of being arrested in false beard and a red and white Santa Claus costume.

Hagen's lament has bored Mo over the years, but that doesn't undermine the sense of his complaint that because people hand over cash for the objects he delivers, they convince themselves they are buying ownership, instead of paying for the services of a proficient team of thieves.

"There's a huge difference," Hagen insists, "But nothing's to be gained by getting into other people's trouble."

CHAPTER 13

The man watching Mo and Inez knows exactly who they are, though not all the information he holds is correct.

According to his sources, subjects number M7514 and I245 respectively are German nationals, one male, one female, aged fifty three and thirty two. There are lots of Michaels and Martins, not so many Iris' or Isobels and only two Indiras, while the Ingrids tend to be a well behaved lot, so the 'M' numbers have outstripped the 'I' numbers since day one. IM's are, of course birds of a different plumage, the Inoffizielle Mitarbeiter, informers of the East German secret police, while the MI's are a peculiarly British obsession connecting the military and intelligence, one, two, three, four, five, six and seven, for all he cares.

He has already read a dossier more detailed than any he has previously encountered and he is hoping to consolidate the compilation of its most telling sections to complete and publish the first credible double biography based only on information obtained using recognised surveillance methods. No talking to friends and family, at least in the open. No newspaper archives. No tv or radio interviews. No autobiographies.

He will rely on his own techniques entirely, listening and watching everything he can access. Having first memorised their physical appearance, he had then spent three days trying to make sense of the jumbled facts about their lives, especially their age. The woman seems to believe her friend is a decade or so younger than he really is.

The long years of practice as a clinical psychologist were surprisingly useful in this new career, a hobby that turned into a profession, when the big mental hospitals were finally closed down. Professor Oswald Bernhardt has always enjoyed watching, spending long hours observing people, the way ornithologists will sit in a hide to watch birds.

The old psychiatric hospitals had provided him with caged up people, whose behaviour was compromised by bemusement at the deprival of free will. 'Caged Up means Pent Up' was the title of his most successful book advocating day care as the low cost solution for most people's mental ills. Long term deprivation, he eventually concluded was only productive with about one per cent of patients. The other ninety-nine went irrevocably mad, angry and frustrated by their sense of unjust imprisonment. Now the contracts that he takes on to pad out his pension, give him licence of sorts to see what these carefully selected subjects, (people), do unmedicated within the boundaries of their own territory.

Had he managed to pass fewer university exams, or gain less exalted professional qualifications, Bernhardt knows he would have been arrested so often that his own incarceration would have been inevitable and permanent. A professional, he prefers the phrase 'intensive observation' to 'pathological voyeur', but he would own up if challenged. Were the real extent of his activities more widely known, the courts would have decreed a prison term, or worse, a life behind the walls of one of the hospitals he knows so well. Instead, down the years he has received regular invitations to attend University colloquia and academic conferences around the world, where he can enhance his reputation.

When retirement beckoned, so came the inevitable commercial consultancy contracts and Bernhardt began to blossom. At last he seemed to have found the niche he craved.

When Mo had begun work in the garden, Bernhardt could hardly believe his luck. Here was a textbook demonstration of thwarted ambition turning to obsession. To embark on the construction of a labyrinth was sufficient in itself to confirm Bernhardt's diagnostic suspicions, (he had written three well received papers on 'Minotaur' and 'Midas' models of male personality disorders and a less successful paper on the rape of Europa'), but to undertake the work using miniature building materials was little short of magnificent in its futility.

The young woman's behaviour, he found equally intriguing. Her willingness to collaborate with the man's expression of psychosis was exemplary. He decided she was quite literally driving him mad. Even more intriguingly, he concluded her encouragement was probably quite deliberate. Whichever way he tried to look at the situation his conclusion was unavoidable, 'this woman knows what she is doing'. What he could not decifer was the nature of her goal, 'what does this woman want?'

As the efforts at construction work progressed, Bernhardt was alarmed in case the diggings would unearth the filament of optic fibre he had run from the cottage to the boathouse, then underwater to his own cottage on the opposite shore of the lake. At the time, he had been careful to conceal the fibre, but the winter had been less harsh than usual and he feared that signs of his handiwork might not have been erased by the frost. In an emergency he could always cut the link, leaving anyone who followed the filament holding nothing more than a loose end of fibre somewhere in the middle of the lake, but the 'subjects' would realise they were under surveillance and the game would be up.

Old, but nevertheless enterprising, Bernhardt had been pleasantly surprised by this latest contract, which, much to his approval, was suggested by a young woman executive from Berlin over a generous meal at the Swan in Weimar, just across the road from the Elephant Hotel. There had been something agreeably academic about the proposal, a piece of research they would like him to take on. The blind listening to the deaf, as she put it. The money was generous without being overly extravagant, but they had paid up on time and gave him enough as a prepayment to buy and install the equipment he needed.

Berhardt consulted his conscience, wrestled briefly with his sense of propriety and professional ethics, but finding nothing to disturb his sense of well-being, discovering in fact that he felt comfortable with the proposal, he accepted immediately, especially since they offered the summer house near Ravensbrucke rent free for five whole years. The only uncertainty in his mind was raised when they admitted their interest was political, that the subjects had somehow disturbed the 'Berlin telephone company' sufficiently to get themselves watched. Berhardt hoped this wasn't sufficient to get themselves murdered, like his old friend and former lover, the equally voyeuristic, Chloe Schaus.

By the time Mo had switched from miniature bricks to the real thing, Bernhardt had already begun to write the case up, enjoying the task of paring down the video material to presentable form for an academic conference in India, "Watched - Watchers - Watching - New Observations in Surveillance Practice - an Overview," which he was hoping to be invited to attend as an alternative to Christmas.

The optic fibre set up gives him pictures from eleven different vantage points, two in each room and three outside. The end of the fibre makes a pinhole-lens, so there's no camera and the video signal is created by computer. Bernhardt's copious notes describe his subjects' speech rhythms and sleep patterns, their posture, movement and gesture, as well as all the usual surveillance detail of woke up, washed, had breakfast, read a book, got laid, took a nap, faked a masterpiece, cooked dinner, ate it, thought about shooting the piano player, phoned the assassin, built another section of wall, got laid, ate dinner, went to bed, got laid, slept soundly.

The fibre also creates its own analogue microphone, vibrating fractionally with every sound, so the computers can assemble a workable soundtrack by analysing the two sources in every room. Outside is harder, but using voice recognition software, he can screen out the intrusive effects of wildlife and weather to make a serviceable, if acoustically monotonous recording of their speech, 'Yew, moth, air, focker, moss, essays, reed, Inga, let, her, hag, hen, rote.'

Things are less stilted in the kitchen, because a pair of microphones long in place are still functioning efficiently. One had been installed by the GeheimStaatsPolizei (Secret State Police) of Hitler's period, the GeStaPo and one from the StaatsSicherheit people, the StaSi (state security) of East Germany's era of 'real existing socialism', creating a stereo pair from right and left. A third was no longer functioning, but Berhardt had been interested to discover that the British Secret Service used standard Varta car batteries to keep their microphones active.

The sixty years of recordings, were they ever to be replayed in their entirety would provide a remarkably consistent set of gripes about the reluctance of the wood-burning stove to provide enough warmth to boil a cooking pot; the smoke that leaked from a crack in the iron flue near the ceiling and the consequent decision made by successive couples to eat their meal, kosher and otherwise, in the main room, because their food has taken two hours longer to cook than they anticipated and the kitchen stinks like a kippering shed.

Now, Mo and Inez were adding to them with remarkable consistency, the smoke, the kippered dinner, let's eat in the main room and Professor Bernhardt was wondering when to embark on the next step of his instructions from the client. He is no professional murderer and he finds the task onerous.

First he decided to take an afternoon walk, setting off through the woods with his usual short strides, a busy badger in his calf length winter coat with its stripe of white fur collar. He imagines it gives him the air of a Maximilian Schell lurking romantically in a Hollywood spy film, but he never once caught an admiring glance that might confirm the illusion. The only person he saw regularly on these walks was a young nurse training for the Olympics, who noticed his symptoms of high blood pressure, poor circulation and general ill health and felt glad she was young and fit.

There are paths everywhere in Federal German woods, with signposts that will lead you to, or from, the next landmark, lake, or café. No matter how isolated the location, it is impossible to claim you are lost, because you are always on the path to somewhere. In these parts it is even possible to follow in the footsteps of the Death March, when the Nazi's had tried to empty the concentration camps in the last weeks of wartime, forcing people out onto the roads to die of cold and exhaustion as they tramped from camp to camp. Of course, they were not lost, it was clear to everyone they were on the road to oblivion.

Bernhardt chose a path leading in the opposite direction to the abandoned concentration camp, which, after three and a half kilometres through the forest, promised to lead him to Alt-Graben, a set of large rocks, which were all that remained of a group of bronze age burial mounds.

After ten minutes strolling through the quiet rows of trees, the path runs along the side of a cobbled road marking the edge of the forest before turning back on itself to continue beneath the canopy of trees, a beautiful mixture of oak, ash and conifer.

There's a field of wheat on the other side of the road and a line of big old elms. Bernhardt knows he's facing south-east and the trees were planted to give shade for dray-horses as they pulled carts and wagons from village to village along the long straight road.

He notices a cross and a small wreath of flowers tacked to one of the elms. Then the path leads him away from the road and back into the gloom. He hears the groan of a lorry gear-box as it picks up speed and a car drives past, blaring its horn at the slow moving truck. Hoping no-one will recognise him, Bernhardt steps behind an oak.

Seconds later another car approaches from the opposite direction.

The screech of brakes is foreign to the insulated quiet of the big trees. The thud, when it comes a few fractions of a second later, is unmistakeable.

In their ignorance, the country boys have taken up two sports.

They race against each other in their hire-purchase cars and spout neo-Nazi slogans at anyone they think of as foreign. With astonishing predictability, they also die by driving into the roadside trees, which are then blamed for murdering village youth.

Though he finds it preposterous, Bernhardt knows that all Embassy staff in Berlin have been officially warned that the German Government cannot guarantee their security outside the city, advising them not to visit the small towns and villages round Berlin unless they are accompanied by a full security escort.

He fully expects there'll be a fresh cross nailed to another of the trees by the time he passes this way again next week, but he doesn't let his stride falter and he doesn't turn to look. There may be vengeful passengers, uninjured but intent on retribution for their driver friend's stupidity. His mother had been born in Louisiana in the days when lynchings were a commonplace and he never forgotten her advice. "Whatever kind of trouble they're in; with people like that, don't get involved. They'll turn their hurt and their rage on you for sure. Don't get involved and never forget the colour of your skin."

Bernhardt knew that the Government's advice to 'Embassy Staff' didn't apply equally to everyone in the 'Diplomatic Corps', but because Federal Germany is a liberal and democratic country, and that's official, they weren't going to say the warning really only applies to anyone of African, Asian, or Middle Eastern (Israeli in particular) appearance.

Though he had been walking for forty minutes, Bernhardt never reached the Alt-Graben. Instead he hid himself in a hollow tree which gave him a convenient vantage point overlooking the cottage and its garden. The oak was one used by generations of spies. When Bernhardt began his watch, Mo was collecting twigs and cutting them into bundles of different lengths.

Bernhardt's presence went completely unnoticed, so much so that when he fell asleep, grew cold and suffered a fatal heart attack, his body simply slumped into the hollow and lay undisturbed till mid-summer, when a long haired black and white mongrel refused to obey its owner's calls to fetch the tennis ball which had been thrown for it to chase.

This delay had interesting, if minor consequences in the academic world, when Bernhardt failed to appear at a university ceremony to bestow him with an honorary degree and the obituaries, when they were eventually published, all noted a controversial debate which arose about his work at several conferences that summer. Had his death been known earlier, a young professor from Wisconsin would probably have toned down her attack on his work at the Tangledance 'Summer of Surveillance' Colloqium and her career would never have taken off. Although Inez noticed the articles in the newspapers, it never occurred to her that the famous old academic even knew that she and Mo existed.

At the moment of Oswald Bernhardt's death, Mo was strolling back to the cottage garden, with a bundle of the thickest twigs under his arm. A dry branched cracked under his feet and this was probably the very last sound Bernhardt consciously perceived, before slipping into eternal oblivion. Mo let the twigs fall in a heap, then, as he stood by the north end of the wall, he started cutting them into finger long sections. His whistling disturbed a duck which quacked and flapped away, but by then Bernhardt was gone forever.

Once he had cut and whittled a handful of pegs, Mo set them in the earth, like a twin row of miniature staves making an arrow pattern leading towards the little gothic tower. Next, he stripped the bark off the more flexible slender pieces of twig and wove them between the pegs creating a double line of very loose wicker fencing. Taking a ball of twine, he knotted the twigs together using a darning needle and began to weave the string into a simple net along the fence.

He worked for three hours without a break, until feeling the cold creeping into his knees and half wondering if he was going to rick his back by standing up, he cautiously got to his feet and looked down on the arrow shaped model. It was about right, or so he felt. People had been building these funnel shaped fish traps along the shores of the Baltic and the North German rivers and lakes for thousands of years. The staves are often whole tree trunks and cormorants perch along the line of the trap watching beady eyed as their dinner arrives, fish by fish.

There's no water in the garden and no fish to flounder in the trap, but Mo has no trouble visualising the oily black cormorants with their wings outstretched like Protestant washing on a line.

While Bernhardt had been walking through the woods, Inez was busy coating sheets of glass with photosensitive chemicals.

She was using a 'History of Photography' from 1905 as a manual and it didn't help much. Hoping to recreate one of the early processes used to make colour photographs, the task defeated her and she settled for a mixture of silver carbonate and ammonium bromide. The silver bromide which precipitated out could be mixed with gelatine, before coating the glass plates. Eder's account was comprehensive, but historical and didn't include precise instructions for the methods he describes.

On the other hand he does mention a Latin poem Pope Leo XIII wrote in 1877 after having his photograph taken in the Vatican gardens.

Ars Photographica.

Expressa solis speculo
Nitens imago, quam bene
Frontis decus, vim luminum
Refert et oris gratiam!

O mira virtus ingenii!
Novumque monstrum! imaginem
Naturae Apelles aemulus
Non pulchriorum pingeret.

She skimmed through Eder's book while her emulsion was ripening after she'd added the last of the gelatine. Later, with the plates drying, she turned to the book again. The actual business of coating the glass is one of those tricky kind of knacks that some people never master and others succeed in a sweat. Inez has never met anyone who finds it easy. According to Eder, the first Berlin factory to produce these 'dry plates' started business in 1879, under the name 'Glaserei für Photographische Trockenplatten'. By 1893, the Allgemeine Gesellschaft für Analin Fabrikation (Agfa) went into production and Inez was surprised to discover that a course for Berlin women to learn professional photography was begun as early as 1890.

Her big plate camera was an antique and came with three detachable wooden legs, held in place by wing nuts, to make a tripod. The bellows let you tilt both the lens and the plate holder forward and backwards to eliminate parallax problems when photographing architecture, which Inez likes a lot. So, the simplest of cameras is sophisticated. They had bought it at the Sunday flea market near the Technical University in Charlottenburg. While the lenses were nothing to write home about, the large format meant it was a serviceable camera and the only problem she had was soon solved when another stallholder provided an external shutter she could clip on the front.

The real pleasure of working with the big glass plates is that once they are developed it is easy to make full-sized contact prints, without having to bother with an enlarger, though if she's really desperate to blow up an image, she can use the camera itself to make a copy from the print, adjusting the bellows until she gets the detail she's interested in. If she spoils a plate, or it cracks, which happens fairly regularly, they'll serve as cloches for fruit and vegetables in the garden.

In fact, this is what happens to the first plate she exposes that afternoon. She had asked Mo to pose by his fish trap and the mock-gothic miniature, which he did by lying next to them, much as a child at play might fool around with his building bricks. Another exhibition title had occurred to her, 'My Man-Child'. She will have her work cut out to complete all these portfolios before Mo's fortieth birthday.

Diving under the black velvet hood at the back of the camera, Inez got the image into focus and tilted the lens so that the little tower didn't loom too menacingly towards the front of the picture. Then she attached the shutter to the front of the lens, swung the focussing plate out of the way, slotted the plate holder carefully into place, then slipped the protective metal sheet out and using a cable release, she went to lie down next to Mo, told him to smile, grinned herself and took the photo.

A whoosh of flash powder exploded in a rush of light. She should have waited. The plates needed more time to dry.

That evening, when she developed them, she discovered the gelatine had failed to set and the silver black negatives had a curious waviness, as if the world had wobbled when the pictures were taken. She decided to clean the plates and start again, but the first one cracked just as she was about to wipe the image away, so she put it one on side to use as a cloche for the rhubarb, one of her favourite springtime treats.

Making photographs in the simple surroundings of the cottage, without electricity, without filters and timers or an automatic printing machine, brought Inez back to the roots of her craft. This was the way that everyone had worked till the advent of roll film and small format cameras. Of course, most of the real pioneers had used the wet plate collodion method and before that calotypes, or the original Dageurreotype. Now, people have stopped using film. It all goes straight into the computer. Like necromancy, the days of darkroom magic are numbered.

Strangely, the French government had paid the Dageurre Brothers for their discovery, then 'donated' the invention to the world, a sense of philanthropy that baffled Inez, who wondered what would have happened had the American government bought out Bill Gates' Microsoft and allowed the Windows computer operating system to enter the public domain, which was the thought occupying her mind when almost unnoticed Hagen arrived.

CHAPTER 14

Inez expected Mo to throw a fit when Hagen turned up at four o'clock in the afternoon, but he didn't seem to mind, even when Hagen poured gentle scorn on his efforts. The words he used most were unusual, "fascinating" and "intriguing", but the tone of his voice was perplexed, rather than encouraging.

"I left my car by the main road and walked through the woods," Hagen explains, after tapping Mo on the shoulder and giving him the shock of his life. "Hello, old son."

Grinning lethally, Hagen walks round the little building site and surveys the work from various angles, as he's trying desperately to think of something to say without offending Mo, who is standing expectantly by the overgrown rhubarb patch.

"Brings a new dimension to the word edifice, Mo, an enhancement for sure," he says with a conciliatory smirk, as he kneels down to get a better look at the gothic arches without getting a crick in his neck. "Without doubt Corbusier will be left spinning in his proverbial, once he gets wind of this one. Tell me, old pal, what on earth have you been dreaming about? I have never seen a miniature cathedral with a doll-sized fishtrap for its Lilliputian alter. In fact I've never seen a full sized cathedral with a fish trap stuck in its navel, so to speak."

Inez wonders whether this might be theologically acceptable, but can't make her mind up. Even when she opens a bottle of Canadian whisky after they've finished off the crispy roast duck that she's cooked for dinner, Inez is wondering whether Hagen is unwittingly correct. A new dimension to the word edifice. The word, she asks herself, or the thing? Then the three of them get down to some serious drinking and a few homes truths.

Business, which should be booming, is doing exactly the opposite, ie, "beginning to suffer a little in the quantity and quality departments, old fellow, not to mention the dreaded word delivery," mainly because, as Hagen tries to find a friendly way of saying, Mo has been unaccountably absent.

Hagen tells them he has had to hire a snoop to track them down, once he had realised they'd fled the coop in Berlin. "I drove all the way from Hamburg to Steglitz to find you were out, so I came back the following day and it was clear, you were not just out, you had gone, left, departed, run away."

He is not pleased.

"You remember Klaus-Dieter Keil, used to be Head of Department in the St. Pauli Tax Office. He took retirement last year and has turned himself into a private detective. Rented himself an office, bought a raincoat, a hat and changed his name. Calls himself Sam Bogart and gets drunk at the Black Bear. I like him, always have, so when we run into each other, I buy the drinks and he tells me all his gossip. Keeps me up to date on the turbot war and the unpredictable wanderings of the great herring shoals. I think he's a blackmailer really, watching what goes on at the homes of those lucky people, your average drinker calls the idle rich, your average bank manager calls 'lucky sods' and journalists describe as 'conniving bastards'. Not that I think Klaus-Dieter should be blamed. After all he has all the addresses and a pretty accurate notion of who is worth what in northern Germany. Keil says there were hundreds of cases waiting to be prosecuted, but they didn't have the manpower to bring them all to court. Now they get a visit from him and cough up unofficially. Has a red haired secretary called Gabrielle, from Ghent. She collects."

Hagen pauses, wondering how much he should reveal.

"I think finding you was the first real detective job he's had, the rest was just snooping and prying, blackmail and extortion, but I don't hold that against him, no I don't mind that. A man has to take the work that comes, though if he ever tries it on me, it will be the last thing he does. You can tell him that next time you meet and mention it to the flamed hair temptress too, if you would be so kind."

It had taken the private eye about a week of diligent searching to pinpoint the cottage and the job had cost Hagen a couple of thousand marks he resented having to spend.

"Look at it this way, Mo," Hagen said with a streak of resentment in his voice, though he was mollified by the pleasures of the duck. "How long have we known each other? And do you really think I would jeopardize your privacy, so why didn't you send me a post-card saying you wanted a bit of peace and quiet?"

"I did," says Mo by way of an answer. "Why don't you read your post?"

Hagen brightens, as though a weight has slipped from his shoulders and he takes a happy gulp at the whisky, "Oh, that was you? Thank God, I thought Willy was serious! The picture of the statue in Copenhagen, right? Why did you write that message, 'You will die, fucking bastard, I'm coming to get you. Willy.' I almost set Götz on him."

"Mine was different, Von Gogh Daffodils, fake of fakes. Japan '93, Sapporo. Don't you remember."

"Shit!" Hagen grows pale. "Then Willy really is after me, shit, I'll have to..... Excuse me Inez, I don't like to talk about these things, especially not after a good dinner with old friends."

"Yes, Hagen," Inez commiserates, enquiring, as if of a social call, "And do you expect he will drop in on us here? Do we, by any chance, risk being blown away in a moonlit firefight?"

"No, he'll try to strangle me at the Sauna. Old habits die hard, he's a sauna and wet towel man, maybe a browning studio once in a while. Doesn't mind sweating away his toxins, but he's scared of the lamps, I know that much. He thinks he'll get skin cancer."

"Who is to say he's wrong?"

"Will he really try to kill you?"

"No, he won't, but he really wants to kill me. There's a difference between trying and wanting, but I'm not sure which is worse, someone lethal but indifferent, or someone essentially harmless, who wishes from the depths of his being that he could consign you to your one and only coffin. I feel bad about that, he's not such a bad type, Willi. Never hurts a fly, except when he goes fishing."

"So why all the trouble?" says Inez in a puzzled kind of way. Had she decided to do away with someone, they wouldn't have time to ruminate about the problem over a glass of imported spirit. They would be dead. Doornail dead, whatever a doornail is, but that's what the English say, don't they, 'Dead as a doornail' and the better off people in Hamburg always try to pretend they are more English than German, though this doesn't really apply in Hagen's case, who is still much more Neuköln than St. Pauli, even after all these years.

"I sold him something that wasn't mine to sell, that's all. These things happen you know. A genuine error. You have something, somebody says they would like it, and you forget that it isn't yours to sell, a hazard of the profession, an honest mistake, like politics."

"Like what?" wonders Inez. "What kind of mistaken politics are honest?"

When Mo asks him what it was that he'd sold, Hagen explains that the statue he'd sold to Willi was a copy, a fake, though one so good he thought it should really be called a facsimile. What

Hagen had forgotten was that he had bought the original off Willi many years before and what Willi hadn't told Hagen then was that the hollow core of the original bronze statue, which was itself little better than a good copy of something mediocre cast for the '36 Olympics, had been lined with thirty five kilos of bullion quality gold, which would bring him a quarter of a million dollars on the black market.

"It was," Hagen explained, "What used to be called Nazi gold. Willi had helped someone on their way to Chile after the war and decided to hang onto the precious. So instead of sending the statue, as he'd promised, he'd arranged to have a copy made, same weight, same antiquing and shipped it off in place of the one that was entrusted to him. Now I'd done the same to him without even realising the bloody thing was worth more than a kitschy bronze of some woman slinging her discus. Like a prop from Leni Reifenstahl's Olympic film, I'm telling you, kitsch. He should have had more confidence in me to begin with. Anyway, I can understand why he's upset, though gold isn't what it was, I mean the price is like nothing nowadays and the stuff weighs a ton. Of course Willi wouldn't see things that way, even after tax and depreciation."

There is something unexpected in Hagen's avuncularity, which Mo finds suspicious.

Hagen has never really been friendly in the demonstrative sense. He isn't that kind of person. From time to time he may be considerate, occasionally kind, but his manner is usually rather cool, even reticent, especially since the move to Hamburg. It all has to do with his name. Known as Hagen by everyone who meets him, he was 'christened' Solomon. He had rejected the name by the time he was three years old, refusing to respond whenever his teachers called him by this proper name, or his friends used the excruciating diminutive 'Solly'.

Hoffman knows they would never have been friends were the two of them a Mo and a Solly, a begel eating pair of Neo-New

York bretzel knitters.

"So, what do you want?"

"Me, today, nothing," Hagen mumbles, "You know that. Tomorrow is another day, as the girl in the movie threatened."

Then he notices one of the contact prints Inez had made the day before, a group of trees reflected in the calm waters of the lake with a distant figure walking along the bank, and he admires it, not only for the pleasing composition, "looks really like something from a hundred years ago, when our great-grandmothers were graceful young girls." But he's also interested in it for its technical quality. "Big original," he summarises. "We've got so used to blow ups and stuff grabbed from video, or ground up in a computer that you forget how a one to one copy from these glass plates has such astonishing atmosphere and clarity, soft tones and fine resolution, really fine. That's a beautiful print. Inez, you should be proud of it. Good work, the best, in my opinion."

Inez acknowledges the compliment with a regal inclination of the head and the faintest of nods. She'd spent hours copying her mother's technique of polite brush offs.

Why is Hagen being so nice? It is out of character. She is unimpressed and unconvinced. He wants something which he knows they won't readily let him have. He had arrived unexpectedly, so Inez hasn't had time to ask Mo if he'll tell Hagen about the book, but it looks as if he'll be staying the night, so they can confer later.

Anyway, Hagen has something else he wants to discuss. The story about Willi and the statue was no more than a diversion, dinner table chit chat, or so it seems, when Hagen becomes his usual curt self over coffee and tells Mo about the problem, not just a problem, but THE problem, the one and only problem that would set the seal on their future in the world.

Hagen had been visited, he claimed, by the Managing Director of a big company in Hamburg, household name stuff, with a genetic engineering department over the border in Denmark.

"Why Denmark?" asks Inez.

"Because the regulations about experiments in Germany restrict the kind of work Genetic Engineers are allowed to undertake. Dates back to the holocaust and the bad reputation German scientists made for themselves under the Nazis. Now almost all German firms have laboratories in Denmark, or Belgium, where those kinds of restrictions don't apply."

Somehow, or another, the Company had discovered a series of telephone calls to Hagen's number, then traced his address.

"When I told him I was an antique dealer, this guy from the company relaxed a little, not much, but he seemed relieved and told me they had been wondering if I was in industrial espionage, or a head hunter poaching their people. My problem was I still didn't know what he was talking about. You remember the job we did in Wüppertal? I thought maybe that, or the people in Leverkusen, they would have every right to be pissed off, if they found out who our clients were."

Hagen reaches for his glass and searches for a platitude.

Mo looks at his old friend and wonders what has really got him to leave Hamburg. He knows Hagen hates the countryside even more than he does. Too many open spaces and hidden corners. They'd agreed that years ago. Either he's running away from something, or he's about to drop a major problem in Mo's lap.

"You remember the Genetic Engineer, what's his name, the one with the discovery he wanted stealing, the print out, all those A's and G's and C's and T's. He's disappeared. That was what the Company man wanted to ask me about. Do I know his whereabouts? Did he have a lover, money problems? Had he mentioned leaving? No, no, no, I replied. I told him we'd sold him a couple of pictures, which he'd paid for in cash, which is true. Minor Dutch genre paintings, eighteenth century. Not very good. A Bohemian miniature of 1636, worth every penny he paid for it, which was fifteen thousand marks. This boss man didn't seem to care, he told me the rest of his story just the same, like he thought I could do something about it, which maybe I can, but that isn't the point. I'm an antiques dealer, antiques don't have anything to do with genetic engineering, or has the world changed more than I noticed? This guy had obviously got the impression I could provide the key to his problem, whereas I hardly really understood what he was going on about."

Hagen throws his hands open, in a gesture of exasperation and sits back heavily in the chair.

"OK, so they haven't seen their man in three weeks and he's not answering their messages, so they go to his house and he's not there either and the car, a company car, can't be traced. So what the hell has that got to do with us. I asked if the paintings were still there, described them. Attractive, but harmless. They're there, says the man, on the inventory his people have made. Then he tells me, they're going to the police to find him and my name will be on the visiting list."

"And what did the police have to say?" says Inez, resigned to the fact that Hagen is determined to drag them into his crisis.

"Phoned me. I told them about the paintings, that was all."

Then Inez came to the point, "And what are you going to do now?"

"That's a good question, I think I have to find him, but I don't really know why. He's no different to a hundred other customers who have their problems."

Inez has been listening as much to the tone of his voice as the words he's been saying. There's a hint of fantasy, a whiff of paranoia, a veneer of sincerity covering a mask of self deception, but she doesn't know Hagen well. Maybe he's always that way? Could be that is what you get for a career in crime?

"Sounds to me as though you're trying to invent a conspiracy theory," says Inez, with a twist on the word 'invent'. "Or, you could be lying to us. Building up a perverse invention of crisis.

Maybe it is one of those European things? I don't know."

"Inez, what has Europe got to do with Hagen's missing body?" interrupts Mo.

"I didn't say he was dead, there's no body," Hagen insists quickly. "This guy said one of his engineers, one of my customers is missing. We aren't talking about murder, you know, or hiding the body. The man needs finding, that's all."

"Missing, presumed..." wonders Mo.

"Presumed nothing," says Inez determinedly. "Hagen what were you going to say."

"A European thing? Why not? The guy knows something. A strange dynamic. People in influential positions want him silenced. Is that it? He is calling their bluff and they're furious. All these European initiatives imply stability, a system that is steadily developing. There's an invisible barrier between this system they're creating and the way we all live. Our society is full of fractures and instability, but there's a European label on almost everything, from food to money, though when you look for the address, it isn't there. All you get is some local office where people do things the way they always have done. The Europe thing is somewhere else, called a 'Programme', or a 'Directive', or a 'Fund'. A product of inequality and self interest hidden by an illusion of complexity. It's important, but it's out of reach."

"A wall," says Mo, predictably.

"No, Mo," Hagen disagrees almost automatically, "Not a bloody wall. Or, if there is a wall, then it's invisible, which could be part of the problem." For a moment he looks puzzled.

"Sure," says Inez sceptically. "Your problem, or my problem?" Then she stops talking too and carries on with her own thoughts in silence.

"You're beginning to sound like Holga Nierbaum," says Hagen, without eliciting a reply. He looks over to Mo, who returns his gaze with a gentle smile.

Eventually Inez says something, turning her attention to Hagen's problem and speaking slowly, "So when things go wrong, this Danish Managing Director guy thinks his man has gone missing because of some weird and complex plot aimed against the Commissioners of the European Community, or their underlings. You're wrong Hagen. I know you're wrong. I think he just got bored with his job and took a walk. Admit it, Hagen, he did a runner. My version is far more probable, when you think about it, even though I've never met the guy. Why should anyone in Brussels care? They simply deny anything they don't want to take responsibility for. Make believe merchants, a criminal bureaucracy right down to the last expenses claim."

"So you think I've got nothing to worry about?"

"I didn't say that, but comparing your lost boy to this fucking book business we've got round our necks, oh shit, I wasn't going to tell you about that."

Like a dolphin that's been worrying about the proximity of a killer whale, but notices a juicy little mackerel wandering past his nose, Hagen snaps to attention.

"Which book would that be, Inez?"

"I thought you sent it me?" says Mo, sincerely, trying to cover Inez, "It's over there on the table, nicely produced, good condition. I should thank you for it, I've never read anything quite like it."

Hagen gets to his feet, steps over to the table and takes the book in his hands, turning the binding between his fingers, before he carefully opens it, " 'Ars Muralis' neat title for a present to our old friend Moses Hoffman wouldn't you say, my dear Mo? Arse against the wall." Then he laughs, opens the book and carefully checks the inside covers front and back.

"What are you looking for?" asks Inez.

"Printers' marks," Hagen replies in his usual professional manner, "In times of strife and turmoil, books are often used to convey messages as code. Worth a look."

"Do you think this is a time of strife and turmoil?" asks Mo innocently.

"Depends where you are in the world. Always somewhere condemned to suffering. On the other hand it also depends when the marks were made and where," Hagen replies under his breath, muttering to himself. He take a pocket magnifier to study various pages in detail as he leafs through the body of the book. Eventually he asks them how they got hold of it.

Then Mo lies.

"I found it at an antique dealers in Schwanebeck, near Bernau."

"Had you been expecting it there?"

"No, they're furniture people, there was a whole room of family heirlooms, medals, books, engineering drawings, model railways, you name it. It was lying at the bottom of the proverbial cardboard box."

"Moses, you're not telling me the truth. It came by post, right?"

"Right," says Inez, not bothering to prolong the confusion.

Hagen looks first at the book, then at Inez and finally lets his eyes settle on Mo, "So now we know we've got a problem."

Mo's reply surprises Inez. She'd never thought he had the willpower to stand up to Hagen.

"No," says Mo. "You think you have a problem about this missing man. You also think I have a problem about this book. That doesn't mean that 'we' have a problem. In fact, I don't think I have a problem about the book and Inez doesn't think you have a problem about the man, so you're the only person here who thinks anyone has a problem at all."

"But I am right, dear Mo and Inez," Hagen grunts, "And the two of you are wrong. Let's open another bottle of the Italian to celebrate."

Reverting to the light Italian red they been drinking with the duck, they talk long into the night and as Jupiter slips below the horizon, they turn to port.

Hagen agrees that the book is a kind of masterpiece. "It hardly matters who made it. The work of an editor, rather than an author, though an editor who understands the history of printing like a master, or a mistress. I think this is almost certainly a woman's work. Someone who knows you better than you remember. Who was that American girl you lived with in, when was it, late seventies, the one from Los Angeles. What was her name, Byron something or other, Hofmeister? Had a friend called Tyrone, slim girl with thick black hair. Wasn't she a printer, or an editor?"

Inez is already dozing on the horse hair chaise-longue, but she opens an eye at the mention of Mo's old girlfriends.

"You might be right," says Mo, sleepily, "But I still don't know what it's supposed to mean."

"This book, old dear, is what Mr. Hitchcock used to call a MacGuffin. It's a precious object with no practical use, but something interesting enough for people to fight over. There's a mystery about its purpose, even its origin, an unknown, yet tantalising 'object of desire'."

Hagen looks rather pleased with himself and suggests that he makes them some coffee.

As he lumbers his way into the kitchen with the bottle of port under his arm, Mo turns to Inez and asks if she's awake. She gives a muffled response, "talks so much bullshit," then Mo admits that he still hasn't clue what Hagen is driving at.

"I think what he's trying to say," Inez mumbles, "Is that we've reached the point where someone should probably get shot."

"Oh," says Mo, "I hadn't realised that."

"Yes," she mutters, "The dark night, the isolated cottage, the old microphones in the kitchen recording every word, then some-one gets shot. It's logical, Mo, even if improbable."

"Do you think the microphones could still be connected?"

"Not unless the Stasi are still in business."

"A shot, funny you should talk about shots," Mo says, "but in thirty years, I've only heard shooting once or twice and no-one has ever aimed a gun at me."

"That's not true. My Mother had a gun trained on you every time you came to visit, but you didn't notice, that's all."

By the time Hagen returns with the coffee, Mo and Inez have both fallen asleep. He pours himself a generous slug of blended Scotch into the mug of Blue Java and tops it up with cream, then sips it in contented silence. If Mo and Inez had a cat (and if they did it would be a white cat with a thick mat of hair) it would be purring at his feet. The night is very quiet and dawn not far off. Three deer are standing silently in the garden munching mouthful after mouthful of fresh green leaves.

When he's finished drinking the coffee, Hagen puts on his overcoat, the book 'Ars Muralis' goes in his pocket and quiet as a cat on its night-time prowl, he unlatches the door Then, just like the deer, Hagen slips away into the darkness.

Ten minutes later, Mo stirs in his sleep, wakes, hears the grunt of a wild boar off in the distance and realises Hagen is no longer sitting where he should be. Inez is woken by Mo's roars of anger, "The thieving bastard, he's nicked my bloody book!"

CHAPTER 15

New York always looks good from the air, especially as cloudless night becomes clear morning sunrise over the glass canyons of Manhatten.

On the ground its a different story and your impressions depend very much on where you look and how much you care to notice.

The man sauntering across Washington Square is Moses Hoffman, who is taking as close a look as he can without actually cutting and pasting the city in a different, more convenient order.

He's been wandering the windy streets since before daybreak, trying to memorise the layout of this corner of the city and the quickest routes between various addresses that interest him. Mo has sneaked down half forgotten alleys, through subterranean car parks, in and out of hotel kitchens. He has chatted with security guards on the Avenue of the Americas, tipped the wink to vagrants on Broadway and sneaked unseen between innumerable Greenwich Village garbage bins. The local people have decided he's an undercover cop and point him out to one another with a gentle warning. They'd like to know who he's really after, so the rest of them can carry on as usual.

A zero tolerance Precinct Captain has already been commended for the appreciable drop in street crime in the neighbourhood, since Mo arrived ten days before, though his officers are reporting a heightening of tension between the garment industry gang-members. They are getting nervous, readying themselves for the big raid; battle lines drawn, illegal furs hidden, waiting for a tip off to say when the skirmishes are going to begin.

After a week scouting the lie of the land, Mo is swimming in America, 'putting the con in renaissance' as Hagen says, Mo is almost ready and drops into a café for a breakfast of scrambled eggs, bacon and hot buttered toast with milky coffee to settle his nerves. He can sense the way people are watching him, wondering about his next move. The floor plan is indelibly fixed in his mind and he knows exactly how many paces and turns he will take from the beginning to the end of this experimental little subterfuge. It is a good plan, a secure plan, but the local people are showing signs of suspicion and Mo decides he must act before someone informs the police.

In a nearby Library, one of the Librarians, a woman in her early thirties, is describing her professional nightmare to a visitor, a polite man, well past retiring age, who listens patiently to everyone who wants to relieve themselves of guilt.

"I have this dream every half year or so and it's always the same," she begins with a replica of the helpless-little-me smile she'd learned at school, which the man does his best to ignore. "One day, someone walks into the library with a box of stuff they've found in their grandfather's attic. No-one knows how he came by it and it's too late to ask, because the old boy died a couple of weeks before, which is why they've been sorting out his things. As soon as I see the stuff, I know that the bundle of rubbish is four or five thousand year old papyrus, written in several languages that no-one can read and will probably never decipher. It could be Asian, Egyptian, or South American. The old man had lived his whole life in Green Bay and never even got to Canada. There isn't the slightest clue to its provenance.

As I'm sitting there looking at the stuff, all I know is that it is both worthless and extremely valuable. If we accept it, the conservation work will blow a hole in our budget for years to come, the media people will come asking stupid, but unanswerable question and jealous colleagues will begin to bicker and argue worse than ever before, while all I will get is the blame."

"Has anything like that ever happened?" asks the patient visitor in a slight but noticeable Mexican accent. He is not a tall man, but has gentle blue eyes that remind the Librarian of her Uncle Matt, whose eldest brother had left the family home after an argument about girls, cars and Christian morals half a century before. Her Uncle Lonnie had never been seen again.

The Librarian decides she can confide in the old man and confesses that yes, just once, something arrived unexpectedly. A cardboard box had been delivered by post from Peru and the Librarian had discovered it was filled with old papyrus. It was in terrible condition, crumbling into hundreds of minute fragments.

What did you do?" the Visitor asks, with the gentle manner of a doctor asking where the patient has a pain and does that hurt?

The Librarian takes a deep breath, crosses her arms over her breasts and decides to confess. His eyes are so trusting. "I scrunched the whole bundle into a mass of fragments and flushed them down the staff toilet," she says quickly.

The Visitor shakes his head, "You don't expect me to believe that, do you?"

"Why not?"

The Visitor say he thinks that so much papyrus was most probably the unwanted part of some robber's haul, stolen goods, but then he says she's made the story up as a twisted expression of frustration with her career, "You should have phoned the police."

"Why should anyone want to steal indecipherable papyrus for

God's sake?" the bewildered Librarian wants to know.

"There are thieves everywhere," says the Patient Visitor, "and everything has its price, however for a surprisingly large number of items and even people, that price is zero, even more often it's a minus number, a liability, a price that must be paid. This simple fact is ignored by most of us most of the time, until we decide to sort things out and discover that getting rid of things is almost as expensive as acquiring them in the first place. Have you never had to pay someone to take your old washing machine, or fridge away? It is a most unusual thief who interests themselves in such objects. If you know of one, I'd like to meet him. I have the key to my cellar for him."

Then Mo walks past them, out of the library. He's carrying a heavy shopping bag.

"Good morning, Mr. Hoffman," says the Librarian with a smile.

"You know that guy?" asks the Patient Visitor.

"He's writing a book about walls," explains the Librarian, "spends hours down in our stacks, searching out old documents. We have a noted collection of tracts in Arabic about Jerusalem. He told me he's found unique information about the construction of the Wailing Wall."

"Interesting, I'm sure," he replies unemphatically.

The Librarian thinks he's going to leave, but the Patient Visitor isn't finished yet. He places a small attaché case on the counter, opens it and reveals a mass of old documents.

"They're for you. They are to be placed in the library's care. I think they're very old, but I don't know what language they're written in."

The Librarian looks downcast at the discoloured papers, gives the man a weak grin, wonders whether she's about to hiccup and reaches for a form - 'Gifts, Loans and Bequests'. "Gifts are best. Presents. Everybody likes presents," she says, "Loans get you into trouble and bequests means you're dead. And we wouldn't want that would we?"

"Let's settle for 'gift' then," he agrees, amicably, without mentioning that 'gift' is the German word for poison.

Just then, Mo comes back in and approaches the counter as if he's forgotten something, "Excuse me, a moment, this is for you."

He hands the Librarian an envelope full of dollar bills.

"Why thank you, Mr. Hoffman," she says, smiling broadly as she's counting the money.

"Your lucky day," says the Visitor, "Looks like there's several thousand dollars there."

"I hope so," says the Librarian, as she starts to fill in the form, "And what was your name, sir?"

"Marlon E. Hepburn, with a 'p' for the 'hep' in Hepburn."

"There's just one more thing," the Librarian continues, "would it be possible for me to have the attaché case too."

"Oh, I was intending to hang on to it."

"Pity," she says regretfully, taking a bundle of dollar bills from the envelope, "You see I collect old luggage. The fine aroma of antique leather bathed in the sweat of distant climes and long forgotten bodies is a refined, yet little appreciated facet of connoisseurship. I'll give you six hundred bucks for that weather worn little sweety."

The Patient Visitor pauses a moment for thought. He never takes decisions with undue haste and wonders how anyone could have learned this prissy way of talking with its 'little appreciated facets' and 'sweat of distant climes', then concludes he's just being curmudgeonly and decides to let her have the bag, which has never been further than Cincinnati and would fall to pieces soon anyway.

"If it really means so much to you, why not? Everything has its price and you obviously have a fetish to succour."

He takes the money, leaving the Library as fast as dignity allows. As he's about to go through the door, he turns and makes a final remark, "You know, young lady, your professional nightmare is really an expression of your guilt. You should acknowledge your wrong doing and make amends. I will let you into a small secret before I leave. You know, my professional nightmare is meeting a librarian like you."

Marlon E. Hepburn was a paper restorer by profession and had spent too many years working for museums and archives in every state of the union, apart from Arkansas and Nebraska, until finally he had been forced to accept that his eyesight was no longer sharp enough for the long hours of concentrated work. Down the years papers had come into his possession, which his clients had lost interest in, or decided were not worth the cost of restoring, or were downright unwilling to pay for, once the work had been done and the time had come for them to settle their bill. He had never stolen anything in his life, but he had a powerful sense that the majority of the documents he was donating to the library had never really belonged to him.

Now he has made the inevitable decision that he is finally going to retire, he can see no further justification for hanging on to them.

A couple more steps through the door and this final good-will gesture will be complete. There's no point lingering. His long working life will officially be at an end and he can visit his accountant's office across the road and tell them to begin paying out on the stocks and bonds, the pensions he's been investing in these thirty years.

All the same he is surprised as he sees the Librarian reach into her desk drawer and take out a pistol, which with an uncanny degree of precision, she aims directly at his heart.

"Fuck off, old man, and don't come here again," is all she says.

Five minutes later, as he's going down the steps into the subway underpass to cross the road, the old man remembers where he has seen the man who gave all that money to the Librarian. That rascally fellow Moses Hoffman had been little more than a child when Marlon ran his antiquarian bookshop in Charlottenburg, a stones throw from the SavignyPlatz where Georg Grosz was living and the whores rattled along to the sound of passing trains.

It gives him a warm sense of satisfaction that the street urchin has grown up to be someone with such an interest in books and documentation. A historian? Some kind of academic, a teacher? That is a good thing to be. Perhaps the world isn't such a terrible place as he'd felt when he woke up that morning. Perhaps it isn't so terrible a place that Librarians need pull a gun on people who try to give books to libraries. Perhaps the German would be able to decifer the Medieval Sorbish dialect in the most interesting of the documents he had given the Library, especially the builders account of raising the new city walls in the little town of Jüterbog, a document he'd always treasured.

When Mo settled into the economy class seat of a Lufthansa 747 at Kennedy, his thoughts were more prosaic.

'Another day, another dollar,' he sighed to himself and promptly fell asleep, dreaming of the United States Postal Service and its postmen and women, who, even as he sleeps, will dutifully be consigning his booty to addresses all over the world.

CHAPTER 16

In the weeks following Mo's highly effective little trip to America, there's only one real question on his mind. How can he get the wall book from Hagen, especially since Hagen has denied taking 'Ars Muralis' in the first place, or ever having had it in his possession?

"Moses, what are you saying? How can you say that about me? Do you honestly believe I took your book? Come now, we shouldn't be talking this way to each other. Did you enjoy yourself in New York? What a wonderful city. Everybody should spend more time there, one or two weeks a year, should be obligatory. The book? Mo, Mo, Moses, you know you don't need to ask me a second time. Please? Give me a break. How long have we known each other, fuckhead? You're worse than soupy thighs Polanski?"

Stealing it again would be easy. Mo is sure he knows where Hagen has hidden it. There's a boathouse behind the cottage on Sylt. In the boathouse are several lockers where the waterproofs hang and behind one of them is a small cupboard with secured locks. However irrational it might seem, Mo also knows that Hagen will raise a hue and cry the moment he knows it is gone and Mo will risk losing his livelihood. They would never trust one another to work in partnership again and Mo knows he will never find anyone else.

The solution to the problem, Mo thinks, will only become clear if he can understand why Hagen got it into his head to purloin the book in the first place. The most likely explanation is that Hagen has no particular desire to have the book, he simply wants to keep it out of Mo's hands, some childish kind of jealousy.

If Hagen was responsible for creating the book in the first place, perhaps he has got cold feet, realising that his joke is in danger of backfiring and he wants to cover his tracks. If that was the case, then why not simply say so when he'd been at the cottage? "Mo, I was joking, give me the book back."

That was all he would have to say. Mo might even have agreed.

Even Inez would have forgiven him. Then they could all have relaxed, teasing each other about their mutual lack of trust and move on.

There are half a dozen other plausible answers, but without Hagen's co-operation, Mo has no way of knowing which could be more likely.

Alone at the cottage, Inez has been worked on improving her home made photographic glass plates. The results are impressive. She can now produce a passable colour image with a gentle range of hues that give her finished pictures the impression of washed out pastel illustrations. The pale lake and delicate birch trees bring an impressionist hint of Czarist Russia to her prints, though the cottage kitchen stinks like a Stalinist chemical works. Settling into a simple daily rhythm mixing chemicals, making plates and taking photographs out in the woods, Inez spends the evening hours at work in her darkroom, printing up the pictures she thinks are worth a second look.

Mo is also working consistently, adding to his drawings and steadily defining the details for the ever more intricate structures he's building in the garden. His days have acquired a different kind of rhythm. After a week and a half of steady digging and carting, Mo has almost completed a set of terraces by banking earth up against the east and west side of a double retaining wall. A row of fresh molehills have appeared in a line across the old lawn, which Mo interprets as a compliment. The muscles on his forearms are toning up and his skin is beginning to darken under the sun, making his eyes seem brighter, more inquisitive, alert. The combination of hard work and fresh air is helping him become fitter and healthier than he has been for years.

He has built the walls to the height of Inez shoulders and they are wide enough apart, so she can walk between them, yet still see over without stretching, or jumping up. Luckily the coconut- shy effect does not arise, because of steps and platforms that create room to sit down, or step up and lean over the walls like a parapet. Beneath the humus where border plants will grow, the terraces are constructed as a set of hollow boxes. A cunning catacomb too small for anyone to enter, but remove a particular couple of bricks from the walls and the hollows reveal perfect hiding places for treasures of all kinds.

Six of the hollows have been filled, proofed and sealed, so they are as secure from interference, as any safe deposit box. The seventh is for the book, "when I get it back" Mo explains, as he's munching through a bowl of corn-flakes and the eighth for Hagen's head, "when I've finished boiling it". Inez tells him to get on with his breakfast and stop being gruesome.

Though several weeks have passed, no-one has yet discovered poor Bernhardt's remains in the hollow tree. By the time spring officially turns to summer, the garden has begun to bloom and he to rot. A wave of new growth is flooding through the countryside. Snowdrops and daffodils spring into full flower, just before the wild garlic blooms, then as lily-of-the-valley and bluebells are almost ready to flower, the trees break into blossom and early butterflies risk adulthood.

Part of Inez' family lore is that once the first chicks hatch and begin to cheep day-long for food, the rhubarb will be ready for picking and this season it proves right.

On the morning she decides the first stems are pink enough to cut, the ripe rhubarb, which for Inez is the most tangible sign of spring becoming summer, has a surprise for her. The big leaves have grown hard pressed against the glass cloches she had made from her rejected photographic plates and on one she found a wavy picture of herself and Mo, in the green and white of chlorophyll and cellulose. She can even see the little gothic tower, as it had been on the day when she first tried to work with the old plate camera.

Now the leaf has been moved, she realises that the image will begin to fade as an even spread of chlorophyll builds up green throughout the leaf, so she cuts the stem and takes the leaf inside the cottage away from the sun, wondering whether the image can be preserved. She doubts whether so thick a leaf can be pressed and dried successfully, but taking two sheets of Mo's thickest drawing paper, she lays the leaf between them in the darkest corner she can find, heaps a pile of books on top and trusts to luck. Maybe the pattern will be preserved. For a moment she hesitates, wondering whether it might be more effective to keep the leaf in a tank of dehydration fluid, but she decides to stay with the nineteenth century methods she's enjoying with her photography. She doesn't want to risk extracting the chlorophyll and ending up with a pool of green solvent and a limp leached leaf. She will press the leaf in darkness, then hope to fix the image once it has dried. First of all, she makes a contact print of the leaf onto another glass plate, so as at least to preserve an impression of this improbable impression.

Despite his concern about the missing book, Mo is happy at the cottage.

He doesn't want to leave.

Inez does.

She's worried about the risks they are running.

The book came from an unknown source.

It has been lost to an unknown destination.

Mo disagrees, "No, a I'm hundred percent certain Hagen has the damned thing."

There are mysterious agents at work laying claim to Mo and Inez' lives, of that she's both convinced and discontent.

Mo says she's getting things out of proportion.

As Inez listens to Mo's conversation, she decides he is the one evading the real issues, bolstering the pretence there is nothing amiss; but Mo has the strange feeling that he's going no-where, as though he's driving without moving, that unnerving sense of hours travelling by car across a wide desert plain. Somewhere on the horizon, hardly visible at first, is a range of mountains. They're probably Australian, but could be Rockies. Take your pick. Slowly, slowly they come closer into view, as though it is the mountains that are creeping across the plain rather than the traveller driving for all he's worth, until all in a moment the plain is at an end and the traveller is in among the land of ice and avalanche, danger all around. These are real peaks and precipices, mountains of the mind and they are looming into view. Mo is pretty sure of that. It's just that he hasn't seen them yet, because of the trees and he knows that by the time he does, it may well be too late, because they won't necessarily be Australian, US or even Canadian, though they might easily be Dutch, or Polish.

"I always identified the countryside with space, the openness, and never before with place, the precision of distinct location," he tells Inez at the end of a day he's spent levelling the terraces.

She's concentrating more on the glass of Soave she's been drinking.

Mo explains that he'd been hoping to start paving round them with carefully cut pieces of old roofing tile, but he hasn't got as much done as he'd hoped and the levelling isn't quite finished. A

chaffinch is noisy and busy. Inez sips and smiles, relaxing.
"Comes of growing up in Berlin," he grumbles, "Countryside.
The very thought of so much space was overwhelming, almost
incomprehensible. The Wall stopped us even thinking about
countryside and our reaction to the Grünewald and the lakes
was entirely, psychological, all about sensing the illusion of
space without any real clues about reality. Our minds craved
freedom of movement, an animal sense of territory, like the
wolf running along the wires of a zoo-cage, where they'll trot
for years in loops and circles. Berlin Zoo. I remember the
careful way we planned a walk to last two or three hours, by
turning back and forth without actually being in the same place
more than once. West Berlin was twenty kilometres from one
side to the other and most of that was city streets. It takes, what,
half an hour to walk from the PfauenInsel to Nikolskoe and
down to Glienicke Brücke, but I've made that walk last a whole
afternoon, passing from path to path, turning in our tracks to
make yet another way through the woods, by the radio mast,
then deciding its time for a coffee and half a minute later
walking across the car park into the log cabin café by the
Russian Church and if we were really tired just picking up the
bus that looped us back to the station at Wannsee in ten minutes.
You know, when the woods were crowded, groups of people
would pass one another either side of a tree to preserve the
illusion of space. You go that side, we go this. A path to wander,
all to ourselves. Private madness, a psychotic need for privacy
in the open air. Me and Hagen played little mind games as we
walked, to persuade ourselves there was somewhere we were
going, an undiscovered corner, that was really just an imagined
sense of privacy. We were surrounded by the forces of history,
not abstract lessons from the schoolbooks, but real armies,
Kalashnikovs, disco bombs, battle-tanks and fighter bombers -
the weaponry to spark off mutually assured destruction.
Counting odd numbers from 19 to 23. Those were my regular

everyday battle ready MIGs, followed by the tantalising firepower of the SS26. Down by the Glienicke Brücke were signs declaring we were leaving the American Sector, though 'leaving the American Sector' was physically impossible, what with East German gunboats on the water and the bloody Wall right down along the water's edge on the opposite riverbank. There were houses behind the wall where attic windows had a view of the river and lakes, but the living rooms faced a dirt track patrolled by border guards in Warsaw Pact jeeps.

People from West Berlin could visit the East for the day, but we couldn't go beyond the city limits. We weren't allowed in the countryside. We were denied all sense of space, but the Kennedys and the Nixons and the Reagans tried to pretend that we were free, that we somehow symbolised freedom."

As ever, Inez knows she must hear Mo out, learn a little from what he says and let his thoughts pass on.

"By the age of twelve, I'd had enough of history and the grand illusions, even though I didn't know what they were. No-one was going to trap me in a uniform, or get me marching on the streets to cheer the willing sacrifice, or fight for change. If I ever had a childish dream of heroism it dissolved the moment I saw a sad American soldier watching my Uncle coming for him and glumly wondering why he'd been sent here to get beaten up and robbed."

Since Mo's agoraphobia has been one of the few stumbling blocks in their relationship, Inez wants to encourage this gradual acceptance of the countryside. Maybe someone should have shown him the open country when he was young? Then the problem might never have arisen.

Even now, he hasn't ventured far from the cottage and she realises that the woods form an effective barrier with the outside world. The trees themselves serve as the wall of security Mo always craves. In his imagination, there is no 'outside world'. His universe is simpler than that. There are places to go stealing, an abundance for obvious reasons, and places to be at home, which are equally obviously at a minimum. The places where he steals are by definition dangerous. Only home is safe. Hagen's house in Hamburg enjoys a special neutral status, neither home, nor place to steal. With his acceptance of the cottage, the home count has just risen from one to two, while the count for places to steal now stands at infinity minus two and a bit. In some unconscious way, Mo can sense the immense, almost infinite, disparity between these numbers, a difference from which the intricate pathology of his neurosis stems.

Watching him at work in the garden is a big relief for Inez, but the stress is slowly building up in her as well. She never expects the improvement in his condition will be better than gradual. Soon it will be time to go. Another week, or ten days, then she'll have to get Mo back to Berlin, or, whatever the circumstances, his old cycle of euphoria and depression will start to accelerate all over again. If that happens, she is almost certain, he will resume the dangerous habits of a psychopath and were that to happen, she doubts if she would be able to help him through it again.

When the yellow van draws up outside the cottage, Inez recognises the tall driver from her previous visits. The postman is resigned about his life driving round the same little knot of villages, but cheerful, because he gets laid twice a day, enjoys good home cooking and is free to vary his attentions between the ladies of half a dozen outlying farmsteads. On Sundays, Hermann plays football for the village team and gets drunk.

He gives Inez the package, then asks for a signature with a friendly smile. For a moment, she thought he was going to ask Mo what he was building, but the puzzled expression on his face as he looked at the structure was enough. He had immediately decided it could only be the work of an eccentric, a budding madman, the product of an obsessive and probably deranged mind.

"I'll be off then," he says, with a wave and half a laugh. Then he reverses the yellow van back up the lane to the point were he can turn onto the forest road proper and drives away in a crash of gears and a cloud of dust, which is the loudest noise Inez hears all day, until a low flying Polish jet screams over the treetops in late afternoon, a NATO exercise, or might that be part1 of World War III?

"What has he brought?" Mo asks, wiping the sweat from his brow with the back of his left hand.

"Package," says Inez, "Shall I open it?"

"Why-ever not?" he wants to know, "Maybe Hagen's decided to return the bloody book."

"You never know," she replies, "Oh well, here goes."

Inez fishes a small black and red tin out of the padded envelope. There's gold writing 'carré de guanaja', Grand cru de chocolat noir amer, but she doesn't open it to try one of the chocolates.

There's a note taped to it.

She unfolds the flimsy computer paper and reads aloud, 'The four phials in this box contain samples, which I have removed from the company laboratory for safe keeping. Do not open them under any circumstances. The results would be fatal, not only for yourselves, but for the people and wildlife of Northern Europe and in time, the entire planet. Botulism, Bubonic Plague and two recently developed hybrids - an inhalant form of AIDS crossed with influenza, accelerated Pneumo-HIV and a water born form of rabies. Neither occur in nature, but will run rampant if they are released. Also, please, keep the phials cool in your fridge, but please do not freeze as this may adversely affect the virus' potency and encourage further unforeseeable mutations. If the seals on any of the phials appear to be broken, or damaged in any way, start praying and place yourselves in voluntary quarantine at the nearest isolation hospital. The virus' are all highly infectious and contagious, each of them fatal diseases capable of wiping out whole cities, entire populations, no survivors, no hope, no more. I do hope you appreciate my dilemma and forgive me for the predicament I have placed you in. You are completely safe, so long as no-one is aware that the phials are in your possession. Tell no-one. I will be in touch as soon as I can to pick them up, but thanks anyway for looking after my diseases. 'safe keeping' and stay cool.'

"Oh shit," says Inez. The note wasn't signed. The package had a return address that was obvious false, Inventia Portano, c/o 'The Golden Dog Casino', Lake Tahoe.

"We don't have a fridge," said Inez, as Mo examines the note.

"What a diabolical liberty," he exclaims, throwing his hands up in despair.

So this was the mountain, he'd been waiting for. Like something out of a white dwarf, or the middle of a black hole, this little tin is unimaginably weighty matter, a biomass filling of thousands of millions of tonnes of rocks and stone. He picks it up and lets it sit on the palm of his hand. Is this mankind's destiny? To be destroyed by the contents of a small chocolate tin?

Sometime or another it's bound to happen, in Mo's opinion, but not now, hopefully and not this, no certainly not this. Mo found himself wondering what Inez' mother would do in such circumstances, she being more likely to face such a situation, than anyone else he knew apart from Hagen and Hagen's reaction would be entirely predictable - find the bastard who sent the package and ram its contents down his, or her throat, then stitch their lips and nostrils together using a staple gun. Given the contagious potential of the virus', the victim will inevitably exhale, so this is not an option on Mo's list of alternatives. Unfortunately, neither is any other.

Should he open the box, to see what is really inside?

What if one of the phials has already broken and the virus' were free?

It could be a bluff. It could be the end.

"What a complete and total cock up," says Mo, "The first phase of my wall ready, bar the pointing. Now this. Inez, go outside for a minute."

As she closes the door behind her, Mo calmly slides his finger through the band of black tape that keeps the lid shut, takes a deep breath and opens the box. Inside there are four sealed glass tubes, lying in a nest of tissue paper. He stares at the little phials and the straw coloured liquids inside.

"Has to be a bluff," he said loudly to Inez, who is looking in through the window.

"That would be a relief," she says with sincerity, but she doesn't sound convinced.

Neither is he.

"In the immediate situation, perhaps," Mo mutters, "but what of the long term. What manner of a madman would even pretend such a thing? And if not this, what next?"

"Hagen?"

"No."

"The barmy bio-chemist, this genetic engineer who disappeared?"

"Could be? But, could equally be what we are expected to think. What kind of a proposition is that? Are we expected to take the possibility seriously that a mild mannered researcher in North Germany is threatening to outdo Saddam Hussain in the surreptitious deployment of biological weapons. I doubt if the UN will send weapons inspectors to Mecklenburg-Vorpommern. Possible, of course, but by no means the only possibility."

"What are the others?"

"I don't know yet."

"Oh. That doesn't get us very far."

"We don't need to get very far. We're already here. We've got the tin."

"At least close it, will you, and tape the thing up again."

"I'll bury them outside."

"Then we leave. I'm not staying here to keep his virus' company, even if they're fakes."

Inez starts her packing, while Mo buries the tin box and its four glass phials. He considers immuring them in the monument, but the network of walls he has so far completed are beginning to assume a kind of ill-defined significance in Mo's mind that he doesn't want to besmirch. It was out of the question, he decided, to hide the phials in the secret hollow within the labyrinth. The old myths of sympathetic magic cast a long shadow in the imagination and he's frightened of stirring up tree spirits and half remembered gods of the forest. Mo tries to evince the possible consequences, then decides against.

So he adopts a highly traditional approach and looks for a cake tin, or biscuit tin, in which to bury the virus'. He finds three in the cottage. One still contains a Christmas pudding made by Messrs Wilkins of Tiptree from England and bought from Strauss Innovations in Berlin, but the other two are perfect, one small enough to fit inside the other.

Mo fills the round biscuit tin with concrete, then puts the flat little chocolate tin inside. Then he fills the square cake tin with concrete and sinks the concrete laden biscuit tin inside. He then pops the lid on the square tin, wonders what kind of cake it had held and tries to work out a good place to bury them. Would an atom bomb solve the problem, Mo wonders idly to himself? A battlefield warhead? The area is pretty sparsely populated. People could be evacuated. At least it's a possibility. The geometric garden would make an easy target for a cruise missile.

Eventually he chose a spot on the north east corner of the hexagon, well away from the construction work and the molehills, where there is a bed of stinging nettles. Ironically, the spot lay on a line linking the tree where Bernhardt had suffered his heart attack and the roadside tree, that the local boys had used as an organic column when they chose to kill themselves by driving too fast in their father's second hand BMW. Extend the line two thousand kilometres and it runs through the core of an abandoned nuclear reactor in the wreck of a Soviet submarine on the floor of the arctic ocean and a further extension would bring you to Minimata, the Japanese town where industrial mercury poisoned the inhabitants and on towards the former island of Krakatoa, (the volcanic one that exploded), East of Java. A Sheng Fui expect would probably advise against the spot on these grounds, but Mo simply gets on with digging a suitable hole.

Once the phials are under ground, safe, or not, Mo lays a heavy stone on the spot, then heaps a mound of earth on top of that. He's hoping the nettles will spread and wishing with every shovelful that a yew tree would take root here and knot the virus' in a millennium long fist of roots until their potency is spent. Mo thinks of pouring a strong alkali bleach over the mess, 'Domestos Kills All known Germs', but he doesn't want to test the advertisers' claims and find them wanting. Taking a careful last look round, Inez notices a pigeon beginning its courtship display, puffing up its neck to catch the attention of the females. As the earth gets warmer, green shoots of new growth will push their way through every crack and crevice in the land.

"Got everything?"

"Yes."

Then they get in the car and drive.

"This is called running away," says Inez.

"Too damned right, let's go," agrees Mo, watching the passenger side mirror, as Inez changes gear and turns onto the main road. A rudimentary cross has been nailed to the elm tree, where the young men rode to their deaths and a couple of wilting wreaths lie fading at the roadside. They don't interest

Mo.

Neither was he interested in the smell that Inez noticed as they were packing the car. "Seemed to be coming from the woods," she'd said, "Sickly, kind of nasty in the nostrils."

"Did you lock the front door?"

"Yes. And I remembered to switch off the gas."

Nor, though perhaps he should have been, was Mo interested in the blue Volkswagon cabriolet being driven a couple of hundred metres behind them.

At the wheel is a slim young woman with dark hair, sea green socks, a charcoal grey skirt with matching jacket and very red matte lip-stick. She is smoking a Gitane blonde, much to her passenger's irritation. He had managed to stop smoking half a year before, now he is on the point of relapsing.

When he complains, she simply laughs at him.

"Why worry, Werner, you're nearly sixty years old, too late to stop now, you'll die soon anyway. Don't torture yourself, have some E, smoke a cigar. Think of Bill and Monika. Relax, I'm driving. Chew a viagra. You're a passenger. Enjoy the ride, but I don't want to hear more of your Hillary fantasies."

Hagen's cousin Werner is so angry at her taunting that he starts to curse and yell, "Scheißdreck, Ulla, pull over and stop the car, now, and get out."

He has been angry with his daughter from the day they set eyes on one another for the first time. She was thirteen years old then and he was fresh out of a Panamanian goal. They were in Columbia, both guests of a cocaine baron, who took a perverse pleasure in their antipathy and an equally perverse pleasure in their perversions. Of course, she had been furious with him since the moment, as a child, when she realised that she had been abandoned. What with her mother being a psychological social worker, who resented his criminal potency, the domestic mix had always been uneasy to say the very least. Now, he loses his temper whenever they meet and she responds provocatively with contempt and derision.

He is also angry with the day, because the newspaper he's read that morning has a headline suggesting there could be a second planet Earth and he feels cheated to be on this one where not only are the Indians and Pakistanis planning to blow each other to Hiroshima style nuclear dust, but he is being chased by a resentful Russian nightclub manager, while everyone else is anticipating a trivial season of Far Eastern football on television.

Werner had suffered a nasty shock, when he discovered the rotting corpse in the hollow tree, which partly explains his aggressive mood, but is no excuse. The sight had been ghastly. Even now, the thought of it made him want to retch. He hadn't said anything to Ulla. Now he wishes he had. Why had he been so curious? He knew something was wrong and he'd stepped up to look. The all too recognisable decay appalled him. He would like to talk about it, but he can't.

"Ulla, there was a body in those woods."

It doesn't sound right as he rehearses the sentence under his breath. He can't bring himself to say it.

"Guess what, girl. While I was taking a leak, I found a stiff stuck in an oak tree near that cottage by the lake."

He can't find a way to say it. Werner doesn't want to die and he doesn't want death for a companion.

If he starts talking about seeing corpses, Ulla will accuse him of exaggeration, which will only make matters worse. Then the only way to resolve their argument will be to return to the place where he could show her the body, which would bring nothing but trouble, because Werner is sure that Ulla would insist they report the find to the local police. Then the police computer would reveal that Werner had left a Munich prison prematurely and without permission during the early nineteen seventies, settling first in Morocco, before moving to Latin America. Ulla, or not, Werner has no intention of returning to spend another five years in Bavaria at the expense of the taxpayer.

Had he realised that the cottage belonged to Inez, or that she and Mo were only few car lengths ahead of them on the road, he would have been in a much better mood. For all their antagonism, Werner is rather proud of Ulla, 'flesh of my flesh' and 'isn't she a .....yes well, good job I wasn't around when she was growing up, I speak in jest, or cest, I'm not sure which.'

Werner hasn't seen Mo in twenty years or more, but they'd shared some hair raising nights breaking into flats and houses, when Hagen and Mo were still at school and Werner was a young policeman, not yet a fully accredited KriminalKommissar.

His contribution had worked like this and it worked successfully for all concerned. After the robbery, where-ever it might be and once Hagen and Mo were well away from the scene of the crime, there would always be someone, who unwittingly found themselves arrested in possession of worthless, but easily identified stolen goods. A watch, cheap jewelry, it didn't matter what. Much more valuable objects would have been lost in the course of the robbery, never to be recovered. Werner termed it the 'known-rogue' syndrome. Of course they would protest their innocence, long and loud, but what is more convincing proof of guilt than possession? Quite. We found the valuables secreted under the accused's bed/behind the sink/beneath the creaky floorboards/in a secret drawer/hidden in the boot of the car/inside a shoebox on top of his mother's wardrobe. The local courts were contemptuous of people's protestations that they had been falsely accused, fitted up by the police. Previous convictions are hard to live down. So it was that Werner rose through the ranks on the basis of a phenomenal arrest rate.

By temperament he should probably have been a schoolteacher, however, deficiencies in his own education mean that he has twisted and turned though three, or four aborted careers, until imprisonment confirmed his unexpected talent as a criminal organiser, line-manager for some of the most spectacular security van robberies on record. If it hadn't been for a flat tyre during a visit by US President Jimmy Carter in 1977, he would probably have been PolizeiPresident by now and the Commerzbank in Potsdamerstrasse would have been a hundred million marks worse off.

By the time Werner has calmed down, Inez has turned onto the motorway running south into Berlin, while Ulla has switched on the radio, skipped from channel to channel until she finds the porno-chat-line station and the air brakes of a lorry hiss as it shudders and slows to a halt in front of them. A tail back soon builds up.

The probability of a chance encounter has evaporated.

The lorry slowly pulls over onto the hard shoulder and the traffic slowly begins to move. Ulla starts the car again and drives away.

Suitably old men's music is playing on the radio, 'I can't get no...', and they travel steadily through the region of racism.

The blue Volkswagon attracts no-ones' attention. Few enough of the microsleeping drivers are paying any attention to anything at all.

197

JOHN CLARK

CHAPTER 17

Inez has driven swiftly towards the city, leaving Werner and Ulla far behind, both thematically and geographically, the distance between them increasing gradually, minute by minute, until after a few kilometres, the gap is unbridgeable.

While they had been living at the cottage, Inez spent a lot of her time listening to the regional radio stations on her Walkman. According to the opinion poll analysis' she's heard, the fascist vote is real and growing. She thinks the notion of a protest vote against the established parties is a myth encouraged by the far right parties themselves, but the media claim that a third of young Germans display confirmed racist attitudes. The thought is enough to darken the thinking of all the major parties and they are disreputably preparing to shed another layer of principles to garner what they regard as winnable votes.

The Berlin schools no longer arrange day trips into the surrounding countryside for fear the Turkish youngsters will be beaten up by country thugs. In the city itself, the majority are reckoned to be fodder for neo-nazi thinking and ultra-nationalist bigotry.

Does she believe this?

Inez doesn't know.

As they're cruising towards the suburbs, she wonders whether Mo has registered any of these changes. Even though she doubts whether all of it is quite as deep seated, or extreme as it is being made out to be, there is a disturbing degree of truth in the assertions. Racist violence is real and the perpetrators are German. People are being misquoted by the newspapers and lying to the pollsters. On the other hand she thinks it might be foolish to ignore the situation. That was what had happened in the early thirties. Most people couldn't really believe that they should take the preposterous Nazi's seriously.

Five, even four years before, such notions would have been laughable. Now they are the sort of thing people don't want to talk about. 'Have you seen young Fritz recently. He's taking after his grandfather. Bald-headed, boot polishing Fascist gits, the pair of them.'

The motorway alternates between sections of lightly worn blacktop on sections where millions have been spent on road widening and stretches of heavily cracked concrete slabs that haven't seen a repair in decades. The car either registers a slight unevenness, rocking along on under-engineered construction work, or threatens to buck right off the road, where frost has cracked the ageing thin beige slabs apart. This is no big deal in a car, scary in truck, but absolutely lethal on a motorbike being bounced aloft like the Yamaha that swerves unseen into a crash barrier only ten seconds after Inez has driven past. Werner and Ulla are caught in the congestion as the emergency services scream along to the scene of the accident.

The Lancia joins the tail of a steady stream of traffic on the Berliner Ring and they drive down the final stretch of motorway into the city with the spiked golf-ball TV Tower at Alexanderplatz in constant view.

Inez is wondering whether to embark on a project to photograph the young Nazis. Then she's doubtful because photographs are so easily manipulated to deny the historic possibility of truth.

Mo hardly says a word until they're on the northern fringes of the city centre, driving past the newly renovated Amalien Park in Pankow.

The tramlines are being dug up on the main road, which slows everything to a crawl, but Mo is puzzled by the renovation work on the old houses themselves.

"Turn off, Inez."

She does and lets the Lancia slow to walking pace.

"Where is number 24?"

"Between 22 and 26, I expect."

"Or 23 and 25, but it's not on this side. We're still in single digits."

The houses are impressive villas, newly repainted a creamy yellow. Someone has spent a lot of money remodelling them. The renovation work is top class, the mortar fine and well finished, probably the finest group of houses in north Berlin. They have been divided up into spacious apartments and the basements have been given over to commercial galleries and an assortment of artists' studios. The solid Tuscan style villas are unusual for the city, because there's a generous band of lawn between the footpath and the houses and only the simplest low wall to divide what is private from what is public.

Mo gets out of the car and checks the names on the bell pushes by the garden gates. It all feels rather smart and unusually private. Pankow has enjoyed a curious up and down kind of history. From its beginnings as a village with a baroque country house and garden for a Prussian King's wife, when small town Berlin exploded a hundred and fifty years later to become a city, Pankow became a worthy, but unremarkable middle class suburb. Under the communists, it garnered a certain moth-eaten caché as a diplomatic district, where Embassy families were housed in well-monitored, but more, or less comfortable quarters. Now, years of intermittent development has created an atmosphere of superficial neglect and deliberate decay, apart from this horseshoe shaped private road ringed by these twenty pairs of large Italianate villas.

In 1983, Mo had spent three months working on a plan to copy documents from an upper floor flat at number 8, then Hagen's client got cold feet and paid them off without him even setting foot inside the building.

Mo scans the doorbells without finding the name he's looking for, so he goes back to the car and suggests Inez drives back alone to the motorway house in Steglitz. When she asks who he's looking for, Mo just tells her, with more than a hint of menace, "Someone who owes me. Don't ask, no lies. My auntie."

And with that she drives away, if not entirely into oblivion, then sufficiently distant for Mo to assume she has either abandoned him forever, or she will be discovered quietly at home preparing their dinner. The don't give a 'can of beans' look on her face, as she put the car into gear, was not encouraging.

By the time Mo has tracked down the right house, a dark blue BMW has silently drawn up across the road and parked, but no-one has got out.

"Oh, it's you," says the reluctant voice from the loudspeaker, a little grumpily, as Mo presents himself for examination before the little video camera by the doorbells, "I suppose you'd better come up."

The door-lock opens and Mo can push into the mushroom coloured hall, where an old metal-grilled lift will take him to the top floor flat, the dachgeschloss, the attic. A maker's nameplate in the lift says it was originally installed in 1922, but checked and overhauled only a couple of weeks ago. When the lift clicks to a halt, he closes the folding doors carefully and steps silently along a thickly carpeted corridor that ends in a white wooden door with two panes of decorative frosted glass.

The house smells clean, but unlived in, which the woman who invites him in says is a consequence of the no smoking policy they've imposed throughout the building.

"I thought of suggesting that the cleaning woman should be asked to smoke a weekly cigar, to soften the pristine edge of things, but my neighbours all protested. Every one of them is a reformed smoker, who lives in fear of starting again. Then I thought, why not a quick splash of cat piss, but the allergy folk wouldn't give it a moment's consideration. I was close to being evicted, might I tell you and I've only been here three weeks. You could have helped with the furniture, you know, Moshe. I have made my move. West to East. Tiergarten to Pankow. I went to school here, grew up here during the war, then I went to West Berlin and a dozen years later they built that bloody wall."

Rather than sidetrack herself with memory loop reminiscence, she returns to the present, "They checked the lift though. I wasn't going to let them get away with murdering the new neighbours in that old rattletrap. They sold me a nine hundred year lease and I intend to have my money's worth."

Her blonde hair sits on her head in an elaborate heap, the wig given extra extravagance by having been hurriedly flipped over the fading remnants of her own hair, beret style, as the doorbell rang. Her teeth are white, but equally false and the flawless complexion a facelifted charade. Hildegarde is eighty three years old, but prosperous and animated. She has unrivalled connections, an up to date pace-maker, a good set of cosmetic surgeons for her face and competent orthopaedic specialists for her new hips. Too all intents and purposes, she is in good shape and twenty percent brand new.

"Sit over there Moses," she says," Where I can see you in the light."

There's the kind of pause, Mo has become accustomed to in the company of old people, as if she had switched off for a few seconds, then switched herself back on.

"And how is your girlfriend?"

The question is mere formality. They've never met. Most likely never will. Inez doesn't even know of this woman's existence.

"We've just come back from the country. She's fine. I haven't disturbed you, I hope."

"No, I was just taking a quiet ramble through the stagnant backwaters of memory, when the doorbell rang and there you were, large as life and just the man I want to see. Now, what is Solly Hagen's address? He owes me money. That was one of life's little cul-de-sac's I worked over yesterday."

"Have you something for me to write on?"

She passes Mo a pad of yellow notepaper and while he's scribbling down Hagen's address and phone number, she says, "I feel sorry for you, Mo."

"Why?" he replies in mid scribble.

"The first half of your life has been rendered historical by a numerical caprice as the calendar passed go on a new millenium. For me it is just another nail in the coffin, but your life has been neatly cut in two. The same thing happened to my grandfather. Born in 1854, he lived to see the end of world war two, but was regarded as old fashioned, an epigone, for more than half his life. It probably saved his bacon during the thirties and forties, when the thugs dismissed him as a weak minded old fellow eking out his existence on a pension of frugality and fresh air. My mother said he was a good amateur violinist and a passable pickpocket, but I like to think there was more to him than that. Who can ever really know?"

She paused for a moment, then gasped for breath.

The pause to inhale was as much of a monument as the grandfather was ever to enjoy. His name was never mentioned in anyone's conversation ever again. No character sketch survives him. All those who had known and remembered him were dead, or dying and evidence of his existence was gradually being eroded as company archivists weeded their files. Records of his birth had been destroyed by tank-fire during the battle for Berlin and his death certificate was being used to line a mouse's nest. A series of Soviet era Latvian microfiches, the Mormon's Olympian catalogues of humanity in Salt Lake City and the Internet would soon be the only repository of evidence for his ever having existed.

"The passage of time is an outrage, Mo, which should anger old people everywhere and terrify the young. It speeds up. Then you die. A disaster. Nothing you can do about it. No-one to protest to. The inbuilt inadequacies are plain for all to see. So much for 'mother' nature, busy obliterating her own. I would like to make a complaint."

"So what are we interested in this time?" she asks Mo.

"Something new," he says to foster her attention.

"Not another more is less?"

Mo smiles generously, "Tante Hilde, what do you take me for?"

She laughs conspiratively in anticipation.

A 'more is less' categorised their early plots, where several small robberies were necessary to finance a big one, until they discovered that the proceeds from the small robberies exceeded the potential gains from their daring 'coups'. Hence 'more' brought 'less' and small was beautiful, east and west, but they persisted and much to Hildegarde's amusement, won themselves anonymous prestige within various authorities and law enforcement agencies, a bonus far outweighing the financial liabilities.

Criminal gossip can be just as catty and riddled with jealousies as any show business clique, but the rumour machine between the preventers and perpetrators of crime never ceases. Whenever one of their raids was complete, she eagerly awaited her colleagues baffled canteen banter, "who are these infernal crooks." Hilde would have dearly loved to have be a confounded 'pimpernel' in their eyes, but no-one ever mentioned her wall evading exploits as a courier between east and west and no-one would have believed her, if she had told the truth.

Mo settles back in his chair and begins to play their favourite game, deploying chance to encourage the level of randomness which characterises their plans.

They try to play about once a month, but sometimes Mo has to cancel and they haven't seen each other since she moved into this new flat.

They visualise together.

First a colour.

The starting point may be quite mundane, a shade of sky blue, the half remembered greens of sea, or lagoon.

Then a place.

Sometimes that is enough to define a town, or a city, often they simple agree on a region, or even a latitude, otherwise they'd perpetually end up choosing Venice, which is both serene and preferred, according to their taste.

The pale charcoal grey she mentions this time, leads to swift agreement, Weimar. Three more hints, including a reference to Fr. von Stein, establishes a group of rooms inside the Schloss, where a variety of Early Renaissance paintings are hung. In particular, there are several Cranach's and a couple of Dürers that Hildegarde has always admired.

They could have simply proposed stealing the Dürers. The paintings are well enough known. Every book about the artist include them in reproduction.

The game-playing ritual provides their decision with a degree of objectivity, as though somehow the decision had been arrived at through the intervention of some external agency, that the challenge they must face has been defined as if by fate, rather than by the mutual agreement of a pair of conniving rogues. They both find this satisfying and sentimentally romantic.

Hildegarde has never been sure and is far too pragmatic to ask which of her ideas for robberies are actually carried out. Mo brings her a bundle of scruffy banknotes whenever they meet, so she consoles herself with the thought that these ill gotten gains might well be the proceeds of crime. This time he hands her a fistful of high denomination Austrian schillings and she wonders if this is enough to buy her nephew the Porsche he craves so desperately.

Even if she can afford to spoil the youth, she decides not to. She had never really liked her husband's relatives. He should have to work harder for his treats. The young man sells property on behalf of others.

Hildegarde had spent the thirty years from nineteen forty seven to seventy seven, working as a judge, sentencing young offenders for crimes and misdemeanours, which she was depressed to admit they had all almost certainly committed. Where-ever possible, she managed to search out the loop-holes of doubt that would allow her to propose a verdict of not guilty to her colleagues at the court. This astonished the defendants, no less that it appalled the prosecutors, who claimed she was singled handedly responsible for the 'events' of May 1968, by having encouraged the worst characteristics of egotism and wilful disobedience in a whole generation of young Berliners. Consequently, her network of contacts is incomparable.

In return for their heavily reduced sentences, Berlin's more calculating criminals remained forever in her debt. One of them was Mo. A small matter of mislaid Hegelian manuscripts from the Humbolt University Library, "lecture notes about the necessity for an epistemological break"; an autobiographical masochist monograph in the hand of Ludwig von Beethoven, "I was born to listen as a form of torture....."; not to mention the six volume diary from Karl Marx' student days, '...having lost money gambling, there seemed little to be done except to adjourn to the neighbourhood brothel. Engels, generous as ever, had to pay off the arrears of our account before the proprietor would let us enjoy ourselves upstairs, but Helga and the commune of 'madels' were, much to our delight, as collectively accommodating as ever. Engels has agreed to organise classes for the young women to improve themselves, though I found them all surprisingly accomplished in the arts of their calling already.'

None of these distinctive documents were ever recovered, though as a matter of academic nicety, Hildegarde did arrange for some selective photocopies to be secreted in the Library archives.

Another of her favourite young talents had been Hagen, who she first met in 1961,when he was picked up in a US Army depot fiddling with the primitive electronics of a Russian surface to air missile. 'The stupid boy almost managed to shoot down a Soviet airliner which was ferrying their Olympic ice hockey team in and out of the Dynamo Sports Centre in East Berlin.'

Calling down these debts of honour is one of life's small pleasures, or so she claims, 'something I must complete before I forget who did what when and what they have become since'. Her Compaq is a loaded weapon primed to discharge its revelations into the internet six seconds after her death is confirmed. When the computer is booted up, the first window presents the question, 'Is Hilde alive, or dead?', before it asks for a password. Enter 'dead' and with hours a mass of Berliners and Brussels-based bureaucrats will find journalists calling with embarrassing questions about the whereabouts of large sums of public money, the contents of specific numbered bank accounts in Leichtenstein and the Channel Islands, and the purchase of various properties in the Caribbean and the murky waters of Arkansas.

Mo is thinking out a set of clues.

Having established the old gallery in Weimar as their goal, little more will be said until the next and often most difficult and dangerous stage of planning, that of identifying the customer. For a moment, the conversation lapses. Then Hildegard changes the subject.

"I had those new drawings of yours hung either side of the Rembrandt in the bedroom," she says enthusiastically. "You remember the little Nebuchadnezzar sketch you brought from Amsterdam when you were a hippie? I almost gave it away for a charity auction, until I remembered it was stolen, so I let them have the Max Leibermann instead. That one I pretended to have bought at an antique stall on the Kollwitzplatz trödelmarkt one Sunday morning. Of course, no-one really believed me. Kind souls, they were all too polite to say anything, especially after the embarrassment of the late Mrs. De Soto's early Picasso. After all, I was giving it away. You can't call a donor a thief, even in Wilmersdorf. Of course, almost any work of art you care to mention has gaps in its history when transfers of ownership are impossible to confirm. God knows how many other crooked, but equally charitable folk might be put off if they thought their misdeeds could be paraded in public. Such questions should be left to the 'experts', though I do sometimes ask myself how much the art world knows about itself. Court is one thing and a certain stage in affairs having been reached, the courts are often unavoidable, but nobody would volunteer to stand accused in a hotel reception room, while moments before it is about to fall under the hammer in aid of the poor and starving, sick and deserving peoples of our host's hobby, that dreadful Indira woman tries to describe the object as something other than that which we all know it is - a symbol of generosity and our good standing in society."

Mo interrupts her apologetically and begins to describe the curious situation which has made him custodian of a set of alleged virus' and a rogue book, which seemed uncannily like the 'holy grail' answer to all his dreams, but had all too promptly disappeared.

Hildegarde starts to take notes, just as she always had professionally, listening carefully to liars lying and lawyers lawyering, or vice versa.

"Human skills are much less diverse than we would like to believe," she surprises Mo by beginning her reply, "Our imagination is aural, visual, tactile, mathematical and verbal. The rest is negligible. Intelligent use of the sense of touch is largely confined to massage, manipulation and fucking, while smell and taste may be refined, as wine tasters and tea blenders might confirm, but seem to lack all potential as a basis for rational discourse at any other level, even to the degree of denying the very possibility. Even pornographers have problems with smell, as you know only too well."

She leans forward and her watery eyes look directly into Mo's, "The few perfumiers I have met all shared a rather abstract quality in their personality, Moses, a certain ethereal presence, as if they lacked the terms of reference for wider forms of debate. Sometimes I sensed a lack of character, in others a surfeit. I may be being unjust here, but hear me out. I may be wrong, but not far wrong, I'm afraid. It's not just aromatherapy, Moses, there's always more to things than therapy."

Her tone is secretive and conspiratorial. Mo has to lean forward to catch every word, as he listens.

"So far as I recall," she declares quietly, "my perfumiers were all poisoners, so their sympathies may have been for things that come in bottles rather than the fine aromatics of the perfumes themselves. Courts of law certainly introduce you to a fascinating cross-section of society, but the criminal fraction hardly merit consideration as a representative sample. You are being lured, liebe Mo, that is the point. You may even be the bait in a trap of someone else's making? Are you the lure itself, or the victim who has walked unknowingly into the trap? That is my only question. The rest is clear. You must strive to wriggle free."

She dismisses the book as a distraction of Hagen's invention and if not him then one of his shadier associates.

"More money than he knows what to do with, that one," she harps, doing her best to undermine Hagen's credibility in her own eyes, because she has always liked him. "He wouldn't have stolen it, if he hadn't already paid for it. Hagen has never actually stolen anything in his life. I remember discussing it with him. He has also been concerned. Though you will think it is nonsense, Hagen claims he has an instinctive aversion to the act of depriving someone of their rightful property, even at the scene of the crime. He expects other people to do the taking, then he enables acts of redistribution, a kind of calculated generosity on his part. I think he almost always thinks he's telling the truth."

Mo tries to look as if he's taking the old lady at her word, but finds it difficult not to giggle at the notion that Hagen might suffer from moral scruples, or ethical dilemmas.

"Once the object has been removed from the private sphere," she continues, "freed, as it were, from the straight-jacket of public ownership, or the bondage of corporate inventory lists, it is a different matter. His self doubt evaporates like the dew of perspiration on a young whore's downy upper lip after sunset."

Mo wonders for a moment how many sunsets Hildegarde has spent watching the downy upper lips of young whores and their evaporating sweat, then remembers that she had spent years dealing with petty criminals and examining their day to day affairs, so her observations, sweat and all, are more than likely accurate. Her notions about Hagen also ring true, to the extent that he probably thinks scruples are a childhood disease and the man's capacity for self deception has been communicated to his oldest confident.

Mo would like to believe that the book was simply an elaborate joke to be enjoyed between friends, though he can't. Hagen is the kind of liar who pulls the wool over everyone's eyes including his own and like all the others, Hildegarde had long ago fallen for the man's charm. That was what rang true. It was a particularly Hagenesque deceit. I am not what I am, nor am I what I seem. Mo has seen Hagen steal chocolate bars from tiny children, wedding rings from the fingers of newly married women and car keys from taxi drivers. So far as Mo has ever been able to tell, Hagen is completely free of all aversions, wholly and exclusively amoral and untainted by the slightest guilts of conscience.

The viral phials, Hildegarde then insists, to Mo's overwhelming disappointment, are probably authentic and deadly.

"I have never met a poisoner who bluffed," she said cautiously, sending a chill of apprehension down Mo's spine, "And I only met one who had a sense of humour. They are willing to bargain to compromise, but it's always the real thing. You can't just walk away. No, it doesn't matter if the sender is a bottle fetishist, or a simple psychopath, your little set of glass tubes are virtually certain to have the capacity to wipe out large proportions of the European population in epidemics of medieval intensity, of that I am convinced. Biological weapons, you know, are more or less uncontrollable."

Mo accepts that this is an 'expert opinion' and prays that experts can be wrong.

"What do you think I should do?" he asks.

The old lady sucks on her false teeth, squints and says, "A very good question. What should you do? An exceedingly interesting question. What should you do? Or should you, on the other hand, do anything? What is to be done? Ah, Lenin. If only....but we are old now. What was done? To be, but not for long? In our case, being is distinctly temporary."

Mo decides not to ask a second time, or the repetitions and permutations might be endless. Thankfully there is a brief pause.

"I do not know if there is anything for you to do," she

eventually declares, "But there are several things you might try to do. Among other things, I think you ought to try and find Hagen a woman. By that, I mean neither a simple lover, nor some purveyor of assorted sexual services, but a real woman, someone with a strong shot of everyday common sense running through her arteries and a liking for old goats. The type I'm thinking of do exist, but they're usually married to the wrong men. Look for an unhappy couple and let Hagen loose. It would do him a world of good and her too. 66% is no bad success rate in the happiness stakes, however temporary."

This is neither the advice he had been expecting, nor necessarily the kind of advice, Mo wanted to hear. Hildegarde was always claiming that women married the wrong men, herself included. 'Do you know', she had confessed one afternoon about her second husband, 'after he died, I shocked myself by feeling a certain sense of relief that our marriage was over.'

"Why?" he asks, returning to the present.

"Why?" says Hildegarde, in a puzzled tremolo, as her hands flutter lightly, as if ruffled by a zephyr blowing across the room, but she doesn't answer her own question. "He was the way he was."

"Why?" asks Mo, now honestly perplexed.

He has always been willing to steal for Hagen, but never imagined would be expected to procure for the man.

"Cast your thoughts over Hagen's life in the last ten or fifteen years. How long is it since Elvira left him for the cheese merchant?"

"He wasn't a cheese merchant," Mo says patiently, "He ran a frozen food factory. We visited it together, I remember the trip distinctly.

"As can I," she cuts in, "Norbert trained as a cheese merchant after he left school. Only later did he complete his diploma in food technology. I recall his thesis on 'freshness and forbidden fruit'. Contrasting the 'fresh and the ripe' was a very cheesy subject, if you ask me, but one which found considerable favour with his structural anthropologist professor."

The old lady turns her head abruptly and glares out of the window, the shakes her head, "Nothing. You know he's running a restaurant in Bremerhaven now, but Elvira is in Surinam. They broke up when Klaus Dieter went to prison."

"Hilde?" says Mo in the gentlest way he knows.

"Yes, Mo?" she replies, wondering.

"You can't really help us with the virus problem, can you?"

"No. I am very sorry, my dear, but no. Unless you think it might be of help to tell the police. I could arrange that for you. They would probably agree to an amnesty, of that you might be almost certain, if it comes to a confession."

"I thought as much."

"But if I think of something else, of course, then."

"Of course."

"I hope we aren't wiped out by these diseases. It would be such a pity. A real shame. Think of all the little ones."

"Yes," Mo sighs, "A pity, something like that."

He is thinking, selfishly, of the walls and terraces, the little half ruined tower and the arches he has been building. If their garden is eventually identified as the source of the plagues that ended civilisation, then the archaeologists will almost certainly misinterpret his efforts and link them ritually to the annihilation. A scene of the crime, unique, carefully, some would surely say neurotically prepared in astonishing detail to summarise the rise and fall of European civilisation. Somehow, he knows that he and Inez would be identified as the couple who destroyed a people and their names stand reviled forever by any chance survivors, like the poor 'de Vil' family from Aquitaine, who were so stigmatised, not only giving their name to the verb 'vilify', but also providing their name for the principal vernacular translations of the biblical character identified as

God's opponent and the source of all evil. This prospect offends Mo's sense of self-respect and for this reason as much as any other, he becomes determined to solve the problem before a wipe out can occur.

"You'd better go."

"I'm sorry we don't have more time."

"Find Hagen a woman, Mo. It won't solve any of your problems, but it will sort out one of his."

There was a certain pragmatic truth, but it failed to stir in Mo's current list of priorities, but lay anchored like an indecipherable attachment to an already lengthy e-mail.

"I'll think about it."

"Oh, did you read in the Burlington magazine. The Dutch have decided my Rembrandt is a fake. Now, they just want to call it Dutch school, first half seventeenth century, unknown master."

"They were here?"

"No, no. They were looking at the picture you left in its place."

"Oh, I'll tell Artur. He'll be flattered, 'unknown master, Dutch School, Seventeenth Century, first half. That makes him three hundred and fifty years old. He'll be delighted his techniques have been authenticated."

"Can you see you own way out?"

When Mo leaves the house, he closes the front door carefully and makes sure the garden gate is properly shut behind him, then checks his wallet to see how much Hildegarde had taken. She has always been such a brilliant pick-pocket. Rather obscurely, the only thing that seems to be missing is his organ donor card. Mo decides to ask Inez about the symbolism. If Hildegarde needs a new kidney, he would rather she asked straight out

Then he walks to the end of the street intending to take the tram into town, but because of the track repairs, it is a ten minute walk to the next tram stop and Mo waves down a taxi before he's half way there.

"Steglitz," he says, siding into the back seat and the driver reminds him to fasten his safety belt.

"When I first came to Berlin in the sixties," begins the taxi driver, "the people here were noisy, but friendly. Berliners always had big mouths and they were always a bit silly, not exactly stupid, just uninformed, badly educated, cheap and cheerful, loud and brash. They were easy people to enjoy. Now, they have all become aggressive. They still talk too much and still they don't know what they're talking about, but instead of being friendly and funny, they've become aggressive, angry about the most stupid piddling little things. I think it's a pity, a crying shame. I used to like this place, now it gets on my nerves. Where did you say you wanted to go, oh yes, now that's another place that gets on my nerves, that is, a nightmare in concrete, that's what I think every time I drive through it, a real old palace of a nightmare. You live there then, do you? I don't think I could face it, to be honest, but somebody has to. I suppose, but I wouldn't have thought that you were the sort really, if you don't mind me saying so."

Once the old lady has moved away from the window and the white lace curtains no longer conceal a shadow, someone starts the engine of the dark blue BMW and slowly, unobtrusively, it pulls away.

CHAPTER 18

"Hello?"

The first voice is neutral, mere enquiry, with a slight uplift at the end of the word.

"Hello?"

The second voice is defensive, dull, characteristically muted.

"Where are you?"

This is a question without literal intent.

Pure ritual. Vaguely repetitive formulae.

A new beginning.

"What? You're fading. Hello?"

Confirmation, as if it were needed, that someone is using a mobile phone, a 'handy' to the Germans.

"Where are you?"

Menacing this time.

The questioner has a purpose.

"Half way across town, in a phone box, near a building site, a noisy building site."

The menace has been registered; defence initiating the vagueness of response.

"Are you trying to be funny?"

Still less a friendly chat-line.

"Speak up, I can't hear you. There's a lorry going past."

Unheard, "I don't think I want to talk to you any more."

A unmarked white twelve wheel rig rolls past on its way to a Government building site with a load of fibre optic cable.

"Why have you decided to call me now? I've been trying to get in touch with you for days. Some madman has been sending me E-mail claiming that you are wandering around with enough biological weapons to end civilisation as we know it and destroy mankind. Such a message, I cannot ignore."

"Calm down, they're not weapons, they're just virus' and bacteria, microbes, plague and stuff, things like that, bio-hazards, it says on the labels. Organic. Natural. I don't have them with me. They're hidden away."

Game.

"You mean it's true?"

Set.

"Yes."

"Are you still there?"

"Yes."

"Must be the same guy who's been e-mailing you. He sent the diseases to Inez and me, assuming that's what they are. Whoever he is, he knew our address out in the country. We were at Inez' cottage. I'm not sure I've ever even met him, though I think he could have been at your place, when I brought the Istanbul pictures, assuming it is the same man. We could be wrong. There was a package, with these glass tubes, vials and a note saying they're a vintage selection of plagues and contagious diseases. He is probably bluffing, but I hid them for safety's sake. Tante Hilde thinks they could be real."

"Shit."

Match.

"Hagen, do you think I'm the kind of person who wanders around with improbable combinations of deadly bacterial cultures and viral infusions in my jacket pocket?"

"Whaaaat?"

"He's your client, isn't he? I'm not responsible. You should have got him the things he wanted."

"How much do you want, Mo? I know the way you think. You, Mo, not him. I can't believe there's anyone else involved. However, I will make sure you are paid whatever you want, so long as you promise me not to release the stuff, ever. Just let us destroy it all, incineration. I'll make sure you get anything you want, Mo. Anything at all, I swear."

"There's no need to try to bribe me. I'm not trying to hold anyone to ransom."

"How much do you want, Mo, just tell me and I'll give you the money, anything you want and we'll sort this thing out, OK?"

"I'm being followed."

"I'm not surprised. Thank God somebody knows where you are. Is there a queue?"

"Across the street. There's a dark blue BMW, just like yours, but it isn't yours. I've seen it two or three times already today. Out in the countryside. I can remember it overtaking us. Then it was parked over the way from Tante Hilde's new place in the Amalien Park. Now it's parked across the road from the phone box."

"What street is that?"

"Mauerstrasse, Wall Street. Ha!"

"I might have known."

"Yes."

"Do you want a lift?" says Hagen with a scurrilous giggle of laughter.

"So it is you, I wasn't sure. I took a taxi, but the driver wouldn't stop talking. I stopped here and got out, decided to walk, then get the U-bahn."

"Mo, how long have we know each other?"

"Nearly forty years."

"And still you don't trust me?"

"No."

"Turn around and watch. I will flash the lights twice. The way you've made a target of yourself in that phone box, I could just as easily roll down the window and shoot you, you realise that? Ping, pong. OK, I'll flash the lights now. That was the first and now I'm flashing them again."

"No."

"What do you mean - no?"

"The lights didn't flash."

"Don't be stupid, I just flashed them twice. One, two, there, again, one, two. You think I can't count?"

"No, you didn't."

Mo is almost as puzzled as Hagen. He had fully expected the lights to flash on when Hagen said they would, but nothing changed, no-one moved, the lights were off. Hagen is sitting behind the wheel of his favourite car wondering whether something dreadful has happened to the electrics and he flashes the lights again and is relieved to see the intense quartz beam brilliantly reflected from the car in front.

"There," says Hagen into the phone, "You saw that didn't you."

"Yes, shit, wrong car. There are two. Right hand side just up the street, from where you're parked, another one, blue BMW, just the same, even shinier than yours, polished, glistening, fully engineered poetry, as you like to say, with darkened windows. You got a twin I never heard about, or something? I'm out of here, you bastard. Bye bye, Go."

Hagen drives, as Mo dives away from the phone and takes shelter behind the last surviving remnants of Berlin's original fortifications.

He waits for the reaction.

Nothing.

No shots.

No-one gives chase.

Not a hand grenade in sight.

Half a minute later, the other dark blue BMW pulls slowly away from its parking place, drives to the end of the street and turns left, leaving Mo lying behind the low wall feeling rather foolish.

As he'd said to Hagen, he's decided to go home by underground. Mo catches a train on Line 2 from Mohrenstrasse which will take him to WittenbergPlatz, near the KaDeWe on Tauenzienstrasse, where he changes and takes the Krumme Lanke train as far as Rüdesheimer Platz, which is only five minutes from home. Without really thinking, he buys a kilo of apricots from the Turkish fruit and vegetable shop on the corner. They cost five marks fifty and are ripe and sweet. He also buys some olives, a big round loaf of white bread and a small piece of feta cheese. The rain begins as he's walking back to the motorway house and the roar of hissing wet-tyres is starting to growl through the air. As he takes the key out of his pocket, the slow throb of a diesel engine distracts him as a lorry changes gear.

When he gets to the flat, Inez is waiting for him.

"He phoned ten minutes ago," she says.

"I don't want to talk to him after that charade in the Mauerstrasse," grumbles Mo, "Drove off and left me, just the way he always ran off when we were kids."

"What?"

"Hagen."

"Not Hagen, I mean 'him', the 'virus man', him. Bloody Hagen phoned a couple of minutes later and asked me to tell you he was sorry," Inez explains, "Now listen, the 'Virus Man' was really jumpy. He is terrified, in a panic. I couldn't get him to calm down and explain. He broke the call off in mid-conversation. He wasn't being rude, he was too frightened to continue."

"Did you tell him we buried the things?"

"Yes."

"And."

"That's when he began to panic," explains Inez, "Says that is the worst thing we could have done. The concrete will distort and expand. The whole thing will split open and roots will take a grip of it all. The diseases will be released into the atmosphere, get washed into the groundwater, a host of vectors, animals, birds, insects spreading infection everywhere. Total fuck up, Mo. I think he definitely wants to kill himself, maybe us too, I'm not certain, but I'm sure he's having second thoughts about poisoning the rest of the planet."

Mo sounds aggrieved and starts hurrying around the flat, cursing and fidgeting with frustration, "Oh, no. That's not fair. First he doesn't tell us what to do with the bloody germ pool, now he's taking the easy way out. Slimy git. That wouldn't be fair, killing himself! He goes and tops himself, leaving us, you and me who have nothing to do with any of this, to sort out his problems and take the blame. What a bastard, I'll kill him for that, if he doesn't kill himself first. I don't even understand why he took the virus' out of the lab in the first place, do you?"

"He tried to explain that, but it didn't make much sense. I suspect he's just another mid-life madman. One of those thirty-five year olds crushed in a career crisis. School, University, Job, Madhouse, Crisis. He's just crazy, out of his mind, nothing exceptional."

Inez' mother had introduced her to a succession of people each individually far more broken and confused than the man she had been talking with, so, she was familiar with the main gradations of madness, from eccentricity via deeply disturbed towards the lurid high ground of criminal insanity. A psychopath somehow reminds Inez of cycle paths, but she knows the similarities are negligible. However dangerous he might prove to humanity at large, Inez regarded the Virus Man as more or less normal. Hazels is nuts and so is you. That the virus' amounted to an unofficial outbreak of biological warfare, a threat to the planet, was a proposition she had yet to come to terms with and was rather unwilling to consider.

"Mo?" says Inez plaintively, subconsciously repressing these unpalatable, yet unavoidable conclusions.

"Yes?" he replies, wondering what she's going to ask.

"There are some photos I have to finish. If you want the bathroom, can you go now, before I set up the enlarger. Yes, I think I'll get my darkroom work done, then we can see each other this evening. Mo?"

"Yes?"

"Can you sort this virus thing out today, please? You see there's your birthday and I shall be really furious if you don't make it to forty, right? It will upset all kinds of plans I have in mind, OK?"

Even now, Mo is surprised that Inez hasn't worked out his real age and happily colludes in this fiction of the lost decade. As he stands on the cusp of a half century, he finds it hard to credit that she still thinks he's only thirty-nine, but he has no problems with her imperial grandiloquence.

This is presidential behaviour of the kind that sees what's next on the agenda, then delegates. Hunger and famine, ah yes, Colin; conflict and armageddon, 'leetza, as ever; slump and despondency, Alan, could you keep your eye on developments. Now, what else have we? That's right, a threat of pestilence and plague. Maybe that's one of yours Tony, but why don't we ask Mo Hoffman to take a preliminary look, while we enjoy a round or two of golf? Thank you everyone. Reports back next Thursday, no wait a minute, Thursday is Chloe's day, let's make that Friday. Never give a sucker an even break.

Inez' retreat into the bathroom serves much the same purpose. She had signalled her concern, then delegated the search for a solution. No-one could accuse her of ignoring the problem.

When Mo hears the key turn to lock the bathroom door from the inside, he knows she will be cooped up with her pictures for the next five hours, so he takes a couple of files into the big room, settles into the grey armchair and brushes up on his knowledge of libraries and antiquarian booksellers in Heidelburg, Freiburg and Tübingen. Just like Inez, he is lying to himself, pretending there is nothing wrong.

When the doorbell rings it is answered by an almighty crash of breaking glass from behind the bathroom door, closely followed by an energetic stream of curses. Mo asks if Inez is alright? She says she is, but a batch of glass plates aren't any more. "Neither a batch, nor plates, just pools of chemical everywhere and shards of messed up glass. I'm putting on the light to clean up." Then he answers the entry-phone.

Once he's come upstairs, the man introduces himself as Michel Marcelle Harfleur of Bremerhaven, "visiting you to discuss the virus question, may I enter?"

Astonished for once, (How the hell does this guy know about the virus'?), Mo leads the stranger onto the balcony without really knowing who he is, though its obvious he is well aware of what has been going on. M.M. Harfleur is extremely tall, very thin, tentative in speech and timid of gesture, which goes with the dark suit and polished black shoes he's wearing. He is also unmistakeably 'official', the unseen hand at work for whoever is supposed to be in charge.

He immediately commiserates with Mo and Inez' predicament, both courteous and thoughtful, well spoken, though characteristically reserved. The privacy of their sanctuary in the countryside has been grievously abused, he concedes, with a subtle display of sensitivity.

Harfleur is a little too well mannered for Mo's liking and he is irritated by his methodical, quietly spoken, explanations. The voice is so soft it hovers half way between a whisper and a lisp. This all worries Mo.

His former colleague, Harfleur claims, had no right to send them what are highly restricted laboratory materials. The items in question, as he refers to the bugs, should never properly have

223

been removed from the bio-filtered storage environments in which they are held like prisoners in a dungeon. Indeed any unauthorised activities are a criminal offence, which should land their perpetrator in an equally uninviting prison. This worries Mo even more. It is beginning to seem as though the glass phials really do contain the biblical plague bugs and their horrible new cousins.

"More than any other beings on this earth, worse even than radioactivity, these micro-organisms are man's worst enemies," he concludes assertively, "Our only purpose at the Institute is to analyse their behaviour and tame them. All else is futile. My life is devoted to these goals. I'm sure you understand that we should like to recover the material and see it returned to safe keeping in its rightful place at our laboratory, while we continue the hunt for Dr. Hahn. This may seem rather melodramatic Mr. Hoffman, but let me assure you that no-one has ever come to harm in the arms of a monster from outer space, or found themselves at the mercy of a malign alien intelligence, while millions and millions of us have fallen victim to virus' every day of every year in every millennia since humankind first trod the earth."

He leans forward and looks gently into Mo's eyes, inviting a tear of sympathy, or at least a sentimental dampness round the eyeball.

"What kind of car do you drive, Mr. Haff-le-ur?" asks Mo, glancing at the card and feigning ignorance.

Much to his disappointment, the man says he doesn't drive, "I came here by U-bahn, then walked. It's only five minutes away." Mo would have been relieved if he'd said he'd just bought himself a brand new dark blue BMW.

"Would you like an apricot?" asks Mo instead.

"Thankyou," says the stranger and reaches forward to choose one of the juicy fruits. "Delicious," he says approvingly, after biting firmly into its golden flesh.

In addition to his job at the lab where the missing scientists works, Harfleur claims to be working for the Science Ethics Committee of the Joint European Regions Research Council, or JERC as he pronounces it.

This might be true, but Mo has no way of checking.

The Director General, Harfleur continues, has asked him, or so he claims, to investigate the case of the disappearing genetic engineer. "This matter is cause for concern at the very highest levels. The young man may be suffering some kind of psychological disturbance and we wish he may receive the necessary therapeutic assistance as soon as possible."

"Oh, really?" Mo says, being cynical, "Have you reported all this to the police?" He really does want to know, but he's hoping his anxiety doesn't show.

"Not as yet."

"Why-ever not?" asks Mo wanting to sound indignant.

"A man who leaves home for a few days, or fails to turn up for work is hardly going to interest the police. On the other hand, if I went to them and described the possible annihilation of the human race, I would probably find myself locked up, rendered unable to act, not only under suspicion, but treated first as a madman, then as a surrogate for the guilty party. I am convinced, infectious diseases or not, our police's reaction would reduce northern Europe to a state of complete chaos inside a couple of days. Imagine all the provincial police chiefs, a dream come true for them and a nightmare for the rest of us. Roadblocks, mass arrests, curfews, riot police on every street corner, media censorship, false alarms and panic, all in the name of public safety and order. 24hour coverage on satellite news. The overtime payments would be enormous and the enquiries into allegations of police brutality, time consuming and expensive. Violence would be inevitable. No, it wouldn't do. Sometimes we face problems, which we must resolve simply and quietly, with as little fuss as possible, no press, or publicity and no expectation of thanks."

Mo decides Harfleur would probably make a good assassin, then wonders if this might indeed be his profession? A cold killer on the prowl, eating other people's apricots.

"Hello," he would say politely. "How are you?" he would ask solicitously. As the victim thinks to themselves, 'what a charming man', he would turn to leave, "Well Goodbye then" and turning again, he would shoot, 'bang'. A freshly filled in copy of the death certificate for the files and the other half of his cheque's in the post. Nasty thought, thinks Mo, wondering whether he should get his retaliation in first.

Having heard what Harfleur has to say, Mo brings the discussion to a halt. "That's as may be Mr. Flaneur, but I do not understand why you are talking to me about all this. I am neither biologist, epidemiologist, nor virologist. I am a printer, a craftsman. I create images and texts. Please sit down. I don't like the way you are stalking round the room. If you want to talk to me, then sit down on the sofa like any other visitor. I do not understand why you have come here to see us. I have no idea what you are talking about. I know nothing about Ethical Committees or virus'. You have 'commiserated with our predicament', but so far as I am aware, we face neither dilemmas, nor predicaments. So far as I am concerned our only untoward contact with virus' happens about twice a year when we catch flu."

"I'm sorry you don't seem to have understood," Harfleur says patiently, his demeanour unruffled, "My enquiries are of a private and professional nature, but we do have access to certain official sources of information. This signature, for example, accepting delivery of the packet containing the virus' phials was signed for here and here, while you were staying at your cottage. That is your handwriting, I believe, 'Herr Oscar Lafontaine?', so to say, Mr. Hoffman?"

Mo knows when it is time to admit defeat and he invites

Harfleur to explain a little more.

The missing engineer, Harfleur says precisely, had received public funding for his research, which was carried out at two laboratories, one near the Technical University in Hamburg and one just over the Schleswig-Holstein border into Denmark, where the rules on experiments in genetic engineering are less stringent than in Germany. Now, even the man's colleagues are starting to deny that their efforts have born fruit.

Harfleur claims that he is deeply suspicious. He doesn't believe the biologists. In fact, he isn't sure what he can believe any more.

Mo agrees. He doesn't believe Harfleur either.

"Belief," says Mo, without intending to sound enigmatic "is getting to be difficult, stretched beyond our normal capacities, shall we say, Mr H?"

After she had heard the doorbell ring, it had taken Inez about twenty minutes to clean up the darkroom. When she finally comes into the living room, Mo is surprised that she's already had time to change and skim on a veneer of make-up.

Well spoken, but reserved as before, Harfleur introduces himself to Inez and she lets her eyes gaze into his a lingering moment longer than he finds comfortable. Her look is glacial.

The contrast between them couldn't be greater.

He mutters and murmurs and mumbles like a real Berliner, while her voice rings out like a bell.

"So, how the hell did you track us down, Misser Haffler?"

"Your name is in the telephone book, Hoffman, M."

"There are lots of names in the phone book and lots of them are Hoffman's, depending how many 'f's and 'n's are involved and among those there are a wide variety of 'm's from Mai to Mustafa and back to Martha via Mohammet. How did you know that ours was the one you wanted?"

She's plain and forthright with her questions. He does his best.

"You own the little cottage by the lake. We checked in the

property registers. Inez Schmidt, born Berlin-Karlshorst, German Democratic Republic, daughter of KGB Colonel Heinrich Heppelman Schmidt, married to Indian Communist Party agent, Indira Muckerjee-Schmidt. Inherited the property from Herrn Arthur Albrecht Schmidt, a German national, of Tel Aviv, Israel. Correct?"

"So what," scowls Inez, "na und?"

"How long have you know Dr. Hahn?"

"Who? I don't know any Dr. Hahn?"

"Frau Schmidt, the Dr. Hahn your husband and I have been talking about. The one who sent you the package."

That she is being obstructive is obviously true, but Harfleur isn't sure whether she has anything to hide. How well might she have known this scientist?

Her whole rigmarole could easily turn out to be a demonstration of typical bloody-minded Berlin stubborness. Dominated by the curl of doubt twisting her lips into a scowl, Inez' expression unmistakeably suggests the latter, an impression enhanced by the mild inflammation of her left eye caused by a stray splash of darkroom chemical a couple of hours before.

"Michel Marcelle," she says accusingly, "I know you. Oh, yes, I can remember everything about you, you fucking bastard."

Like a rabbit caught in the headlights of an oncoming car, Harfleur blinks a blink, but doesn't move a muscle to evade the oncoming juggernaut.

"I don't recall," he protests meekly, while a flurry of half forgotten incidents, minor embarrassments no more, sweep through his mind, "I really can't imagine how we might have met."

"But, I do," Inez affirms, "Indeed I do, liar. In those days, you were too obsessed by your own ego to notice other people, or very much of what was going on around you."

Harfleur glances round the room, as if he expects to chance on some relic to remind him of an earlier encounter.

"You were such an irritating person, my mother told me everything about you. Indira Muckerjee-Schmidt? Sage and guru to the troubled youth of Berlin, right?"

Michel Marcelle Harfleur, then known as Michael Hässler from Wilmersdorf, had been one of Inez' mother's most loyal subjects; a candidate for psychotherapeutic analysis, that is, for which purpose he attended twice weekly sessions at their flat overlooking the Landwehr Kanal in Kreuzberg. Except for a brief pause in the summer of 1983, when he was arrested on suspicion of murder and kept in custody for three weeks on the island of Mallorca, 'Creepy', as Inez and Indira had called him, consulted her mother regularly from 1981 to 1986. He paid his bills regularly too, which also marked him out as exceptional, if not clinically abnormal.

He had displayed a series of deviant tendencies, the nervous twitches all too mild for anyone to recommend incarceration, but sufficiently obvious for people to avoid sitting next to him on the bus. Inez cast her mind back in an effort to remember what he had done for a living. None of the accusations of child molesting had ever been taken seriously, she could remember that, but what had he done for a living? Social work?

Clearly, he is a changed man. Is he still a deranged man?

Gone are the nervous ticks and twitches, the nose-picking, but what has replaced them in the twisted lattice of his personality?

Gripping hold of half a memory, less than a memory, an impression really, no more than a reminder, she recalled that 'Creepy' had studied law and even managed to qualify as someone specialising in property and ownership.

Although she was too young to remember much about the 1980's, it was blindingly obvious that the 'wende', the period of German Re-Unification, when east joined west, must have been a goldmine for types like Hässler, who, even then, was already well on his way to becoming his alter ego, Harfleur. Millions of disputes arose in the New Länder, not only about who owned what, but who had once owned what and who after several generations of births and deaths might have the right to own what.

After the dirty tricks of the property world, Inez decided it was predictable that he should somehow turn his attention to genetics and viral contagion. This was hardly the outcome her mother had expected from her therapeutic endeavours, so Inez assumed, but no-one could doubt the effectiveness of her methods.

Standing before her now, Inez concludes he is a fully fledged malevolence. To her dismay, he does genuinely seem to have achieved some kind of official standing. Michel Marcelle is the least suited of all her Mother's former patients to be given any kind of licence to pry into other people's lives. Indira had categorised him as a class 2 B&H, blackmailer and hostage-taker, temperamentally of sufficient incompetence to endanger the lives of his victims. Might that too have changed?

Michel Marcelle does not see himself as quite so disagreeable a person as Inez implies. The long years of therapy had achieved at least a nominal measure of self awareness, even if it had only served to moderate, rather than alter his behaviour patterns. The simple passage of time had achieved at least as much, maturing and mellowing his less attractive tendencies.

It is almost four years since he had carried a butterfly-knife regularly and six months have gone by without him using the canister of CS gas he still carries in his jacket pocket. The old brass knuckle-duster, which had once belonged to his grandfather lies almost forgotten at his sister's house, along with the key to his special wardrobe which they keep in her dressing table drawer.

Now he can afford better quality suits, Michel Marcelle has discovered bureaucratic methods to inflict pain and distress on his unwitting victims, without resorting to violence, or even the mildest threat of physical intimidation. He simply promises to undertake a thorough procedural examination of the situation and administrators quail.

In Germany, the promise of a thorough bureaucratic examination is enough to make anyone break out in a cold sweat. Wars may be fought and won; children conceived and brought to term; the business cycle may turn from boom to slump; comets may complete whole orbits of the sun and plunge into the atmosphere of one of the great planets, yet in such a brief span, a thorough bureaucratic investigation of the facts and circumstances, participants and consequences, both judicial and paranormal is unlikely to have gotten so far as 'C' from 'A', assuming any measurable progress is achieved at all. Final reports are almost unknown and meetings continue beyond retirement.

Michel Marcelle is, anyway, completely unconcerned by Inez' disapproval. Call him Hässler, or Harfleur, he doesn't care.

Taking a couple of steps towards the balcony door, he angles himself to stand silhouetted against the daylight. This has the odd effect of making him seem like a stand up paper cut out, since the grey of his suit almost perfectly matches the greys of their interior decoration. Mo wonders idly whether to shoot the man and have him stuffed as a trophy, a still life 'a la' early Gilbert & George, or simply to enjoy this unusual lack of contrast between man and environment, a chance encounter between curtaining, a lack of personality and solar alignment - a hyper-expressionist moment too brief to be photographed and doomed to remain forever unrecorded.

"Some questions best remain unanswered," Michel Marcelle begins, as if echoing Mo's thoughts, "I don't think you will approve of what I'm going to say, or like what you are going to hear, but I haven't travelled half way across Europe just to pay a simple social call."

What-ever the reason he's here, Inez is now completely

unsympathetic towards the man and looking for flaws, she notices one of his shoelaces is undone and there is an anonymous stain on one leg of his trousers.

""I am here for a purpose," Hässler Harfleur adds threateningly and altogether serious, "Our concerns are probably a little different to your own. Even so, in this instance, we consider that you will agree with us more than you will disagree. It is also true that we will disagree with you, but, in current circumstances, we are the only people who will take your case seriously. 'They' will simply try to discover the whereabouts of the virus' and take them from you."

Inez snaps to attention.

Who are 'we' and who are 'they'?

If Mo and Inez are 'us', she says to herself, and Michel Marcelle, 'other'; enough you might think; though he thinks of his colleagues as 'we', then 'they' becomes the great unknown, the 'other' to define the 'otherness' of their circumstances. 'Oh, mother', mumbles Inez, thinking of another 'other', wondering distractedly why she never had a brother.

"Who are you talking about?" asks Mo without pausing to dwell on the analytical.

"The domain of genetic manipulation is privileged to suffer the pitfalls of self-regulation," says Hässler Harfleur, sounding reasonable enough without making any sense to them, before he embarks on an even more flowery explanation.

"This little world of competence has but a single purpose, yet we must divide ourselves perchance to undertake a thousand functions. We propose, evaluate, undertake and criticise ourselves in parallel and tandem. One day judge, the next day judged, first this, then that, permissions granted, or refused. We inhabit a world defined by Chinese Walls of disclosure, non-disclosure and self-disclosure, peer group valuation, confidentiality and information sharing, transparency and subsidiarity; the need to know defined and implemented with respect to verticality, horizontality and networking, across the formats, inter, intra and extra. From desk to desk, office to office, keyboard to e-mail address, running unseen between companies, allotting responsibilities and accrediting organisations, government departments, the invisible boundaries of separation, dividing us from ourselves and the others who know us for what we really are. All that is but the complicity of those who look at the same wall from opposite sides and in this abstracted circumstance, our commonality is really the knowledge that the wall exists at all. Our dilemmas exist, therefore, largely in the ethical dimension."

Mo deliberates, then leans forward, ready to ask a question.

"Who determines the form these Chinese Walls display?"

"They are the result of long deliberation and collective effort."

"They are of course abstractions," says Mo, awed by this new addition to the lexicon of walls and walling..

"Naturally."

Inez wonders whether Michel Marcelle has realised, in current company, just how important walls are.

"They too are interested in walls."

"They?" asks Mo, hoping he sounds naive.

"The Masons and Master Builders, Guilds and Lodges, Gods and Mammon, dreams and nightmares, legends of Isis and Osirus. Brothers on the Square, their 'Sekretarius' a man of complete trust, a man who would be King, you know the kind of thing."

Does he?

Mo gives Michel Marcelle a glance of cynical disbelief.

"You mean 'freemasons'?"

"Self and same, all for one and one for ourselves."

"And one for the road," says Inez, almost silently.

Mo laughs.

Michel Marcelle sniggers, "I knew you wouldn't believe me."

Inez grimaces, "Fuck off, creepie. We've heard enough horse

shit for one day. You get your greedy little nose back to your committee, or your company, or your cowshed, or whatever it is and leave us alone."

"She's right," says Mo, "Time to go."

"If that's how you feel, I will take my leave."

"That is exactly how we feel," says Inez, "Go on, creepie, Fuck off."

"Mr. Harfleur," Mo says slowly and deliberately, "stay away from us. Don't try to meddle with the cottage. If you do, there's a dose of bubonic plague coming your way in the post, understood?"

Michel Marcelle looks down at his shoes, as if he's expecting to find a message written on them, then stands up and walks to the door.

"So be it," he says. He's easy going, relaxed, just someone leaving an old acquaintance's apartment, where the corpse is cooling down.

"Inez, we do keep your mother under observation at all times. It would be tragic were she to suffer an accident by the riverside. In winter, there are currents under the ice, deceptively fast and the ice is treacherously thick. Were anyone to be so unlucky as to fall into the stream and get dragged beneath the ice-shelf, their end would be inevitable and swift. Let me give you an address for the dose of plague you mentioned. I wouldn't want it misdirected and dispatched 'return to sender', or re-routed like Paddington Bear to some railway station 'Lost property' office."

He hands her one of the business cards, with e-mail, fax and phone numbers. There's also an address, in Bremerhaven. The company he works for has a name, 'Cross Key and Compass Consulting'.

"Our offices used to be in Antwerp, but we moved to Bremerhaven when the Kaiser abdicated and was forced into exile there. I'm not sure why. Some of my colleagues expected we would move offices again following German Reunification, but it was not to be. Good day to you both. I can see my own way out."

As Harfleur leaves, the phone begins to ring again.

Inez answers, "Oh, hello, I thought it might be you. We've just had a visit from your friend Michel Marcelle Harfleur, if you can believe that's the latest name for our old friend Creepy Hässler. Of course he's changed, but without any noticeable improvement, so far as I could see.

Yes, Mum, he's fine and I'm fine too.

Yes.

So, how are you.

Oh dear.

I see.

Yes, Mum. of course I understand.

Yes. How dreadful.

How could they be so awful. Honestly.

Right then, we'll see you Sunday week, for coffee, yes.

We're looking forward already.

Bye, Mum.

I'll tell him.

Of course I won't forget,

Bye now."

CHAPTER 19

A carefully printed note tacked to the front door of the old house says, 'Ancient Monuments bring Financial Ruin'. The paint on the door has lost its colour and is gradually peeling away from the wood in a series of gentle curls. The wall of the house is a dirty grey. Moss and grasses are growing in the gutters. Out of sight, a liverwort has colonised a downpipe. The sun is shining, but the narrow street is veiled in gloomy shadow.
Number 37.
Number 39.
The virus man had announced that he would leave a message at Number 5.
Given the decayed state of the whole street, an alley really, flanked by ill-matched rows of two-storey timber framed houses, it was obvious no-one had spent a penny on their upkeep since the end of world war two. The smell could be worse, but it isn't, because so few people live here any more.
This is the little town of Nauen.
Inez has never been here before and Mo had trouble with the directions Inez' mother had passed on. It had been Indira who had taken the phone message and her sense of directions usually consisted of telling the taxi driver which airport to go to, then finding the right gate for the flight to India, or San Francisco. She had never bothered learning to drive. Why should she? In

those days, there had been a bloody great wall round the city to stop you getting anywhere, even if you tried.

Some miles west of the city, Nauen is famous for having been the focal point of the Red Army's massive pincer movement around Berlin in the dying weeks of World War II. Having fought for complete encirclement, the northern and southern armies met here. For the succeeding decades, the Soviet battle plan to invade West Berlin depended on tank columns rolling along the Heerstrasse, that broad straight road Hitler had built from the Olympic village on the outskirts, direct towards the Brandenburg Gate.

Nauen has never really recovered, though a spanking new set of regional tax offices have been built since Unification and a rubbery smelling factory closed, or at least cleansed. The astonishing arrays of long wave and Warsaw Pact radio transmitters have been dismantled and the Russians themselves withdrew in a cloud of purloined household goods and thinly disguised stolen cars. A dying breed, the young men of Nauen specialise in dangerous driving, tree impact and 'auto-destruction'.

The houses look uninhabited, but about one in three shows signs of life, historic hovels with dingy net curtains, a rubbish bin, a drooping geranium, flowerless behind unwashed glass.

Inez has knocked on the door of number 5, though there isn't much door left, so she's taken half a step inside already and asks if there is anybody there. She's almost at sneezing point.

"No," says Mo, trying to give her a fright, before a second voice says, "Who is that?"

"Is that you, Dr. Hahn?" Inez asks tentatively, then she sneezes.

There's a brief scuffling noise over their heads, then a shower of dust trickles through the holes in the battered ceiling. Inez pushes the door completely open and looks up, hoping to catch a glimpse of whoever it was, before she sneezes once more.

The air of subterfuge was completely unnecessary and wholly

unsustainable. With a great clumping of feet and more showers of dusty plaster, a heavily built man wearing a charcoal grey overcoat almost demolishes the bannisters as he tramples downstairs. In his late twenties, Mo can remember him from the meeting at Hagen's house, so he's amazed when Inez starts grinning like a circus chimp, bounces up and down, then gives the fellow an all embracing hug.

"Mitch!" she yells a couple of octaves higher than the voice Mo is used to hearing, "What the hell are you getting up to? This is Mo. We live together. He's almost forty. I can't believe it's you. We had Creepy Hassler snooping round our flat, but I didn't tell him anything."

Deciding he needs somewhere to sit down, thus introduced, Mo picks up an old orange box and sets it on end. Before he perches himself on it, he realises that rather than oranges, the blue labels suggest the box was intended for tins of top class Caspian caviar. Mo gives it an optimistic shake, but unfortunately it is empty.

Inez is spluttering before a sneeze, but the words spill out all the same, "Are those diseases real, you son of a bitch?"

Now Mitch is standing in the middle of the room with a big grin on his face. "Sure, they're real. You don't think I'd be firing blanks, do you?"

This is a none too oblique reference to their schooldays together, when Mitch and Inez had provided each other with sexual entertainment and hours of exploratory callisthenics. Exhausting but invigorating, Inez' Mother had said commending their efforts. Mitch was suitably enthusiastic, curious and from Inez' point of view, considerate. Then he left for a Technical University Institute in Karlsruhe and that was that, though he never forgot the tips Inez' mother had explained to him.

As he remembered Inez's vague remarks about old boyfriends, Mo suddenly felt the world contract around him. First the

Harfleur/Hässler, now a 'Mitch'. The plot had been domesticated. He could remember one of Inez' descriptions, which had loosely paraphrased the utterances of a Hollywood movie star.

She had enjoyed lying in the Tiergarten at night, while the border guards trained their night glasses on the sight of him plunging into her under the stars. So this was the one who had done the plunging. Unsurprisingly, Mo is not impressed. It would take an unusual man to meet one of his girlfriends former lovers and think to himself, there goes a better man than I.

The boy she described had suffered from none of the usual distractions, beer, football, drugs, hanging around listening to music, or riding around in his father's car as one of a gang of smelly footed teenagers. Whatever the drawbacks, he liked fucking and became rather good at it by the time she ditched him for an 'ossie' sound technician with a flat on the Schönhauser Allee, a collection of bootleg tapes and a seemingly desirable single of a bald East German actor singing 'House of the Rising Sun'.

Inez never imagined Mitch would get through University and embark on a career. She had expected him to self destruct in a cloud of angel dust. He had always seemed to be the lorry driving type, a roadie, like his father, who was a Sergeant in the French Army, proudly driving a PLUTON missile launcher around Alsace for fifteen years.

"But why did you send the phials to us at all? We don't even have a fridge out there."

"I hadn't expected that, but I knew the address for your cottage and it is the most isolated place I could find. The nearest towns are quite small. The next big city is Berlin and nobody cares about Berlin, so it doesn't matter which way the wind blows. Apart from that there aren't any significant centres of population for thousands of square kilometres in any direction. If there were to be an outbreak, I thought it might just about be containable. The towns could be sealed off. The military could sanitise that area, scorched earth policy, or a carefully controlled nuclear explosion. You can imagine the alternatives, none of them attractive, but several better than nothing. A quiet corner of the world, hidden in a sea of sterile sorrows. No worse than Chernobyl. The Brandenburg sand would turn to glass, but I don't think that would matter all that much. Then, I decided that of all the people I know, I thought you might be the only one who would sympathise with the situation and understand the sacrifice that might be necessary. And the other thing of course was that your Mum had told me about the cottage and explained that the global disaster line runs right through the garden, which set the seal on my decision. Inevitable, once I knew about the global disaster line, it was obvious I needn't look any further. This must be the place. She had surveyed it that summer we used to go walking in the Tiergarten."

"Well I'm glad you thought things out so thoroughly, Herr Hahn," says Mo, without blinking.

As Hahn is about to correct him, 'Not 'Herr' -'Herr Dr', I'm relieved you understand the problem', he doubles up, gasps and drops breathless, an excruciating pain shooting through his body, because Mo has knee'd him between the legs as hard as he knows how. The house shudders as the full weight of Hahn's body drops onto the old deal floorboards.

"Little bastard," says Mo curtly, realising he's seen the man before.

"Stop it, Mo, enough is enough, both of you," says Inez. When they turn to look at her, she says, "I do understand."

What does that mean? I do understand. Understand what, Mo wonders in blank amazement. His stomach churns at the realisation, that merely because they haven't died an excruciating death, Inez can choose to ignore the man's actions. She's standing there wearing an expression of placid toleration as if nothing untoward had occurred, or could occur. Mo looks at his shoes. If they were proper boots, he would gladly kick the groaning creep in the neck.

"Are you hurt?"

"Yes."

"Good. Get up. Explain. An orderly explanation, if such a thing is possible? Motivation, method, objectives. Don't digress. Start."

"My objective is to thwart a plot. My motivation is to save the world. My methods are diverse. I mean no-one harm. I can't get up, it hurts. Please don't kick me again."

"I'll think about that. You're lying."

"But I'm not digressing. Please don't kick me again. It hurts, really it's fucking intolerable."

"Now you're telling the truth."

As he looks down, first at the groaning young scientist, then glancing around him at the teetering frame of the old building, Mo realises that what he does next will represent a turning point in his life. He has a choice, yet before he can make that choice he must question his own motives. As well as repressing the urge to kick the man again, Mo feels like sneezing. If he kicked him, maybe the sneezing feeling would stop. There's a hint of damp and the slow smell of fungus and dry rot announces itself in his nostrils. The rest is moral decay.

Mitch lets himself relax a little as he realises that Mo probably isn't going to kick him again, but he stays down on the floor, anyway, subservient, because any sign of resistance is bound to trigger the old Berliner's wrath. Does she really believe this old wreck is only thirty nine?

He looks up at Inez, hoping for a sign, (Is it safe; Can I get up now? Does he kill people?) but she remains impassive.

Perhaps she's curious about how the pain feels as it flows through Mitch's body?

Perhaps she is curious about the limits to Mo's violence, now it has begun to reveal itself? Does his anger flood over the

241

boundaries of self control?
Is this exciting?
Is she intrigued?
Perhaps she is simply bemused that two of her favourite lovers should be confronting one another on the floor of a ruined house in a dump like Nauen?
Mo seems to have lost interest in the scuffle.
He is thirsty.
Unexpectedly, he is also affected by an odd sense of insecurity. Sometimes, Mo thinks he is thinking like an artist, then he corrects himself and decides his interests are merely obsession, a selfish trick of his worn out psychology, highly personal subjective impressions and expressions of an idiosyncratic temperament. Walls on the brain, the penalty he must pay for being brought up in Berlin. That's it, a walled up mind and a warped personality. He wants to hide, or lock a door and shut the world outside.
A statement of fact, not mood.
Always the bloody wall and all its counterparts across the world.
Now the world is closing in again.
Mo doesn't like Mitch. He is irritating and too big. He takes up too much space. There are worse things in life that Mo has to attend to and Mitch's insistence that they drop everything to deal with his viral suspicions is a distraction, what's more, a selfish, ill-conceived distraction. As a young man, Mo would have been fascinated, but no longer.
Until Mo met Inez, he had been more or less content in his misfit isolation. The deal with Hagen was workable, sometimes awkward, yet enough for him to avoid working-life as a machine minder at the drug factory, or a clerical assistant for the city administration. He could always keep his head above water, but there are times when he wonders if the security of driving a bus, or even more fun a tram would have been a better choice.

Then he reminds himself that Hagen's business has given him the chance to travel the world and explore the detailed symptoms of his inbred agoraphobia. For much of his life, without a passport, public transport would have got Mo no further than Spandau. "I have lived in strange times," Mo concedes to confirm his doubts and Inez looks at him wondering whether he's talking to her or simply to himself.

There are also times when Inez wonders what is going on inside Mo's head and this is one of them. Even Mitch seems to have realised there's something odder going on in Mo's mind than his own, which is a rare example of objective thinking on his part.

Mitch hasn't actually stood up yet, but he's leaning on one arm, half squatting, half kneeling, more or less certain the kicking is over, but absolutely unclear what might happen next. He doesn't want to make a run for it, but he would like Mo to concentrate on the issues at hand. His wishes are ignored.

Mo sinks into a introspective slump, leaning with his back against the door so no-one can come in, or out.

He is not happy. The whole business of walls has permeated his existence for as long as he can remember. Hagen once called them his leitmotif. Now he has the oddest sense of destiny. This old building is crumbling. The walls are decaying so rapidly, that the timber is already being exposed and there's blue sky peeping through the cracks. Actually, this is untrue. There is a sheet of sky-blue gyp-roc board behind the wall. The sunshine has gone. The weather outside has turned dull and grey.

Looking down at the man on the floor, expectant and resentful, Mo then glances quickly across at Inez. She is staring at him with a puzzled expression, distant and removed. It feels wrong. She is distant. Mo always envisages their efforts in personal terms, Mo and Inez. Inez and Mo, walled within the private sphere of their lives together. Books and more books. Paintings, drawings, fantasies, food and photographs, sex. The library.

243

Interiors and exteriors, both equally private. Neither privileged, nor sponsored, until Inez began to make contact with galleries and art centres, it had never occurred to him, or rather he had never taken the thought seriously, that what he was up to had wider consequences. Most of the artists Hagen had introduced to Mo were types who half believe their work will change the world, or at least bring them wealth and fame, whereas Mo had never really considered himself an artist. Like an artist, sure, sometimes, but printing is the trade of a skilled artisan. He'd never looked himself in the mirror and thought, this is the reflection of an artist.

When Mo steals books and manuscripts, he does so without making moral distinctions. The same is almost true when he draws. He is aware of his craftsmanship, but he does not overestimate the subtlety of his talent. He has never been at one with a community, nor will he ever be. That he gets paid from time to time is mere convenience. No-one who has bought one of Mo's drawings has ever shown the slightest interest in him personally, or acknowledged the artistry of his vision, rather than the excellence of its execution.

Everything he does is conducted as part of a private dialogue with himself and sometimes with Inez.

Until now, that is.

Now, the significance of his actions is subject to alarming exaggeration. His life is being robbed of its continuity. Not only has he changed, but the dynamics of that past are no longer relevant for the present. The world of his childhood has ceased to exist, the foundations of all his attitudes and ideas ceased to prevail, yet even if one percent of the virus story is true, whatever he does, active, inactive; fast, or slow; good, bad, or indifferent; his deeds could have massive consequences for other people, for people he has never met and will never get to know. It may even cost them their lives. Nothing has prepared him for this. It feels like politics. Mo has never harboured a single political ambition. Now he is encumbered with an awesome political decision, the kind of decision real politicians hope never to face.

Mo sits down again, hunches over like a Samurai warrior, glaring Mitch straight in the eye, "Now, what was it exactly, that you want to tell us?"

Mitch glances around uncertainly, looking first at Inez, then at Mo. There is murder in the air.

"Well then?" says Inez wondering where Mitch last had his hair cut. It looks as if someone has taken a lawnmower to it.

"One of my closest friends thinks you are probably a poisoner, a criminal psychopath, someone who should be locked away, but not believed," adds Mo gratuitously, "so do be cautious what you say. She has the authority to ensure her wishes are carried out and whatever else may happen, if she has you incarcerated, all your opinions will be ignored for the rest of your life."

"That wouldn't surprise me," Mitch answers, then he tells them a raft of lies, peppered with half truths here and there, which reveal more to Inez and Mo than Mitch imagines, because some of his lies are much closer to the truth than he realises. These aberrations are Mo's favourite form of communication, the inadvertent truth.

Mitch explains, more, or less honestly, how the police raided his house three times. "Said they were looking for materials which had gone missing from the labs." He wonders whether Mo and Inez believe him. Then he describes how the police had turned up at work one day, two in their normal green jacket uniforms with tan trousers, one in a motorcyclist's brown leather jacket and four plain-clothes types. The five men spent the day interviewing most of the people who worked there, while the two women systematically went through all his files. He has started to embroider the story with palpable untruths.

"Did they ask about your paintings?"

"Yes. Though only the Dutch seascapes," (an outright lie), "the rest didn't interest them. I gave them my dealer's address in Den Haag. He's a German guy from Hamburg, but he keeps a shop there, selling over-priced water colours to the suspects' wives and girlfriends."

"Suspects? Who?"

"People in town for the war crimes trials. They all want souvenirs from Belgium to take back to their friends."

As Mo had expected, the man hadn't recognised him from their meeting at Hagen's house in Hamburg.

Then he surprises Mo.

"I didn't buy much from this guy," Mitch explains, "He once tried to sell me some fake Iranian manuscripts. Told a long and complicated story about an academic collector, who'd died. I checked it out. Went to Manchester in England. It was all untrue. You can't trust art dealers, that's a fact."

Where is the story leading, wonders Mo, as he waits for Mitch to carry on.

"No academic. No family. No private collection being sold. No blind girl in Paris," the young man continues, wary of Mo's scepticism and fearful of his tetchiness, "Some pictures had been stolen from the John Rylands Library a few months earlier, but they had been recovered. Someone put them up for auction in New York. A suspected connection to an arms dealer, working from Istanbul, remained unproven, but it doesn't matter much, since this Iranian had been murdered a few days before anyway. I expect the pictures I saw were some kind of fancy photocopy. After that I decided I wouldn't buy anything else from him."

The lies are smooth and accomplished, but the man is a little too flabby, despite his youth, and very out of condition.

Mo wants to ask him whether a false provenance automatically means the pictures themselves must be fakes, or whether it was simply a cover story for genuine material which had been stolen. He doesn't even mention the word thief. Then he wants to ask what became of the genetic code he'd been sent from Denmark, but he keeps the knowledge to himself. Mitch is not worth informing.

Mo is mildly amused that the man thinks that his half forgotten friendship with Inez is the link that has brought them together, an almighty red herring to tangle him up in Mo's thieving net, which may yet prove useful if he's ever in need of an alibi. He would surely confirm that the first time they had met was in the strange confines of a tumble down front room in Nauen.

"About the 'problem'?" is all Mo asks next, because he finds it difficult to imagine why anyone sick, or sane should want to send vials of plague and pestilence through the post to someone's country cottage.

Before Mitch starts to explain, Inez goes to the door and looks up and down the street. If she and Mo had managed to find Mitch, shouldn't Michel Marcelle be trailing close behind?

"Yes," Mitch drawls reluctantly, obviously confused, not quite sure whether he'd mentioned the code in his story or not. "I needed a hostage, not you, please believe me, I mean the bugs. I had no alternative. I took the bugs hostage. They are my bargaining counter."

"Why?"

"I have been working with these people for three years, three and a half years, now. They recruited me with the promise that I could complete my doctorate, a necessity in this industry, but I found myself dragged into work I consider unethical. The laboratory where I work is almost new. Most of our energies go into straightforward biotechnology, working out cheaper ways of making drugs and specialist chemicals for industry. We're not trying find a cure for cancer, or the elixir of eternal youth, but making things cheaper is an expensive game. To make cheap cars you need expensive robots; to make cheap drugs, you need expensive research programmes. That means you need money

247

to stay in the game. You need money from investors, money from banks, money from charities and research foundations, money from governments, money from anywhere you find it, and that's the problem, anywhere and the other problem is you have to try and keep all these people happy all the time, because if any one of them starts causing trouble, within a couple of weeks half your finance can pull out. My boss spends eighty per cent of his time trying to raise more money."

"So what?" says Inez, unimpressed. "That's what bosses are supposed to do, its normal. So who did he end up making a deal with?"

"Nobody."

"Nobody?"

"Exactly. The best way of making money is to produce something no-one has."

"Who?"

"Nobody. I told you. Worse than unethical, some of their projects have the potential to be as destructive as a privatised atom bomb."

There's a break in the conversation as Mo exhales, a sigh deep with exasperation and Inez works out whether she needs to sneeze just once, or to splutter in swift succession.

"Who is no-one? No-one you met," Mo snaps curtly, "or no-one at all, or someone called Nobody, like Captain Nemo? A natural nobody, or a legal nobody?"

"What?" says Inez, momentarily confused.

Somewhere out on the main road, at least a street away, almost a world away behind the hovels, a tractor driver misses a gear. The chug of an old fashioned diesel throbs through the house and a window pane rattles in sympathy with the grinding squeal of wormgear steel in one of those chalk on blackboard moments. The noise makes all three of them cringe as a trickle of discomfort runs down their backs and the conversation has to pause.

After shrugging his shoulders a couple of times, Mitch answers Mo in his own terms, "A natural nobody, legally constituted in the name of a supposedly used-to-be somebody."

"The world and his wife."

"Not far off. Not a wife, but an apostle. I'm not sure which world."

"This, or the next?"

"Precisely."

Mitch makes a submissive gesture of helplessness, as though he's beginning to pray.

"The Church? Luther, Rome, Armenia?"

"A church, a church with as many halls as the Conventicles of Albequerque," Mitch carries on obscurely, knowing full well that neither of them have a clue what he means, "though each of them is no greater than the other, nor less in the eyes of the whole."

"The conventiwhat of Albiwhere?"

"Never mind." Mitch mumbles and tugs at a nail protruding from the floor.

"Where might we find the answer?"

"Not here, that's for sure. I just needed somewhere out of the way, where I could be sure no-one would find me. Nauen seemed as good a place as anywhere."

"OK, then," says Mo, "Where do you want to go?"

"I have a plan."

"Action, at last," says Mo eagerly, "I enjoy a well conceived plan of action."

"No, a plan, a roll of paper with drawings all over," Mitch insists, "The plan of a building. Walls, roof, floor."

"Even better," says Mo. brightening a little, "How old is it?"

"Quite new, a print out, I doubt if they've finished the topping out."

Mo is disappointed, "Show us."

"There's not much to see. Just holes in the ground and half

finished building work. You know what building sites are like. Half Berlin is a building site."

"The plan. Show us the plan."

"Oh, OK. Come with me then."

It is Inez who realises what is going to happen next, though she is uncertain where Mitch wants them to go. She expected him to ask them to follow his car, until he explains that he arrived in Nauen by local train from Spandau, so she suggests he drive the three of them in the Lancia.

"We could take a bus, if you prefer."

Neither of them do.

Mo is still sitting on his caviar box, sulking again, when Inez decides it's time to leave. He gets up without complaining and follows Mitch and Inez to the car.

"You drive," says Mo to Mitch, "I want to keep my hands free, so I can kill you."

Mitch mumbles a reply neither Mo, nor Inez can hear properly. Then Mo turns to Mitch and smiles, but it looks more like a slow grimace and Mitch flinches with apprehension.

CHAPTER 20

Mitch's improbable bio-gesture is a problem in dire need of a solution. Not only that, but Inez expects that, by now, the viruses will probably be trying to find their own way out of captivity. She puts on her Ray-bans, so neither Mo, nor Mitch can see the signs of strain that must be showing round her eyes.

Sitting in the passenger seat of the Lancia with a hint of warm sun on her arm, she can all too easily imagine the little glass phials cooking away contentedly in the sunshine and the day draws nearer when the inevitable crack will spill one, or other of the liquids letting the virus' loose.

A drop in the ocean. A drip in the landscape. Then what?

These powerful brews deserve to be disposed of properly. That much is clear, but how? Does Mitch really know what to do?

"Do virus' starve," she wonders out loud, "or are they cannibalistic? Do they lie dormant waiting for the right conditions to signal their revival, or do they gestate until the moment is ripe, then indulge in multiple orgiastic mutation?"

Neither of the men replies, but the sense of tension mounts as a fearful whiff of nervousness creeps into their sweat.

"What are their chances of survival?" Inez asks rhetorically, "And if they survive, what are everyone else's chances of survival?"

Such has been the success of medicine, that neither Inez, Mo, nor anyone they know, had ever seriously expected to die as just another victim of an mass epidemic, one among thousands, one among millions, merely the smallest unit comprising mortality statistics of infectious disease - one per cent, one per thousand, one per million, just one and the one is you.

Mitch is driving nervously, almost stalling as the car hits a succession of suspension cracking potholes in the cobbled road leading out of Nauen.

The Lancia bumps over the tracks of a level crossing, before he speeds up and they dive past the straggling suburb of Falkensee, on through the dense acres of apartment blocks in Spandau and into the heart of Berlin, where he pulls into the car park in the forecourt of the former royal palace, the Schloss Charlottenburg with its statue of a gilded and improbably naked young girl, which rotates imperceptibly, but erratically atop the palace dome.

Once they leave the car, Mitch leads them across the road past the Egyptian Museum, where Nefertiti is immaculately preserved in stone; then Inez is surprised by the astrological symbols and mythical beasts decorating the Eosander School until it is Mo's turn to be surprised once they've walked past the petrol station on the corner of Kaiser-Friedrich-strasse and a shop window display catches his eye. The shop sells antique bricks and tiles, plaster mouldings, assorted brackets and brass door fittings. It is a muralists' emporium. "Stone the crows," Mo exclaims, looking at the shop window with delight, as one of the local birds flaps off with a protesting caw.

While Inez helps Mitch find the house they are going to visit, Mo stands outside the shop looking at the window. He is impressed by the simplicity of all the objects on display. A tile is something hard and flattish, a brick squarer, a plaster moulding that little bit more complex and less hard. In isolation, a brass doorhandle is a fairly straightforward piece of casting. A steel bracket even simpler. Even the doorkey, a code carrying chunk of metal if ever there was one, is still, for all its potential mystique, a blank with simple elements cut away in a particular order. Replicate, multiply, then assemble a set of objects like these in the right order and you could build a palace with a rotating statue of a naked girl on its dome. Working within more simple ambitions, you could build a wall round a city and terrorise its inhabitants for a generation.

A great deal of human endeavour seems to be related to getting things done in the right order, or working out what the right order of doing things might be. If this, then that, from omelettes to gallium arsenide chips and back to eggs is eggs.

As well as doing the right things in the wrong order and failing to achieve your objective, it is equally possible to do the wrong things in a workable order and quite unknowingly create an abomination. The trick seems to mean knowing what the 'right' order might be before you start doing things, then being able to tell the difference between right and wrong which has never been entirely obvious. Pity the industrial chemist whose brilliance led not only the lead-based 'anti-knock' additives for petrol, but also dreamed up the atmosphere destroying CFC's used in refrigerators.

There's a rather pretty baroque style church just up the street, which is a good example of what can be achieved with bricks and mortar. Not only are the components assembled in something like the 'right' order, they achieve a degree of harmony. Except for the blue columned new school, which looks as though it was built in the late nineteen sixties, or early seventies, most of the houses here are late nineteenth century, also interesting in their own way The school isn't so bad either, given the things you need to link together in the right order to come up with a school, this and that, then another and something else.

There's a wine shop nearby, a bakery and a driving school. The old 'school house' is now used as council offices. No bigger than a normal family house, it gives some idea of the priority general education was given in eighteenth century Prussia. Not far off, there's a street of local shops, the Wilmersdorferstrasse.

Mo is standing in the doorway of a typical apartment house with a big front door that leads onto a wide hall with an elaborate staircase on one side. The hall also opens onto a yard around which the building is arranged. There are twenty five doorbells. Twenty five flats with one, or two, or five, or so many people per family, each with dozens of friends and relatives scattered across the city.

Nothing is in isolation.

While Mitch and Inez still haven't managed to pin down the right address and decide to retrace their steps, Mo suddenly has an overwhelming sense of the holocaust being methodically enacted on these Charlottenburg streets with post redirected, 'gone away' and changes of address officially registered with authorities and scarcely a murmur of protest. There should be different names written on this wall by each of the little bell-pushes. There should be an entirely different community living in these streets.

How many of the people who lived here worshipped at the old Synagogue, by what is now called Richard-Wagner-Platz? The Synagogue was broken into, burnt and destroyed by local thugs during Krystallnacht. How many of them watched helpless as the windows of the business's were smashed and anti-Semitic slogans daubed everywhere? How many of the people who knew this house, also knew the ramp at Auschwitz? How many people who knew this house played a part in sending them there? Did they pass each other on their ways to and from the Wilmersdorferstrasse shops? Did they catch each other's eye during the round ups? Did they face one another, as a train pulled in the goods station at Grunewald to be loaded with human cargo? Did they cast the first stone? Are they still living round the corner?

After the Nazi's came to power, this was one of the few districts where Jewish people were permitted to live in Berlin and families from all over the city had to move there. Along the way they were cheated of their property and robbed of their savings and belongings. Despite their impoverishment and humiliation, none expected to be victims of genocide, to die in a gas chamber. Before that war, no-one had heard of a 'gas chamber'. The concept of a room designed for mass killing lay in the realm of the inconceivable.

Mo knows that almost every house hereabouts could have been lived in by a Jewish family and if they didn't have the chance to emigrate, their fate was inevitable. With hindsight, what happened is familiar enough. The thuggery, the round-ups, the deportations to camps. Brutality and mass slaughter. Railway timetables and camp factories, medical experiments and extermination. Jews, Gays, Gypsies, Political Opponents, the Disabled.

Everything that happened was carried out, step by step, over a long period of time. One thing led to another, then the accumulation of detail was followed by the culmination of events. Each anti-Semitic deed and every anti-Semitic thought had its place in a particular order of perverse behaviour that it is too late to alter, too late to evade, too late to disavow. All that haunted Mo his whole life long.

All over Berlin, there should be different names by the door of almost any house you care to visit.

All over Berlin, a particular order of events had been observed and the outcome is familiar to the whole world, but increasingly ignored, or forgotten.

Mo wonders whether, rather than building a grandiose monument to the holocaust in the city centre, which a lot of architects and self important people want to do, it might be more fitting simply to write the names of holocaust victims near the doorbells of the flats where they used to live. Why not, indeed? The local people would then be reminded of the murder victims who once lived in these, their homes and the visiting dignitaries could pay their respects on a human scale. The records survive. In Germany, records seem always survive, even if people don't. Writing on the wall is familiar enough in Jewish history. Abraham, Bernstein, Cohen, David, Elijah and Goliath..... ......Nabucco....Samson...Zebedee

Mo was straggling behind them as if lost in a dream, when Mitch finally found the address he was looking for. "Number 81, not 18, right, I hope she's in. Sorry, you two. The ransom will be fine."

"What's up?" Inez asks, only half registering the word ransom, wondering whether Mitch' motive is really financial, as she realises Mo has turned pale.

"Flashback," says Mo, uncomfortably, "Tainted by an aura of fear and hatred. The house doesn't feel right. Too many people have suffered here. How can anyone live in one of these buildings without suffering a perpetual sense of revulsion. I'm sorry, I can't come inside."

This annoys Inez. "You mean I'm going to have to go in with 'thingy', all on my own. Honestly, Mo, that's no kind of help."

The house is on the corner of a side street, near the school. The facade is Jungendstil, decorated with elongated female figures, flying fish and grotesque male heads, but the interior is modern, almost post-modern, elegant and glassy, overlooking the pepper pots of the Picasso Museum and the Egyptian Collection of the Prussian Cultural Foundation.

Mo is as good, or as bad as his word and stays outside. "Inez, I can't, it smells of holocaust. The air is full of it. I'll meet you by the fountain in the park."

Leaving Mo to go and walk off his nausea in the palace gardens, Inez and Mitch take a lift to the fifth floor, then walk up another single flight of stairs to the penthouse.

A smartly dressed secretary shows them into a sitting room and asks them to wait. "Madame will see you in a few minutes."

'Oh ho,' thinks Inez, 'Madame is it, then, with a long low 'a' in the dame to follow the mad. Sounds like my mother.

Young Mitch has obviously picked up another strange set of bedfellows since she parted with him. They probably take him for a stray, she decides, like a dog without a home, or a cat that's lost its way.

Inez and Mitch have been sitting admiring the view, nibbled a few peanuts and are enjoying the cuddly effect of the expensive leathery brown furniture they're sitting on, when 'Madame' arrives carrying a green and white plastic bag from Rogacki's fish shop with a loaf of bread and a chunk of smoked turbot inside. "My favourite fish," she declares sniffing the package, then notices there are visitors.

"You are?" she asks and Inez replies.

"I see," she says, once Inez has explained herself, without indicating satisfaction or otherwise, "And why has young Mitchell brought you here to see me?"

Inez does not reply.

"Mitchell, you should take a bath, dear boy."

Inez decides to intervene.

"He thought you might want some photographs."

"Oh, are you a photographer too?" the woman says dismissively, "Well, why not. How interesting of you to think of me, Mitchell."

"But it won't be necessary," Inez intervenes, "You don't interest me photographically. I think we should stick to virus's and do our best to concentrate."

"You photograph virus's? I thought they were too small."

"No. No. The reason for our visit. Mitchie boy here is threatening to destroy the world with a four-pack of genetically engineered bacteria and virus specials which he just happened

257

to have stumbled upon at the laboratory where he works. Having purloined them, he dispatched them by post to my cottage. I would like them dealt with, as soon as possible. I think he has assumed that you will organise the payment of a ransom for their safe return. I do not expect a penny for myself. However, Mitch strikes me as being criminally insane and I suspect he will either put himself entirely at your mercy, in which case you are about to shoulder a massive burden of responsibility, or he will murder you without warning, in which case I need say no more."

Inez looks up at the long legged, blue eyed, dark haired beauty standing before her and watches the skin sag and the eyebrows crunch into a frown, as the make-up cracks and fifty-seven years are exposed in a single expression of disgust.

"Parasites, I've met a few, but virus' are something new. I suppose there must be a first time for everything," the woman says with a convincing frown of concern, as a shower of powder falls to the floor, "Though I fail to understand the logic behind your actions, dear boy. What kind of a ransom were you anticipating, Mitchell, surely you don't expect me to give you money?"

She pauses to take in Inez, again, before saying anything that might subsequently be considered prejudicial, "And what might your role in this ransom business be exactly? I can hardly think of you as the photographer with a predicament? Anyway, I think we've met before, but I can't remember where, so enlighten me, please, if you would be so friendly?"

"My name is Inez Henrietta Margharetta Muckerjee-Schmidt-Hoffman, photographer and hyper-realist of Berlin. I am not interested in ransoms, all I want is that these appalling diseases are removed to a place of safety."

The woman heaves a sigh of relief. "And I am Iris Braun, also of Berlin. Ask your mother, if you want to know the worst. That much I know about you from your name. She is a singular individual. I remember her well from our SavignyPlatz days, before she went to the east. Neither of us ever tired of getting laid. It was the only thing we had in common, apart from Jens, who I'm not going to tell you about. Later, much later, when she had discovered some kind of success, I was foolish enough to buy some paintings from her auctions. Isn't it an encumbrance?"

"The name, or being my Mother's daughter?"

"Quite. Pretend I didn't ask. You know, almost all the paintings turned out to be genuine, not copies, not fakes. The real thing at charity auction prices. It was so embarrassing. I have a Rembrandt drawing here that cost me three hundred dollars. We all thought it was a student copy. Is that what you mean by hyper-realism?"

"No, it's what I mean by a provincial art market. Neither the buyers, nor the sellers, know what they're doing."

The flowering of unexpected friendship has just withered on the vine and Iris returns them to the principal theme of their discussion.

Inez speaks rather quietly and very politely, but her words are daunting enough in themselves, "Mitchell has led me to believe you know something of blackmail, extortion and hostage taking."

"Elaborate," Iris replies, meaning explain, but Inez misinterprets her.

"Plain, or decorated, there's little choice," says Inez without wanting to sound rude, thinking of Mo, who must be sitting by the fountain wondering how long they're going to be.

Iris objects, "No, elaborate - explain, describe, tell."

Inez says it more slowly, "Bribes, Hostages and Ransoms."

"That would encompass blackmail and extortion, true," Iris concurs, giving Inez a condescending little lip curl of a smile, "What I need you to explain is who is trying to blackmail whom, who is doing the extorting and who, most importantly of all, are the extorted?"

259

JOHN CLARK

"Rage and revenge," replies Inez, "I think sunny boy Mitch here is scared of his hostages, the test tube thingies, I know I am, but I also think he is scared of the people he thought were his victims, these business scientists and their peculiar friends, or perhaps he believes they are after him."

"You mean they don't care? Now, that I can understand. If anyone kidnapped my daughter, I would raise a glass and celebrate, 'take her, please, don't hesitate, just don't tell me where I can find her'."

"I'm sure you don't mean that."

"What? This is Berlin, of course I mean it. Have you met the girl? Take her, she's yours, answers to the name of Doris, Doris the Dentist, what a bore. I'll be happy never to see her again. Nothing but trouble, ask your Mother sometime, I'm sure she'd say the same of you. Now, Mitchell. Tell me why you are being so stupid?"

"I can't take them back to the lab. I think the company will sell them as weapons of mass destruction. Some of their customers are dictators."

Iris rolls her eyes with dismay.

"What on earth do you expect me to be able to do about it, you stupid boy? Inez did you know he was so stupid, despite his doctorate to be? Can these people really be as dangerous as you seem to imagine, Mitchell, my dear? After all, even dictators have families and I can't imagine why anyone in their right mind would want to endanger themselves and everyone around them."

"That's what I thought," Mitch claims, "Then I realised it wasn't so. I've seen the paperwork, read the contracts, written down the delivery dates. It is almost too late, already."

"Almost already?" says Inez, puzzled, "already almost might make more sense, but not a lot."

CHAPTER 21

Rather than set off straight away towards the park, Mo had watched Mitch and Inez go inside, then step into the lift together.

Once they were safely out of sight, he decided to linger outside the house and keep an eye on the comings and goings. Who's in, who's out, who's going up, who's come down? The omens were hardly propitious.

A big-boned woman with a green and white carrier bag had given him a suspicious glance, scowled to herself, then disappeared into the building, as Mo decided to wander slowly round the corner and pretended to interest himself in the sculpture gallery studio. The north side of the studio is a single window, a wall of glass. Looking in on the array of classical plaster casts, miniature, life-sized and over-life sized copies of Roman, Greek and Renaissance statues which fill the space, Mo is surprised how white they seem in the greyish green daylight of an overcast afternoon.

Who is the hero wrestling the dragon? Mo realised that Inez would know, just as she would know who the armless woman was supposed to be posing as. In Inez' absence, his ignorance arouses no reaction and they stare blindly through the reflection of the street that he is watching in the window glass.

A Scandinavian tourist notices the sculptures and wants to photograph them, which leads to an argument between the man and his wife, she insisting that it is pointless to use a flash while taking a picture through a window.

"All you'll get is a reflection of the flash," she says in a regionally accented North East Swedish that would have been difficult for Stockholmers to understand.

"We'll see," he says defiantly, and she pretends to ignore him as he snaps away.

As the third flash makes Mo blink, he notices something move under the shadowy armpit of a heroic helmeted warrior. The reflection moves from left to right. A man he half recognises has left the house and is walking towards the Schloss. Mo tries to remember who it is. About fifty-five years old, he is neither well-dressed nor scruffy, medium height, or a little taller and marginally overweight, but neither fat, nor even plump. It's Mr Average, thinks Mo to himself and digs a little deeper in his memory. Who was Mr. Average? A singer, a dancer, conjurer? Mo is sure their paths have crossed before.

Still, he can't remember the man's name, so he decides to follow him.

He doesn't get very far, before the man stops, turns and walks up to him.

"Why are you following me, Moses?"

"Martin!" Mo exclaims, "I know it sounds stupid, been such a long time and I knew we knew each other, but I'd forgotten your name, so I was hoping."

"Ja, ja. Stop making things up. You were following me, pickpocket style. I have already moved my wallet to another pocket. Moses, I am going to the café, the Italian Oper, or maybe the Möhren on Bismarckstrasse, so long as the cakes are fresh. You can come with me if you like. I have no secrets from you. My mysteries are your mysteries, share, enjoy. You can decide, if you like, we'll go to your favourite café. Which is it? Please telephone your people and ask where we should go. Then you can tell me where we're going and I will start walking and you can follow me, if you want to, but it would make life simpler if we walk together, then we can talk. Once we get to the café, we can drink an espresso together, or enjoy a cappucino. You choose which table we sit at. I don't mind, you choose. You can even choose the cakes, if you like, or maybe you prefer croissant in the morning, it is scheiss egale, my friend. Then you can walk round the park with me, we can look at the buzzard's nest down by the stone bridge and avoid the joggers, then we can go to the Dresdner Bank branch on Otto-Suhr-Allée, where I will take some money out, then we can walk back to the apartment together, by which time my wife's sister will have finished listening to the cock and bull story your girlfriend and that little shithead Mitch are spinning, but please, Mo, don't tell me you have forgotten who I am, or try to pretend that you are not following me. I worked as a spy for sixteen years and I know to the very last footstep, when I'm being followed."

"I didn't know you live around here," says Mo apologetically.

Martin shrugs and ignores Mo's insecurity.

"So how are you, Moses and how is that thieving bastard Hagen? Why did he go to live in Hamburg? It seems a waste. My sister was always in love with him. You know, she would have been more than happy to share the villa in the Grunewald, a half dozen doors away from the Kaiser's grandson, the KönigsAllee, Thief Street, I tell you, it is class, but he ran away, foolish and her a wealthy widow at the age of twenty seven. Need I say, she would have been a good woman for him and made him a better wife."

"He regrets it."

263

"Bullshit, Hagen never regretted anything. One espresso and a glass of mint tea," Martin says to the café waitress, then he turns to Mo saying, "We should have gone to one of the Turkish cafés. The tea is better and the coffee sometimes too. I like that Greek coffee they make. You know why I stopped driving taxi? I got home one night and thought I don't need this any more, so I sold the cab to a young engineer from Iran. Talented young man, but nobody will give an Iranian engineer a job in Berlin, even if he has a doctorate, they're all too scared of terrorists, so he ends up asking me about driving taxi. You remember Bozorgnia, one of his nephews, brilliant musician and good poet. My wife says he's good looking. Married, clever wife with a degree in sociology and revolution, pennyless, a couple of kids. You understand. They need the money. I gave him the Mercedes. I like them both. Did you hear? The Grandfather was murdered in Istanbul by his own niece. What about that? Now, tell me. Did you enjoy the book?"

"Which book, what?"

"My Hadrian book. Don't tell me you never received it." Martin flushes with rage, "I sent it by courier, the parcel, the spelling, everything, just like they asked. Oh, it never reached you, oh, my, what a disaster, the work that went into it. You really mean you never even got to see the thing. You didn't get to hold it. I'll sue the courier people, I swear I will. After the bank we go to my lawyer. It's a disgrace. "Ars Muralis" We'll sue the 'ars' off them. I'm insured. My lawyer is a tiger, a greedy tiger, we'll win. He never loses. He has two wives, one current, one ex - a vampire that one, six kids to feed, a mistress in Fulda, three assistants and four secretaries. He has to win. Only then do I pay him."

"Martin. Who were 'they'? Who was it asked you to send me that book."

"They didn't ask me to send it. You underestimate these things. We are talking about a major commission, a formal contract with dates and clauses and guarantees and penalties. The work of a lifetime. They asked me to make it, not just the facsimile work, everything, binding in all the original material they had for me, ageing the leathers, took me months. But if you never saw it, then that's a real tragedy. Some of the calligraphy was outstanding, Mo, the best. I don't know who it was, but the standard of lettering was incomparable. I've never seen better. Now I should kill myself, you never saw it. Mo, I really and truly never thought I would get the chance to work that way again. You know when my father closed down the printing business, I thought that was the end of everything."

Martin and his father. Oscar Faust, the infamous Oscar the Fist, The Weimar Forger. Now Mo's memory began to slot one little snippet of information after another. Oscar had systematically corrupted the Goethe archives from 1935 to 1957, as an act of revenge for the unfortunately clash of names, which had made his schooldays unbearable.

Moses looks up and notices the waitress glancing towards their table.

"I can't help feeling that an incisive moment of decision, or rejection is leading us inevitably towards a conclusion," he remarks enigmatically.

"What are you talking about, Moses, the promised land, already?"

"The book arrived, Martin," Mo says softly, "I read every page; the craftsmanship is unsurpassed, good as your father's work ever was."

"Mo, you're a gentleman," Martin replies, "But why are you stalling, what happened?"

"The book was stolen."

Martin looks puzzled for a moment, then as if he can't understand, he asks, "But how?"

"Hagen walked away with it one night in the summer. We were at Inez' cottage. Of course he denies taking it, but there was no-one else, just the three of us."

"Well, maybe there's an answer."

"No maybe about it, Martin, there is an answer, but I don't have the slightest clue what it might be."

"I don't believe you."

"Martin, I don't even know the question,"

"Alright. You don't know the answer and you don't know the question, but did you read it? That's all I am asking."

"Yes."

"Thank God for that. Thoroughly? Page for page, for example, the story of the latent spell?"

Martin is once more his genial enthusiastic self and he smiles at the waitress, "More coffees."

"Which part was that?"

"Only a short passage, little more than a paragraph really, a long paragraph, but less than a page, bit one of my favourites. Taken from the common place book of a Hungarian lawyer, who was living temporarily in Trieste. "

"Forgive me, I really can't remember the story."

"I've also forgotten the exact words, which were in Hungarian anyway, a language I've never spoken well, though it rolls off the tongue like oysters in champagne. But anyway, the story goes like this and remember I'm the one who's telling it, so quiet for a moment or two, a little respect for the storyteller. Thankyou my dear."

Leaning forward Martin sucked a newly arrived espresso, felt his heartbeat quicken and his blood pressure rocket, before he started to recite the dozen, or so lines of his approximate translation.

"The old man had always known.

The stones had lain undisturbed, since his grandfather's father was a boy, or even longer.

Yet deeper in the mists of time, it had been predicted that seven giant stones, each inscribed with mysterious runes, would

266

appear as if from nothing on that very spot. They would protect the villagers from the curse of the first Mongol King, who wanted to die laughing, but was beheaded before he could remember the punchline to his favourite joke."

"Don't ask me how they knew, but they did".

"So it goes on. The old man stood and watched as one by one the gang of men began to lever the stones out of the ground. He laughed as a spring of the purest water began to flow.

The villagers had always had to dig very deep wells for their drinking water, arduous and dangerous work. However hard they sought, the water was brackish and the supply unreliable.

In fact the village had been named in their language, Moquanbè, the place of sour drinks. Now that they had a steady supply that was cool, sweet tasting and crystal clear, they renamed the village, Moquibé, Whitewater.

Within ten years, everyone in the village was either mad, or dead from the massive doses of mercury and cadmium they were ingesting every day. Ever since, the village has been known as Maqumbiè, the place of latent curses, though many years have past since anyone lived there."

"And?" asks Moses.

"Well," Martin finesses, "The story impressed me, even if it's not much of a folktale, from a Proppian perspective. I like irony, always have, and I was persuaded to collaborate. I'll tell you the rest, while we're driving there."

"Hold on, where is there?"

"Don't you want to meet the people behind all this?"

"Of course."

"Then why are you waiting, don't hesitate, the game could be lost before it has commenced."

"Martin?"

"Yes?"

"Do I have a choice?"

"I'm afraid not."

"Can we wait for Inez."

"I'm sorry, old friend, that won't be possible."

"You fucking bastard."

"There are worse things in life, as you know only too well, than fucking a bastard. The car is across the road."

Martin paid the waitress and led Mo across the road to the waiting car, a dark blue BMW.

"Get in."

Martin chatters away as they shuffle along with the traffic queue from one junction to the next, red light after red light. On the road from Rudow to Schönefeld the whole stream of cars and lorries drags to a halt. There's nothing special happening, just a road that's too small for the volume of traffic. The BMW slowly fills with black smoke as the lorries crash in and out of gear and Mo complains of a headache from the diesel fumes, as a set of air brakes gasp and hiss.

"It will pass," Martin assures him, "All things will pass, just give it time. Eventually, you won't notice a thing. That's how bad it is. Could you look in the glove compartment and see if there's any chocolate?"

Inez left Mitch by the car and went looking for Mo in the gardens behind the Schloss. Of course, he was no-where to be seen.

In fact the gardens were deserted apart from three gardeners pruning the topiary and a skinny girl in a red t-shirt, who grinned mischievously as she jogged swiftly by, 'Guten tag'.

CHAPTER 22

The place-name sounds grandiose and the moated Schloss is fine in its own way, but the cumulative impression is oddly inconsequential, a landowner's folly de grandeur, the symbols of plenty erected in the shadow of country poverty. The square is like a muddy farmyard, with estate offices on one side, the Schloss facing and a brewery steaming away to the left. They have arrived in a village called Preyna.

A mouse raised black and white cat sprang onto the bonnet of the BMW as soon as Martin pulled up. It waits until the doors are locked and the men walk away, then springs up to sleep on the engine warmed steel and scratches neatly as it stretches before curling up.

"Don't worry, Moses. I'm not going to drag you into the midst of a masked orgy."

"Good," say Mo, relieved, but also slightly disappointed, as though, he had always wanted to be involuntarily entrapped in an orgiastic conclave.

"Oh, there may well be such gatherings in the Schloss, now that the renovation work is nearing completion. I know they had problems deciding on an eventual use for the place, so the rental business may be their bread and butter. The village has done quite well with motor-bikes. Did you notice the cyclo-cross track they've built by the main road?"

"Leather?"

"What?"

"Motorbike leathers, S&M, orgies, leather. It's a pattern."

"I wouldn't know. Moses, would you like me to ask about the orgies? You sound enthusiastic. I can ask for you. Do you have a credit card?"

"No, really. I'm only here, because you brought us."

"Then shut up and stop distracting yourself, Moses, try to concentrate, please, and watch you don't step in the muddy bits."

Martin opens a door in one of the old stable blocks and reaches up for the light switch. In the daylight, all Mo can see are the first few steps of a stairwell leading down, he assumes, into some sort of a cellar. As the men go inside, the cat opens one eye, notices a patch of sunshine falling on a window-sill and realises the engine is cooling faster than expected. With a brief stretch it extends its claws and makes another set of fine parallel scratches in the expensive paintwork, then springs lightly away to its next favoured spot and wonders (being in its own mind a superior being of superlative feline quality) how long it should wait for the next mouse (small furry delicacy sent by God purposely for my nourishment).

Martin footsteps echo as he treads carefully down the spiral stair. "I was brought here as a new recruit," he explains, "when the Russians began training us for clandestine operations."

"What?"

"Informers. I was trained here, so were a thousand others, over the years. Some of them I taught myself. They didn't want the East German authorities to know, so we were brought here. Out of sight, no-one to notice apart from the old printer and he thought we were working for the Americans, which was the most stupid piece of self-deception I have ever come across. All over now, thank God. Take a seat, I'll be back in a moment. Need a piss."

The room is a simply furnished office, with a drawing board, a couple of wooden plan chests, a desk and a couple of filing cabinets. Apart from the fact that they are deep underground, the room is a typical workshop office. There's a second door, with frosted glass, and one wall has a big window, but Mo can't see anything apart from his own reflection and the room around him. When he hears the sound of a toilet flushing, Mo notices the familiar smell of printers' ink and relaxes. This is home territory, a tradesmen's confederacy of workplace and practice. He knows what to expect, or rather, like a doctor walking through a new hospital for the first time, he thinks he knows what to expect.

"The whole point of a moat, like the one round the Schloss here," says Martin, when he returns, "is to create the impression that the buildings are surrounded by a river."

"A wall of water."

"Something very like that," Martin agrees, "However most moats are little more than a broad ditch that is quite easy to tunnel beneath. Which is what we have here, a network of cellars on which rests brewery, schloss and estate offices, all part of a single set of foundations, the same structure really, one and the same building subdivided according to use. Above ground, of course, they look quite distinct, contrasting styles, work from different periods, though that doesn't matter. It all connects."

Somewhere off in the distance, Mo hears a lorry changing gear. It must be something to do with the brewery, he concludes. There is also the faint hum of electric motors and conveyor belts, the brewery machines stirring away their tea of malt and hops.

"The problem with these vaults is seepage. The brewers are always complaining their hops get fusty. They really are damp and once a decade there's the danger of flooding. The lower levels are permanently under water, but other areas are quite dry. Follow me?"

"Good for nothing then."

"Not exactly. Potentially the water can be used as a barrier, a wonderful security system sealing whole sections of the cellars off from one another. First it would be necessary to swim under water, then surface at precisely the right place. Any isolated space would be dark, almost certainly airless, very inhospitable."

"What have you been hiding here, Martin?" asks Mo suspiciously.

"A minotaur, of course, the local wight and other abominations. We include sinners of all kinds, those who sin and those who are sinned against."

Then Martin turned on the lights in the next room and led Mo into a workshop which had been kitted out with vintage range of printing equipment, rotary and flat-bed presses, typesetting machines, a foundry for casting type, guillotines and numbering machines. They were all tools that Mo had used at one time or another. Not a computer in sight, along one wall he noticed three ancient wood presses and a set of tanks and moulds for making hand-made paper.

"Let me show you some of the proofs."

Another door leads onto a corridor. Mo follows, as Martin beckons him on. After a right turn that's not quite a right-angle, then few steps down, another turn leftwards, but again not quite a ninety degree corner, until a flight of iron stairs lead up once more. "Water main for the brewery. The passages have to dodge around all manner of immovable objects. You get used to it after a while."

Martin points out the passage is covered with a powdering of fine brick dust, "We're near the bottom, you can see how much pressure the brick is under."

"Martin?"

"Yes?"

"The boy said he had a plan."

"Who?"

"Mitch the boy with Inez."

"What does he intend to do?"

"Not that kind of plan, a chart, diagram, that kind."

"Oh, where of?"

"I don't know."

"Then why are you telling me?"

Martin opens a heavy wooden door that leads them towards the foot of a cast iron spiral stair. The circular walls are lined with shelving. Closing the door behind them he switches on a hand lamp and beckons Mo to start climbing.

"Most people imagine these stairs must be part of the Schloss, inside one of the turrets, but they're wrong. Don't mislead yourself, Moses. They lead somewhere else. Up you go. Watch your feet. They're quite safe."

Mo can just about see enough from the lamplight. The shelving is filled with grey storage boxes. Lying through his teeth, Martin says he has no idea what they might contain, or whether if fact they are full or empty. When they reach the next pair of doors, turning to the right, he is more forthcoming about the archive cabinets which lie along one side of the curving corridor.

"This collection has been established as a repository of memories. One day a select group of historians will be invited to examine them and establish which are to be regarded as true and which are false. The task will be never ending and controversy will be inevitable, the issue beyond our wit to resolve."

Mo looks around. There must be millions of pages stacked

away in the files.

"What kind of memories, Martin, whose memories?"

"Human experience. Written. No video discs, or films, or tapes. Simple written evidence."

"No pictures at all?"

"Occasional illustrations, but only in exceptional circumstances. You provided us with a group of Persian illuminations, which we were delighted to accept."

"Are they here?"

"Where else? Would you like to see them again?"

"Of course."

"Mind your head," says Martin as he shows Mo through a low doorway into a reading room.

"Sit down. I'll be back in a moment."

Alone for the first time since entering the labyrinth, Mo tries to take stock. There is a broad shelf running the whole length of one wall, a couple of readers' stools and the rest of the room has plan chests, filing cabinets and a massive apothecary's cupboard. There's a camp bed in the other corner. Everything is military grey, even the carpet, which Mo recognises as the same simple weave as the one in their bedroom at home. He has never felt threatened by Martin and can't think of a good reason why he should now. Then he admits to himself that he is frightened. The place makes him nervous. Though he is usually agoraphobic, here under the ground, or shut in a tower, or where-ever this secret room really is, Mo feels shut in, claustrophobic and nervous. Is this to be his prison? He, a printer, entrapped, yet surrounded by millions of documents?

Martin comes back carrying mugs and a pot of coffee on a tray. "There's no milk, but there should be sugar in the filing cabinet, third drawer down, if you want some. Here, have a piece of apple."

While Mo pours coffee, Martin goes to the plan chests and searches through until he's sorted out a set of papers for Mo to look at.

"This was one of the originals," he says, showing Mo a flimsy fragment mounted on a leaf of acid free rag paper.

"The powdered lapiz had been mixed in an odd medium of poppy oil and a blend of plant extracts I couldn't pin down. Smell. There's still a reminder of opium, but the others I don't recognise, you?"

Mo shakes his head, "I suppose I ought to know."

"After four hundred years," Martin mutters, "I doubt it. The most difficult part was deciding what these marks had once represented. It's all so faint. Scarcely a single figure is intact and all you can really see of the buildings are the outlines the original artist drew before he started working with colour."

"How many were there to begin?"

Martin picks up a pen and begins to doodle on a piece of scrap paper, then he answers Mo's question.

"None of them were complete. I had three half sheets and a set of scraps, which someone or other had decided were probably part of the same group. I wasn't really convinced. That was all I had to go on, until Hagen came up with a similar set from the library in Manchester, which we borrowed for a few weeks then dumped on the market in New York. The paper was a funny mix too, linen, cotton and strands of all manner of plant fibres, but I think I did a good job. Eventually I had four large sheets of a quality that would fool the gallery people. You can't carbon date everything. So I set to work. I cut the sheets into eight, so we were looking at a maximum of 32 images. Well, that soon came down to 18, because I had to settle into a technique and feel comfortable with the story, especially because it was all direct from the original, these were real people, with real histories, an authentic journey through the fantastic world of a sixteenth century actor. What astonished me most were the descriptions of the fights scenes and executions they staged. Somehow they convinced the audience that his head could really talk, even

275

after it had been severed from his body."

Mo too has begun to sketch as they talk to one another.

"Here," says Martin, "there's a block of Ingres paper behind you."

"The stage," he explains, "was very like a Japanese 'No' theatre. Portable, with a fixed set of interiors and exteriors, with a place for the band and enough room to act out any manner of meetings and disputes. These people were travelling from city to city, so you can understand the convenience of a portable theatre. The layout is simple to establish, a perimeter wall, a copse with an open glade, then the house and garden. The colours and architectural style varied from region to region, according to local tradition, but the great epic of live theatre was faithfully re-enacted where-ever the groups performed."

"The pictures were part of a theatrical performance?" Mo asks, confused.

"More than that. The plays were the first example I've been able to find of a play within a play and the only example I know where a whole theatrical tradition was built around the experience of a single theatre group and its history. A kind of creation myth, if you like, but a myth about the recreation of performance."

Martin stands up and begins to circle slowly around the room. In a single flowing move, he reached into one of the plan chests and pulled out a sheet of illustration manuscript, which Mo immediately recognised as one of the series he had picked up in Istanbul.

"The story begins," Martin declares, "as a band of defeated soldiers return to their homelands after years of deprivation when their now dead prince-general led them from campaign to campaign in ever more inhospitable climes. The soldiers arrive home in their village to find their youngest children are thirteen years old, yet without exception, every one of their wives has betrayed them. There are babies in every cradle and the streets are filled with young children at play. This is the moment all the women have been dreading, but the sad truth is that of twenty seven young men who left as volunteers to fight alongside their Prince only nine have returned. The warriors have lost their appetite for violence and much to the women's relief they accept the situation. However, instead of returning to the simple routines of village life, the nine warriors resolve to create a theatre, so they may recount their exploits and win back the respect of their wives and children.

Each of the episodes they recount concerns the story of a different warrior. In a way it reminds me of the story of King Arthur and the Knights of the Round Table, where each knight has his own tale."

"Anyway, once I'd managed to bring the various stories together, it was fairly straightforward to paint the illustrations."

While Martin was explaining, Mo had been trying to remember the story he and Inez had deciphered from the three images from Istanbul. Hadn't the young man been the one to lose his life? The girl had been hung naked from a tree, then there had been lovers, then she stood over the body of her dismembered lover.

Martin laughs.

"I know. The girl. One of the knights was a transvestite, a girl masquerading as a man. Look at that picture a little closer and you'll realise that it is she who is the warrior and the young man her foe who must be vanquished. So it was."

"You're making it up."

"Of course, some of it, but not all of it."

"So, why the dog and the severed foot still in its shoe?"

"Oh a gruesome detail, strong enough to distract a buyer from my technical failings. The stronger the sense of narrative in a picture, the more people are willing to believe they are genuine. My technique is good, but not that good and there could well be elements of technique I don't know about."

"No, Martin, I won't accept that as an explanation."

"So be it, I cannot tell you what to believe." Martin smiles benevolently. "Let's go join the others."

He reaches for the light switch by the door and shows Mo into the next room. They're back in the workshop once more. Mo laughs, as he looks at one historic printing press after another. The majority are made like a wine press, with a handle to turn that creates the pressure. Few are made wholly of wood, most have a cast iron frame, even though many of the moving parts are still made from hardwoods.

"Even the one's I didn't have to build from scratch, I still restored myself," Martin says proudly. "Dad bought this place from the organisation that privatised government property when the East German regime collapsed. The Treuhand were happy to be rid of the bunkers. They neither knew nor cared what these buildings were for. I took it over when he died, in ninety three."

"Is this where you created the 'Ars Muralis'?"

"Created would be the wrong word. The bulk of the book was genuine, absolutely authentic material. I just added nuances here and there to complete the illusion and to enhance the sense of falsehood and fakery. I seeded and salted the anachronisms."

"Why?"

"Good God, Moses, its taken you long enough to get round to asking. Why, indeed?"

"Not just business, Martin?"

"Business, or the affairs of men, push and shove, there's little enough to distinguish one from the other. Consider your own part in the duplicity, though I should say, the price they paid was too small. I doubt if Hagen saw a profit. The prices were far too low when you consider all the running around that had to be done. First Manchester, then Mykonos and Philadelphia, the deal in Istanbul. There should have been a lot more money for all the work involved."

Without giving Mo chance to begin a reply, Martin led him

away from the presses, back in the direction they had come.

"I'd like to tell you how I went about faking up the Ars, but there's not enough time."

To Mo's surprise, the next door led them into a comfortable drawing room with a spectacular view looking down over the lake, while off in the distance massive excavators and draglines plunder the hillsides for brown coal, swallowing whole villages, which are wiped from the face of the earth, then carefully reconstructed as a substitute for themselves away from their original site.

The drawing room looks much as it might have done before the first world war and the two women taking tea look like a brace of overdressed Russian Duchesses of similar vintage. Sitting side by side on the vermilion red sofa are Iris and Inez' inimitable Mother - Indira. There are two fresh cups and saucers for the men.

"Do be seated," Indira says regally.

" 'Darjeeling', or 'Johnnie Walker'?" asks Iris more prosaically, brandishing a teapot in either hand.

Martin prefers whisky, while Mo decides to stay sober,

"Thankyou. A cup of tea would be most refreshing."

"Now, Moses," booms Indira, "My daughter had the good common sense to tell us about the troubles you've made for yourself and, as loyal parents, Iris and I would like to help in any way we can."

"Poor Mitchell is beyond himself."

"My daughter has been ordered to rest and prescribed sedatives."

"You, then, must assume responsibility for this nonsense."

Martin looks anguished on Mo's behalf, but says nothing.

"What do you want?" Mo asks.

"We think the right thing to do would be for you to recover the package which was sent to you."

"You mean fetch the virus'?"

"Quite."

"But why?"

"A precautionary measure. We are almost certain that the phials contain nothing more harmful than coloured water, but we think it is best to err on the side of caution. My son has never distinguished himself for honesty. I can't believe he would do such a stupid thing. There again, I can't entirely rule such foolishness out. I would readily order him to return them himself, but, of course, and, well....you are the only one who knows their precise whereabouts, are you not? We don't want to risk disturbing them by accident, just, er, in case."

"Where is Inez?"

"Oh, I think she and Mitchell are practising their calisthenics."

"Then, I suppose I'd better go."

"Take the BMW," says Martin, "here, have the keys."

Martin does not volunteer to drive Mo, or even to accompany him on this peculiar expedition.

When they finally told her that Mo had been sent back to the cottage, Inez shook herself free of the drug induced torpor and took the keys to the Lancia. Driving north alone, the sun was slowly sinking in the west.

As the autobahn rutted and clattered the little cars, evening slowly turned to night and high above her, the stars began to shine.

She arrives at the cottage to find the BMW had been parked with its headlamps on, the harsh light scouring the cottage garden. Leaving the Lancia in its usual spot, she walks past the building, calling Mo's name two or three times, but he doesn't reply. The woods are equally silent and so are the moons and the stars. The only sound she can hear is the gentle lapping of the water against the boathouse jetty.

Then she scrambles over the earthworks to stand on top of the terraces that Mo had built. The low beams of light create eerily long shadows which melt into the dark lake's gloom, but the fishtrap church was flooded in a pool of halogen blue from the car headlights. The shadow of the fishtrap is projected and enlarged onto the brick walls, a confusion of straight lines of taut rope and strained gnarled boughs.

The miniature bricks have lost their colour in this strange illumination, but every crack and blemish on the surface is etched clear by the substitute sunset.

From her vantage point, the shadow of the whole building stretched across the garden towards the boathouse, an amalgam of towers and spires, as the haphazard combination of shadows from shrubs and grasses combine with the building's detailing to create a fortuitous impression of gothic grandeur, a city of the darkest night.

Then the shadows lurch and Inez almost loses her balance as everything around her seems to tremble and wobble. One of the car tyres has sunk a little into a muddy rut. The model ruins are plunged into darkness, the magnificent shadowplay lost forever.

The conifers and bushes spring into view in their place and there, a few yards away from her, where a new hole had been excavated lies the figure of a man, a pickaxe by his side and around him chunks of harshly broken concrete. Inez jumps down from the terraces and starts to run across the garden.

Then she stops fearful and begins the retreat to her car.

She had never seen anything so slow as a dead Mo.

Unsure what should be said, Inez was bemused by a death notice that appeared the following morning in the local paper: "Born in 1951, Moses Hoffman died while celebrating his fortieth birthday party, at the age of 53".

-END-

JOHN CLARK

Acknowledgements:

Pope LeoXIII poem 'Ars Photografica, page 122, is quoted from
J.M. Eder's 'History of Photography', trans Epstein, Dover
Press, 1978.

Erwin Panofsky comments and his translation from Albrecht
Dürer on page 22 are from: "The Life and Art of Albrecht
Dürer", Erwin Panofsky, Princeton University Press, 1971

Afterword.

In the later nineteen nineties, when 'Lone Hunter' was being written, the internet and the whole structure of networked services were in their infancy as systems of digital mass communications. Of course, all kinds of networks were already in existence, some digital, some analog. Messenger services are nothing new, recall the Marathon runner. Swapping data between businesses, banks and industry was part of the enormous established telecommunications framework that included traditional landlines, telex and telegrams, or the transmission of tv signals via cable, satellite and terrestrial broadcasts. The capacity of these existing systems was often determined by peak levels of usage, which might only be needed for a few minutes a day, or for a few intensive uses such as reports from weather stations for meteorology and weather forecasting. This environment was completely different to the emerging framework of networks accessible to all, which the emergent internet promised and indeed fulfilled.

Having a personal computer that could be used to communicate via a modem, accessing websites, chat rooms and emails was a novelty that increasingly large numbers of people all over the world took advantage of via services like Compuserve and AOL, accessing an entirely new domain of interactive communication. Many of the most popular mobile services, such as Facebook and WhatsApp, or Twitter are more technically sophisticated versions of the same generic features - a personal profile, a set of contacts, or 'friends' and open communication based on interests, events and memes, with the ability to search for more.

The emergent internet was seen as being divided into 'walled gardens', such as AOL, or direct online access via 'browsers' such as Netscape Navigator. AOL users accessed a system

283

managed and maintained by AOL and at that stage did not make use of HTML, but relied on their own protocols. This is in many ways the true precursor of the services now accessed via mobile devices and the various generations of mobile technology, with Google's 'Android' providing the same determining framework of access to services via pre-installed 'apps'. The other alternative was for users to subscribe via an internet provider, then select a particular browser to call up individual websites by their IP address, navigating the internet via recommended links to other sites. The potential attraction of a search engine enabling users to search thematically, were gradually emerging, but were at that stage fairly rudimentary. With so many websites being created, the notion of a simple catalogue was unwieldy and the analytical approach adopted by Google would soon become dominant.

For 'Lone Hunter', however, the key notion was the potential to give something a virtual existence through the process of making a search request, even if there was no corresponding object to the term being search for. A book title can be sought and not discovered, yet the book concerned now has acquired the potential for its existence. Having been sought, a plausible absence was quickly and easily established, whereas the process of building a legend, a myth, or establishing an implausible object, might take years or even centuries. Our histories are filled by tales of lost and missing objects, from Treasure Island to the search for the Grail itself - the Holy Grail of much sought objects. For Moses Hofmann, no sooner has he entered a search term, its non-existence is affirmed online, despite his having had the desired object in his hands before the loss then confirms his role as a hunter.

As 'Lone Hunter' became the initial volume of a trilogy rather than the single novel originally planned, the very rapid development of a digital culture was emerging and evolving almost month by month, as new capacities were explored, including audio and images with increasingly ambitious websites and the massive growth of the basic infrastructure of the web providing extraordinary increases in bandwidth and the levels of potential connectedness.

Quite fortuitously, a project I became involved with to establish a new tv channel based in Berlin brought me in contact with electronics engineers and information technologists for the first time in many years and I realised the approach they were taking to bringing programmes from a server to the digital tv bouquet for cable and satellite services was little different to that needed for a version of TV via the internet. Not only had transmission and playout become server dependent, but low cost versions of digital video cameras and edit systems could achieved similar technical goals to the established professional systems. An astonishing technological convergence was revealing itself in a timescale of months rather than years. The speed of this transformation outpaced the perceptions of media professionals to the changes sweeping through the technical structure of communications at every level.

What seemed initially to be a novel new entrant to the range of available media was soon revealed to be so disruptive as to become a dominant technology once the mobile revolution superceded the classic 'internet' in the mid-'noughties', overwhelming landline telephony, analog broadcast radio and television, photochemical film and photography including medical imaging, recorded audio media on cassette, CD and gramophone records, printed newspapers, magazines and specialist publications and many aspects of publishing especially updated standard reference works, while relatively new media like computer games, were quickly adapted for online purposes as potentially massive simultaneous online presences.

Recognising the potential impact of this huge shift in the techno-cultural framework of contemporary society created a wholly new context for any fictional work in this period.

The underlying theme of 'Lone Hunter' is authenticity and people's relationship to aspects of authentic or inauthentic factors, whether in relation to objects, ideas, or events.

All my characters are intended as people who consider themselves to be behaving normally within the context they find themselves. To this extent they reflect a contrast between the era of traditional media and the new digital environment. They are members of a generation bridging two distinct cultural eras, the epochs of analog and digital communication. That will progress much much further as the trilogy develops.

LONE HUNTER

Publishing History.

'The Moses Hoffman Trilogy' was originally available in three parts. An earlier version of 'Lone Hunter' was published by the AVINUS Verlag in 2004 as an English edition for German. Early drafts of ANIMAL SELF and The SWOOP were available online at our websites.

berlinpicturecompany.com

Other Works by John Clark

Novels

CIAO CHARLIE (2015)

URBAN WEATHER (2016)

GAMING WITH ATTITUDES (2018)

THE PEOPLE THAT NOBODY WANTS TO MEET (2020)

MOVIE
"WRITERS BLOCK" (2013)

JOHN CLARK

The Author.

John Clark is a British born writer based in Berlin.